Meeting

Wednesday

by Willie S.

Dedication

To every underestimated intern, caffeine-driven coder, stressed HR manager, and gloriously chaotic boss—this book is for you. You're the unsung heroes who survive office life with resilience, sarcasm, and bewildered determination. If you've ever cursed a rogue semicolon, endured mind-numbing meetings, or explained tech to the tech-averse, your struggles and triumphs deserve celebration.

Here's to the late nights, shared deadlines, lukewarm coffee, cheap wine, and the friendships forged in the trenches. May this book bring you a smile, a laugh, and a nod to the wonderful absurdity of work life. May your coffee stay strong, your wine stay full, and your bugs be few. Cheers, cheers to absurdity!

This book has been inspired with debt and gratitude given to my family and extended family. The Highest God is in my heart and all else is in my dreams. You are in my prayers, my friends.

Contents

Chapter 1: The Great Grape Escape

Max slammed his fist on the table, scattering crumbs of a half-eaten croissant across the already chaotic expanse of papers, coffee rings, and empty wine glasses. "Grapevine!" he announced, his voice booming across the open-plan office. "It's going to revolutionize the way we code!"

Lily, the perpetually unimpressed HR manager, raised a perfectly sculpted eyebrow. She was filing her nails, a task that seemed to require far more concentration than any of Max's pronouncements. "Revolutionize it how, exactly?" she asked, her voice dripping with the subtle venom only years of dealing with Max could cultivate.

Max, oblivious to her thinly veiled sarcasm, launched into a passionate explanation. "Imagine this," he enthused, gesturing wildly with a half-full glass of what looked suspiciously like Merlot, "an AI so sophisticated, so nuanced, that it can analyze your coding patterns, your stress levels, even your current mood, and then recommend the *perfect* wine to accompany your digital endeavors!"

Dave, a developer whose coding skills were only surpassed by his cat's Instagram following, barely looked up from his phone. He was engrossed in a particularly adorable video of his ginger tabby, Mittens, batting at a feather toy. "Sounds... interesting," he mumbled, more to himself than to Max. "Mittens just posted a picture of her new scratching post. It's getting a lot of likes."

Sophie, the wide-eyed intern, stared at Max with a mixture of awe and confusion. The sheer audacity of the idea was breathtaking. "But...how would it work?" she finally managed to squeak out. The words hung in the air, fragile and questioning, dwarfed by Max's exuberant vision.

Max, energized by Sophie's innocent query, practically vibrated with excitement. "It's all about algorithms, my dear Sophie! Sophisticated algorithms that analyze keystrokes, mouse movements, even the subtle nuances of your facial expressions captured by your webcam! We'll use biometric data, sentiment analysis, and a whole host of machine learning techniques to identify your current coding state and tailor the perfect wine recommendation. We'll call it 'Code & Sip' - or maybe 'VinoVerse'? No, 'Grapevine' – that's perfect!"

Lily sighed, the sound barely audible above the clatter of Dave's keyboard and the occasional "meow" emanating from Mittens' video. She envisioned the potential PR nightmares: "Imagine the liability if someone gets drunk and accidentally deletes a client's database! Or, worse, if the AI recommends a wine that clashes with someone's prescribed medication. Max, this is pure madness! It's technically unsound and a massive legal risk."

Max waved her concerns away with a dismissive flick of his wrist. "Details, details, Lily! The vision is what matters! Think of the possibilities! We could have a whole new market: 'WineSoft Pro' with personalized wine pairings for each coding project! We could even create a 'WineSoft Premium' tier with exclusive access to rare vintages!" He leaned forward conspiratorially, his voice dropping to a near whisper. "Imagine the marketing potential. 'Code Smarter, Drink Better' or perhaps, 'Debug with a Cabernet Sauvignon'."

Dave finally looked up, his gaze drifting from his phone to Max's increasingly animated face. "Cabernet Sauvignon? I think Mittens would prefer a Sauvignon Blanc. It's lighter, you see, better for her delicate palate."

Sophie, meanwhile, was diligently scribbling notes, her initial bewilderment replaced by a quiet fascination. She found herself unexpectedly captivated by Max's boundless enthusiasm. There was something endearingly absurd about it all. The juxtaposition of high-tech algorithms and fine wine was, in its own peculiar way, strangely compelling.

The brainstorming session that followed was, as Lily would later describe it in her detailed HR report, "a spectacular display of controlled chaos". Ideas flew faster than the empty wine bottles being tossed into the overflowing recycling bin. There was talk of AI-powered wine cellars that could anticipate your needs, of self-stirring wine glasses that synchronized with your coding progress, and of a revolutionary new programming language written entirely in wine-tasting notes.

Dave, fueled by a surprisingly potent blend of caffeine and cat-related inspiration, suggested integrating a virtual wine sommelier into the program – one that could provide tasting notes and pairing suggestions in real-time. This, he insisted, would add a level of sophistication unmatched by any existing software. Lily, however, was having none of it. "Dave," she stated, her tone sharp enough to cut through the cacophony, "your cat's Instagram is not a viable software development model."

Sophie, however, had a breakthrough. While wrestling with a particularly stubborn piece of code, she discovered a way to integrate user preferences into the wine selection algorithm. She'd found a way to incorporate the user's individual taste, building a user profile and predicting their likely wine preferences, something that Max hadn't even considered.

The prototype they eventually cobbled together was… unique. It was an ambitious mix of cutting-edge algorithms, slightly off-kilter AI, and what could only be described as a healthy dose of accidental genius. The initial testing phase involved a copious amount of wine, a surprisingly effective debugging session triggered by a near-catastrophic wine spill, and a series of hilarious glitches that unexpectedly enhanced the program's quirky charm. The cat filter, a result of Dave's unintentional coding mix-up, unexpectedly became its most popular feature. The board presentation, scheduled for the following week, promised to be, to put it mildly, eventful. Lily shuddered inwardly at the mere thought. But despite her apprehension, even she had to admit a strange sense of excitement. After all, who could possibly predict what absurdities WineSoft might unleash next? The possibilities seemed as endless and intoxicating as a well-stocked wine cellar. And in the heart of that intoxicating chaos, they just might have stumbled onto something truly special.

Lily tapped a perfectly manicured fingernail against the overflowing recycling bin, a small mountain of discarded wine bottles looming before her like a testament to Max's unrestrained enthusiasm. The air still hummed with the lingering scent of Merlot and the faint echo of Max's pronouncements about revolutionizing the coding world with AI-powered wine recommendations. She sighed, the sound a delicate counterpoint to the persistent clatter of Dave's keyboard.

"This is insane," she muttered, mostly to herself, but loud enough for Sophie, who was organizing her notes, to hear. Sophie, ever the optimist, simply smiled faintly and offered Lily a sympathetic glance. Lily knew the intern saw the inherent absurdity, the sheer comedic genius of the situation, a perspective Lily, unfortunately, couldn't quite adopt.

Lily's first intervention was subtle, a carefully worded email titled "Project Grapevine:
Scope Refinement." She suggested they focus on a more manageable Minimum Viable Product (MVP), something less ambitious than a fully-fledged AI sommelier integrated into the WineSoft coding environment. She proposed a simpler user interface, one that offered wine recommendations based on the coding language being used – a JavaScript Sauvignon Blanc, a

Python Pinot Noir, perhaps. The email ended with a cautious yet optimistic tone, aiming for a balance between professional concern and an avoidance of completely stifling Max's creative impulse.

Max's reply arrived less than a minute later, a single sentence brimming with undiluted enthusiasm: "Lily, darling, you're thinking too small! We're not just recommending wine; we're crafting a holistic coding experience! Think synergy, think ambiance!" Attached was a hastily drawn flowchart, filled with arrows, annotations, and what appeared to be a cartoon depiction of a dancing grape.

Undeterred, Lily tried a different approach. She organized a meeting, cleverly titled "Project Grapevine: Risk Assessment and Mitigation Strategies," ensuring the seriousness of the title would somehow penetrate Max's exuberance. She outlined potential legal issues: liability for alcohol-related incidents, data privacy concerns related to biometric data collection, potential conflicts with existing health and safety regulations. She even cited a case study of a similar AI-powered coffee recommendation system that went spectacularly wrong, resulting in a series of caffeinated-induced coding errors and a major lawsuit.

Max listened, a patient yet slightly bewildered expression on his face. When Lily finished, he simply smiled and said, "Yes, Lily, you raise some valid points. But these are mere minor hurdles on the path to true digital enological enlightenment! Think of the brand awareness! We'll be the first software company to have its own line of WineSoft-branded wines! 'Debug with a Chardonnay' – I love it!" He jotted down the slogan on a napkin, already envisioning the marketing campaign.

Lily tried reasoning. She explained the financial implications, the potential for budget overruns, the need for additional resources – both human and financial. She even used charts and graphs, carefully crafted to highlight the potential for project failure. Max, however, remained unmoved, his enthusiasm proving impervious to any kind of logical argument or fiscal reality.

His counterargument was simply this: "Think of the fun, Lily! Think of the team-building opportunities! We could have themed wine tastings, blind tastings, even a company-wide grape stomping festival!" He envisioned a series of quirky team-building activities centered around wine, from blind tastings to grape-themed scavenger hunts. The image conjured in Lily's mind was not of collaborative spirit, but of chaos bordering on complete pandemonium.

Frustrated, Lily resorted to her final weapon: the threat of HR intervention. She explained the company policies on workplace safety, the importance of maintaining a professional environment, and the potential consequences of excessive wine consumption during working hours. She subtly hinted at the existence of workplace conduct guidelines, the implication being that Max's actions were dangerously close to breaching them.

This strategy, however, backfired spectacularly. Max, instead of being intimidated, merely laughed. "Lily, my dear, you're taking this all too seriously! It's all in good fun! Besides, a little wine never hurt anyone... well, maybe a little. But think of the creativity it unlocks! Dave just wrote an entire module in Python while sipping a Riesling – and it works flawlessly!"

Dave, momentarily distracted from his cat's latest Instagram post, nodded in agreement. "It's like the wine unlocks a hidden level of coding prowess," he mumbled, absentmindedly petting Mittens, who was now perched on his keyboard. Mittens, in a display of feline solidarity, stepped on the enter key, causing a cryptic message to flash across the screen.

Lily stared at the trio – Max, his face flushed with enthusiasm, Dave lost in a world of code and cat videos, and Sophie diligently taking notes, her eyes wide with a mixture of wonder and bewilderment. She knew then that her interventions were futile. Max's vision, as ridiculous as it seemed, was infectious. The entire team was caught up in the intoxicating swirl of AI, algorithms, and an unusually large amount of wine. Lily, though initially horrified, felt a strange sense of reluctant admiration. Perhaps, she thought, there was something to be said for embracing the madness. After all, who knew? Maybe "Grapevine" would revolutionize the coding world, one glass of wine at a time. She just hoped there wouldn't be another HR report filed, perhaps one about recovering from the chaos that was about to follow. The board presentation loomed large, and

Lily's crafted nerves were frayed to the point of breaking. She needed a glass of wine. A very large glass of wine.

The air in the WineSoft office hung thick with the aroma of slightly burnt coffee and the faint, lingering sweetness of Merlot. Dave, oblivious to the escalating tension surrounding the "Project Grapevine" deadline, remained engrossed in his world: a carefully curated blend of code and feline-themed social media. Mittens, his ginger tabby, sat regally perched on his keyboard, a tiny furry overlord overseeing the development process.

Mittens, it seemed, had developed a penchant for the enter key. Every few minutes, a random keystroke would send a ripple through Dave's code, resulting in a flurry of cryptic error messages and the occasional, unexpected burst of whimsical functionality. This latest instance produced a peculiar effect: the entire user interface of the "Grapevine" prototype was suddenly overlaid with a whimsical filter, bestowing digital cat ears and whiskers upon all the wine bottles displayed.

A collective gasp echoed through the room. Sophie, ever the observer, let out a quiet giggle. Lily, however, looked like she was about to spontaneously combust. Max, initially startled, stared at the screen with a mixture of confusion and growing fascination. The wine bottles, once elegantly displayed, now sported a variety of amusing feline attributes – a Cabernet Sauvignon with jaunty whiskers, a Riesling sporting a charmingly crooked pair of ears. The whole thing had an undeniably absurd, yet strangely endearing quality.

"Dave!" Lily exclaimed, her voice sharp with a mixture of exasperation and disbelief. "What in the name of Bacchus has happened to our project?!"

Dave, startled from his cat-induced trance, blinked slowly. He glanced at the screen, then at Mittens, who was grooming a paw with an air of supreme indifference. "Uh... Mittens did it," he mumbled, pointing a slightly trembling finger at the cat.

Max, however, was already beyond the initial shock. His eyes were gleaming with an almost manic intensity. "This," he declared, a wide grin splitting his face, "is genius! Pure, unadulterated genius!"

Lily's jaw dropped. "Genius? Max, this is a glitch! A catastrophic, cat-induced glitch!"

"No, Lily, my dear," Max countered, his voice brimming with uncontainable enthusiasm. "This is a feature! A unique, cat-tastic feature that will set us apart from the competition! Think about it: 'Grapevine,' the only AI wine recommendation system with an integrated cat filter! It's quirky, it's memorable, it's... purrfect!" He paused, admiring his own pun with a childlike glee.

Dave, encouraged by Max's unexpected endorsement, began explaining how the filter worked, a combination of accidental keystrokes and a poorly commented line of code. He admitted that Mittens' involvement was significant, adding, "I think the cat's improving my code, actually. She's got an uncanny ability to find and fix bugs — or at least, to add delightful, if somewhat unexpected, new features."

Sophie, meanwhile, was documenting the whole incident, her notes filled with exclamation points and doodles of cats wearing tiny sommelier hats. She saw the potential for viral marketing gold, a quirky edge that could capture the hearts and minds of the internet.

Lily, however, remained unconvinced. She launched into a series of reasoned arguments against the integration of a cat-themed filter into a professional wine recommendation system. She brought up brand image, potential user confusion, and the possibility of negative reviews from wine connoisseurs who might find the feature frivolous.

Max countered with passionate arguments about embracing unexpected creativity, fostering a unique brand identity, and capitalizing on the inherent virality of anything remotely cat-related. He even presented a hastily sketched marketing campaign featuring Mittens as the face of WineSoft, complete with a tagline: "Uncork the Purrfection!"

The debate raged on, a fascinating clash between rational pragmatism and unbridled creative enthusiasm. Dave, meanwhile, had returned to his code, Mittens once again supervising from his keyboard. He even added more cat-related embellishments to the filter: hats, bow ties, and the occasional whimsical pair of monocle.

The next few days were a whirlwind of activity. The cat filter, despite Lily's initial objections, unexpectedly became a massive hit with early testers. People loved the quirky, unexpected twist. Social media went wild with screenshots of wine recommendations adorned with digital cat ears and whiskers. Max, predictably ecstatic, ordered custom-made WineSoft branded cat collars for the office cats (there were three now, after a stray showed up, apparently drawn in by the aroma of late-night coding sessions and spilled coffee).

Lily, reluctantly, had to admit defeat. The cat filter, initially viewed as a major setback, had somehow become the defining characteristic of WineSoft's "Grapevine" project. It was a testament to the company's unique, chaotic approach to innovation. The "Grapevine" project, originally conceived as a sophisticated AI wine recommendation system, had morphed into something completely different, yet undeniably successful. It was a testament to the power of accidental creativity and the undeniable appeal of cats.

The presentation to the board was approaching, and the tension, although still palpable, was laced with a strange sense of exhilaration. The board had no idea what to expect, but they were prepared for anything. After all, nothing in WineSoft's history had been predictable, and this was no exception. Lily even found herself wondering if she should prepare a contingency plan involving a large quantity of Chardonnay, just in case the board members needed a little liquid courage. The impending presentation hung like a ripe grape, ready to burst with the intoxicating, chaotic energy of WineSoft. And somewhere amidst the lines of code and the flurry of feline-inspired designs, a new chapter in WineSoft's unpredictable history was being written. A chapter where cats, wine, and code magically intertwined, producing a result that was completely unexpected, utterly delightful, and undeniably successful. Who knew? Maybe even the stuffy board members would get a kick out of the cat filter, after all. The thought, bizarrely enough, gave Lily a small surge of hope, and possibly a craving for a glass of Pinot Grigio. After all, she was part of WineSoft, and embracing the chaos, as absurd as it often was, was simply part of the job description.

The hum of the server room was a lullaby to Sophie. Outside, the city thrummed with the energy of a Friday night, but inside, the only light came from the flickering screens and the faint glow of the emergency exit sign. Around her, the usual Friday night chaos reigned – Max was attempting to build a miniature vineyard in the breakroom using empty wine bottles and some suspiciously sticky substance, Lily was battling a particularly stubborn spreadsheet, and Dave was, predictably, engrossed in a livestream of his cat, Mittens, attempting to navigate a complex obstacle course made of yarn.

Sophie, however, was locked in a battle of her own. She was grappling with a particularly stubborn bug in the "Grapevine" project's algorithm. The bug, a seemingly insignificant glitch, was causing the system to randomly misidentify wine varietals, resulting in some hilariously inaccurate recommendations. A Sauvignon Blanc might be identified as a robust Zinfandel, a delicate Pinot Grigio as a full-bodied Cabernet Sauvignon. The results were both amusing and terrifying. Amusing because they were absurd, terrifying because they threatened to derail the entire project.

Hours bled into one another. Sophie hunched over her keyboard, her fingers flying across the keys, her eyes glued to the monitor. Coffee cups littered her desk, each a testament to her relentless pursuit of a solution. She tried everything she could think of – rewriting the code, debugging the algorithms, even resorting to some decidedly unorthodox methods involving a rubber duck (for debugging purposes, of course).

Nothing worked. Frustration gnawed at her. The deadline loomed, and the pressure was mounting. She felt the familiar sting of self-doubt. She was just an intern, after all, a wide-eyed newcomer to the chaotic world of WineSoft. Was she really up to the task? The thought hung heavy in the air, as thick and cloying as the smell of old coffee and spilled Merlot.

Just as despair threatened to engulf her, a strange thought struck her. A wild, almost reckless idea, born out of desperation and fueled by copious amounts of caffeine. It was unorthodox, unconventional, even bordering on absurd. But it was the only thing left to try.

Sophie's idea was simple, elegant, and utterly unexpected. It involved harnessing the existing, albeit flawed, functionalities of the system, twisting them to her advantage, leveraging the existing chaos to her benefit. Instead of attempting to fix the bug that was causing the misidentification, she decided to exploit it, transforming the error into a feature.

It was a risky move. One wrong step, and the whole system might crash. But she saw the potential for brilliance in her audacity. She felt a thrill of exhilaration, a rush of adrenaline. It was a crazy idea, but it just might work.

With a mixture of trepidation and excitement, she began to implement her plan. The code flowed from her fingertips, the lines blurring together in a harmonious symphony of logic and ingenuity. She worked late into the night, her focus laser sharp, her determination unwavering. The server room hummed, a steady rhythm accompanying her tireless efforts.

Finally, as dawn painted the sky with hues of orange and pink, she finished. She took a deep breath, and hit the enter key. Her heart hammered against her ribs as she waited for the results. The system started up. The code compiled. And then...silence. A silent, expectant silence that stretched out, filled with the tension of a thousand unanswered questions.

Then, it happened. A series of data points appeared on the screen. The algorithm worked perfectly. Sophie's unconventional approach had successfully identified the wine varietals without fixing the initial bug, creating a completely novel algorithm in the process.

She stared at the screen, her eyes wide with disbelief and a dawning sense of exhilaration. It worked. Her seemingly reckless, almost absurd idea had worked. She had turned a potentially catastrophic bug into a surprisingly elegant solution. It was a small victory, but it felt like a monumental achievement.

The next morning, Sophie walked into the office with a spring in her step. The residual effects of the late-night coding session were evident – her hair was a mess, her eyes were bloodshot, and she was wearing yesterday's clothes – but she radiated a quiet confidence. She had conquered the bug. She had proven her worth.

Max, ever the exuberant leader, greeted her with an enthusiastic hug and a spontaneous shout of "Eureka!". He immediately seized upon her unconventional solution, declaring it "pure genius, the kind of lateral thinking that only a true WineSoft innovator could achieve!"

Lily, though initially skeptical about the strange lack of error-fixing in Sophie's approach, quickly recognized the brilliance of the solution. The new algorithm, while not entirely conventional, was incredibly efficient. It was the kind of unexpected innovation that WineSoft was known for – a blend of chaotic energy and unexpected brilliance.

Dave, still recovering from Mittens' latest yarn-based escapade, simply stared at Sophie with wide, admiring eyes. He even managed to suppress a triumphant meow in response to her success.

Sophie's accidental genius had not only solved a critical coding issue but had also profoundly impacted her own self-perception. She had discovered a knack for thinking outside the box, a talent for finding unconventional solutions to complex problems. The experience had given her a newfound confidence, a belief in her ability to navigate the chaotic world of WineSoft and contribute meaningfully to the team's success. The late nights, the spilled coffee, the seemingly insurmountable challenges – all of it had led to this moment of triumph, a testament to her resilience and her unexpected brilliance.

The presentation to the board was still looming, but the atmosphere in the WineSoft office had shifted. The earlier tension had given way to a quiet excitement, a shared sense of accomplishment. They had faced a daunting challenge, and they had overcome it, thanks in no small part to Sophie's accidental genius. The quirky cat filter might have been a happy accident, but Sophie's solution was pure, unadulterated brilliance, the kind that came from embracing the chaos and finding the unexpected beauty within it. The "Grapevine" project, once teetering on the brink of disaster, was now poised for success. And it all started with a late-night coding session, a stubborn bug, and a young intern's unconventional brilliance. The success felt sweeter because of the unexpected journey they had all shared, a testament to the power of unexpected creativity and the beauty of accidental genius. The aroma of burnt coffee and Merlot now carried a distinct undertone of triumph, a potent blend of chaos and success. The impending presentation wouldn't be just a presentation; it would be a celebration of WineSoft's unique brand of chaotic innovation. And somewhere in the background, Mittens purred contentedly, her contribution to WineSoft's success, both direct and indirect, undeniable. The unexpected success of the project was a testament to their ability to transform chaos into opportunity, a cornerstone of the WineSoft ethos, and a tribute to Sophie's quiet brilliance. The world of wine and software had never been so delightfully intertwined.

The air in the WineSoft office crackled with a peculiar energy, a heady mix of anticipation and the distinct aroma of a dozen different wines. The "Grapevine" project, Sophie's accidental masterpiece, was finally ready for its first official taste test — a euphemism, of course, for a somewhat chaotic and decidedly boozy internal review. Max, radiating an almost manic energy, had transformed the conference room into a makeshift wine cellar, complete with fairy lights strung haphazardly across the ceiling and a collection of mismatched wine glasses that looked like they'd survived a particularly boisterous game of Jenga.

Lily, armed with a clipboard and a distinctly unimpressed expression, surveyed the scene with the air of a general inspecting a battlefield. She'd already warned Max about the potential liability issues of an office wine tasting, but her concerns had been met with his usual enthusiastic dismissal – a combination of hand gestures and mumbled pronouncements about the importance of "synergy" and "organic workflow." Dave, true to form, was live-streaming the event on Mittens' Instagram, narrating the unfolding chaos with the same level of seriousness he usually reserved for his cat's daily yarn adventures. The caption read: "Wine tasting at WineSoft! Will Mittens approve? Tune in to find out!"

The tasting itself began with a flourish. Max, acting as the self-proclaimed sommelier, launched into a flamboyant presentation of each wine, his descriptions growing increasingly fantastical with each passing glass. A simple Pinot Noir transformed into a "ruby nectar of the gods," a Sauvignon Blanc became a "liquid embodiment of spring's awakening," and a Merlot morphed into a "velvety embrace of autumnal bliss." His pronouncements were punctuated by theatrical gestures and dramatic pauses, eliciting a mix of amusement and bewilderment from the rest of the team.

Sophie, however, kept a relatively clear head amid the swirling chaos. She observed the reactions of her colleagues, noting their feedback on the app's accuracy and user interface. While the others were gradually succumbing to the intoxicating effects of the wine, Sophie's focus remained laser-sharp. She sipped her wine judiciously, making mental notes on the functionality of the algorithm while simultaneously assessing the team's response to her innovation.

The initial stages of the tasting proceeded relatively smoothly, though the room's atmosphere was infused with the kind of relaxed yet focused energy that only a workplace wine tasting could generate. But as the evening wore on, and the wine flowed freely, things began to take a decidedly unpredictable turn. Max, fueled by a particularly potent Cabernet Sauvignon, suddenly had an epiphany. He declared that the algorithm needed an integrated "mood-matching" feature, one that would recommend wines based on the user's current emotional state. He envisioned the app analyzing the user's social media activity to determine their mood, then selecting the perfectly paired wine accordingly. The idea, though initially met with stunned silence, quickly gained traction as more people joined in the discussion, intoxicated by the wine and the excitement of creating the impossible. It was the kind of outlandish yet strangely brilliant idea that only came about through a combination of copious amounts of wine and the inherent chaotic energy of WineSoft.

Meanwhile, Dave, engrossed in capturing the "peak chaos" moment for Mittens' Instagram, accidentally deleted a significant portion of the "mood-matching" code. The joyous camaraderie of a few moments before turned into a silent stare-off, as the reality of the situation sunk in. The room went silent, except for the faint clinking of wine glasses and the hum of the computers. An uncomfortable silence followed. Sophie, however, maintained her composure, quietly suggesting a workaround while calmly restoring the deleted code.

The subsequent frantic coding session was punctuated by the sounds of frantic typing, frustrated sighs, and the occasional outburst of laughter from a suddenly sobering Max. In the midst of the chaos, Sophie's clear-headedness proved invaluable, guiding the team through the crisis and preventing a complete catastrophe. While others lost their focus, Sophie remained calm, her logical thinking cutting through the intoxicated fog that pervaded the room. She subtly adjusted her code, subtly improving the functionality and efficiency of the algorithm without interrupting its core workings. Her work paid off.

As the evening finally came to a close, the WineSoft team looked upon their work with a peculiar mix of relief and accomplishment. The taste test had been far from perfect. Indeed, it could generously be described as a controlled disaster. But amidst the chaos, something truly remarkable had occurred. The "mood-matching" feature, while initially accidental, had injected a degree of innovative spirit into the project. It added a layer of playful absurdity that perfectly embodied the company's quirky personality.

Max, having finally sobered up, admitted that Dave's accidental deletion may have been a blessing in disguise, prompting him to consider a completely different perspective on the algorithm. Lily, while still maintaining her professional composure, acknowledged the unexpected efficiency of Sophie's coding. Even Dave, amidst the post-event editing of Mittens' Instagram feed, managed a grudging acknowledgment of his contribution to the project's unique flavor. The taste test was officially a success, despite the unexpected hurdles and the generous flow of wine. It was a testament to the team's resilience, their ability to adapt to the unexpected, and their uncanny knack for turning chaos into a creative springboard. The "Grapevine" project, once a simple bug-fixing endeavor, was now evolving into something far more ambitious and wonderfully absurd. The aroma of Merlot, burnt coffee, and success hung heavy in the air, a fitting testament to another day at WineSoft. The presentation to the board was still looming, but the team, fortified by shared laughter, accidental genius, and a surprising amount of leftover wine, felt ready to face any challenge. After all, what could possibly go wrong?

Chapter 2: Code and Cabernet

The morning after the chaotic wine tasting dawned, not with the usual groan-inducing alarm clocks, but with a deluge of notifications. Phones buzzed, emails pinged, and the collective gasp of the WineSoft team echoed through the still-quiet office. The source? An unexpected viral sensation: the cat-ear filter.

It had all started as a coding error, a bizarre glitch in Dave's "mood-matching" algorithm. Somehow, instead of suggesting wines based on emotional states, the app was slapping cartoon cat ears onto users' profile pictures. A completely nonsensical, utterly random function, yet one that had somehow captured the internet's collective imagination.

Max, ever the optimist (or perhaps still slightly tipsy from the previous night's Cabernet), saw this as a stroke of genius. "It's disruptive!" he exclaimed, pacing the office with the energy of a caffeinated hummingbird. "It's innovative! It's...cat-tastically brilliant!" He grabbed a half-empty bottle of sparkling wine from the fridge (a leftover from the tasting, naturally) and poured himself a glass, his grin as wide as the Cheshire Cat's. "This proves our unique brand of chaos-fueled innovation works! People love the unexpected, the absurd! We're not just making wine-pairing software, we're making *experiences*!"

Lily, however, approached the situation with her usual pragmatic cynicism. "Max," she said, her voice dripping with a carefully measured level of exasperation, "I think we need to assess the potential legal ramifications of this before we start planning a celebratory parade." She tapped a finger against her clipboard, a stack of legal documents already prepared for review. "Copyright infringement, potential brand damage, unwanted attention... the list goes on. We may not just be dealing with a viral trend; we could be facing a lawsuit."

Sophie, ever the level-headed coder, analyzed the situation with her usual calm. "The filter itself is harmless," she pointed out, her voice quiet but firm. "It's a simple overlay; no personal data is being compromised. The viral spread is likely due to its unexpected nature, the humorous absurdity of the whole thing. The fact that it seems so random is what makes it fun."

Dave, meanwhile, was basking in the glow of his accidental masterpiece. Mittens' Instagram account had exploded with followers, and the cat-ear filter screenshots were flying around the internet like digital confetti. "My cat's going viral!" he exclaimed, a wide grin spreading across his face. "This is bigger than the time Mittens won 'Cutest Kitten of the Month' at the local pet store!" He adjusted his cat-themed tie, which had a subtle pattern of miniature cat ears, a fitting accessory to the moment.

The entire day unfolded in a whirlwind of media inquiries, frantic apologies (from Max, who'd managed to accidentally tag several high-profile wine critics in his early celebratory tweets), and frantic attempts to contain the viral spread. The press

release Lily had drafted had taken an unforeseen turn. From "WineSoft Launches
Innovative Wine-Pairing App" became "WineSoft Apologizes for Accidental Cat-Ear Filter, but Secretly Delighted by Unexpected Success."

The board meeting, previously a looming shadow of dread, now felt oddly... optimistic. The cat-ear filter, in its unintentional genius, had somehow transformed WineSoft from an obscure startup into a quirky, meme-worthy sensation. The board members, initially expecting a straightforward software presentation, were instead greeted with a slideshow showcasing the filter's global reach, peppered with screenshots of surprised celebrities, confused political figures, and Mittens herself looking serenely indifferent amid the digital pandemonium.

Max, armed with his newfound confidence (and a fresh bottle of Sauvignon Blanc), delivered his presentation with an untamed energy. He explained the filter's accidental origin, highlighting its inherent absurdity and its unexpectedly positive effect on brand awareness. He framed the whole incident as a triumph of unconventional thinking. "We didn't plan this," he declared, "but we embraced it! And the world embraced it right back!"

The board members, initially taken aback, were strangely charmed. The filter had somehow imbued WineSoft with a personality, a unique brand identity that resonated with a tech-savvy audience weary of sterile corporate images. The chaotic energy, the accidental brilliance, the adorable cat ears – it all coalesced into something unexpectedly endearing.

The meeting concluded not with a formal assessment, but with a flurry of laughter. One board member even asked if it was possible to incorporate dog-ear filters in the next update. Lily, ever the voice of reason, suggested they carefully assess the potential legal ramifications before making any hasty decisions. But even she had to admit that the cat-ear filter, as bizarre as it was, had changed the game.

The next few weeks were a blur of media appearances, collaborations with cat-themed influencers, and a desperate attempt to understand why a simple coding error had catapulted WineSoft into the global spotlight. Dave, unsurprisingly, was still milking the situation for all it was worth, transforming Mittens' Instagram into a high-fashion cat blog. Max, in a moment of sheer brilliance (or perhaps mild intoxication), decided to monetize the cat-ear filter by introducing a customizable version where users could choose their own animal ears – from cats and dogs to pandas and unicorns.

Lily, initially concerned about the potential legal battles, found herself surprisingly amused by the whole affair. The viral success had overshadowed the original wine-pairing app's shortcomings, making it almost irrelevant. Sophie, ever the rational coder, worked diligently on fixing the original algorithm and adding the requested features, her calm precision a stark contrast to the general mayhem unfolding around her.

The unexpected success of the cat-ear filter was a testament to the unexpected power of happy accidents. It proved that sometimes, the most unexpected glitches can lead to the most unexpected successes. WineSoft, a company built on quirky personalities and chaotic energy, had somehow stumbled upon a viral phenomenon. And as the team looked back at the chaotic journey, they knew one thing for certain: their brand of chaos-fueled innovation, as absurd as it may seem, had struck a chord with the world. And it all started with a simple coding error and a very photogenic cat. The future of WineSoft was uncertain, but one thing was certain: it would never be boring.

The celebratory mood following the cat-ear filter fiasco was short-lived. The aftermath of Max's "innovative" wine-tasting demonstration, meant to showcase the company's new Grapevine software (a supposedly revolutionary wine-pairing app built on an algorithm that, ironically, seemed to have more bugs than a vineyard in spring), had left Lily with a headache that even the finest Cabernet Sauvignon couldn't cure.

It all started, as most workplace disasters do, with a spilled drink. This wasn't just any drink, though. This was a particularly robust Cabernet Sauvignon, the kind that stains like a vengeful artist, and it had been spilled not on a tablecloth, but on Bernard, the lead software architect's, pristine, brand-new laptop. The perpetrator? None other than Kevin, the intern who'd yet to fully grasp the concept of "professionalism" in a setting that was already teetering on the edge of utter chaos.

The scene unfolded with cinematic slow-motion grace. Kevin, overwhelmed by the sheer number of wine samples and Max's overly enthusiastic explanation of the "synergy between tannins and digital interfaces," had tripped over a stray power cord, sending his glass, and a significant portion of its crimson contents, arcing towards Bernard's laptop. A collective gasp filled the room, followed by the unmistakable hiss of electronics meeting Merlot.

Bernard, a man whose coding style mirrored his organized desk, let out a strangled cry that rivaled the screech of a dying server. His face, usually pale with the glow of a dedicated coder, was now the same shade as the Cabernet that had just murdered his machine. The air thickened with the scent of spilled wine and simmering rage.

Lily, ever the observant HR manager, watched the scene unfold with a mixture of dread and a strange, dark amusement. She knew this was going to be a paperwork nightmare. The potential legal ramifications alone were enough to make her contemplate a career change – perhaps to something less... explosive. She already had a mental checklist forming: incident report, witness statements, damage assessment, potential disciplinary action (for Kevin, mostly), and, oh god, the legal fees.

Max, however, was surprisingly unfazed. He'd already begun rationalizing the incident as a "team-building exercise gone slightly awry." He even suggested that Bernard could write off the laptop as a "business expense," which, given the company's peculiar financial practices, might actually be possible.

"Think of it, Bernard, old boy!" Max boomed, waving a nearly empty bottle of Chardonnay. "A baptism by Cabernet! A rite of passage into the WineSoft family! Your laptop is now one with the grape!"

Bernard, still staring at his ruined laptop with the same expression one might reserve for a deceased loved one, did not find this particularly comforting. His response was a low growl that suggested he was contemplating more than just disciplinary action against Kevin.

Sophie, the intern who was more sensible than Kevin, quietly retrieved a box of tissues and attempted to soak up the wine spill with an expression of
near-apocalyptic despair. Her attempts were about as successful as using a tea cosy to stop a runaway train. The Cabernet had infiltrated Bernard's laptop with the determination of a seasoned spy.

The rest of the Grapevine demonstration, predictably, was a complete disaster. The software, which was supposed to effortlessly pair wines with emotions, seemed to be malfunctioning even more spectacularly than usual. It suggested a Bordeaux with feelings of existential dread and a Riesling with overwhelming joy. The audience, comprised mostly of skeptical investors, were less than impressed.

Lily spent the next few days wading through a sea of paperwork. Witness statements varied wildly, from Kevin's rather unconvincing claim that he'd been "magically tripped by an invisible force" to Dave's surprisingly detailed account of the spilled wine's trajectory (Dave, it turned out, had a hidden talent for physics). Bernard, predictably, remained inconsolable. His laptop had contained years' worth of code, research, and, according to him, "the secret to achieving true digital harmony with Pinot Noir."

Adding insult to injury, the incident had attracted unwanted attention from the media. A particularly sensationalist blog had already coined the phrase "WineSoft's Cabernet Catastrophe," and Lily was bracing herself for a wave of negative press coverage. The cat-ear filter, previously viewed as a stroke of luck, now seemed like a distant, utopian dream.

The board meeting loomed, a storm cloud of doom on the horizon. Lily knew that explaining this incident was going to be a lot more challenging than presenting the success of the cat-ear filter. The difference between an accidental viral success and a disastrous wine-soaked malfunction was vast and, unfortunately for Lily, increasingly noticeable.

In an attempt to salvage the situation, Lily prepared a presentation that carefully avoided mentioning the "invisible force" theory, while strategically focusing on the company's overall progress, subtly glossing over the recent setback. She crafted a narrative that emphasized WineSoft's commitment to innovative technology and work-life balance, while carefully omitting the parts where that balance involved precarious stacks of wine glasses and a surprisingly athletic intern.

The meeting was, predictably, a mixture of awkward silence and strained laughter. The board members, while still impressed by the cat-ear filter's unexpected success, were clearly concerned about the company's overall stability. One even asked if there was a company-wide policy against wine-induced incidents, a question that left Lily speechless.

Despite her best efforts, the shadow of the Cabernet Catastrophe hung over WineSoft. The incident served as a stark reminder of the delicate balance between creative chaos and professional decorum. Lily, however, was determined to restore some order. She implemented a strict "no-wine-near-electronics" policy and added a mandatory "Workplace Safety 101" course to the company's onboarding program.

The future of WineSoft, it seemed, remained as uncertain as ever. But one thing was clear: Lily's job as HR manager was about to get a whole lot more complicated. The cat-ear filter might have brought temporary fame, but the Cabernet Catastrophe was a reminder that even the most innovative companies need a healthy dose of common sense—or at least a very effective spill-proof wine glass. And perhaps a dedicated intern to ensure that nothing went amiss during the next company wine-tasting. Or, more precisely, to ensure the complete absence of wine at any company events for the foreseeable future. Lily decided a new policy was in order. The only acceptable beverage at future WineSoft events would be… sparkling water. With a tiny, lemon-shaped slice. No cat ears this time. Just tiny lemons. For maximum, and most importantly, spill-free, impact.

The aftermath of the Cabernet Catastrophe hung heavy in the air, a miasma of spilled Merlot and simmering resentment. Lily, armed with a new arsenal of safety regulations and a severe caffeine addiction, was attempting to steer WineSoft back from the brink of utter chaos. But the universe, it seemed, had other plans. Or, more specifically, Dave's cat, Mittens, had other plans.

Mittens, a fluffy Persian with an unnervingly expressive face, had inadvertently become a social media sensation. Her initial appearance in the cat-ear filter demonstration had been a happy accident, a fleeting moment of furry-faced charm amidst the technological mayhem. But the internet, that fickle beast, had embraced her wholeheartedly.

Images of Mittens, sporting a digital crown of feline-themed filters, began circulating online. Memes blossomed, fan accounts proliferated, and hashtags like

MittensTheMagnificent and WineSoftKitty took over Twitter. Mittens had a more dedicated following than the Grapevine software itself.

The attention, at first, was a welcome distraction from the lingering embarrassment of Bernard's ruined laptop and Kevin's near-apocalyptic wine-spill. Max, ever the opportunist, saw a chance to leverage Mittens' unexpected fame. "Think of the branding possibilities, Lily!" he'd exclaimed, eyes gleaming with avarice. "Mittens merchandise! Mittens-themed software updates! Mittens... Wine!"

Lily, however, was less than thrilled. The thought of WineSoft becoming synonymous with a cat's unexpected internet stardom was not exactly what she'd envisioned for the company's future. She imagined stuffy board meetings punctuated by meows and purrs, investor pitches interrupted by demands for catnip, and financial reports adorned with feline-themed emojis. The image was enough to give her another migraine.

The endorsements started pouring in. A cat food company offered Mittens a lifetime supply of salmon-flavored kibble, a plush toy manufacturer wanted to create a line of Mittens-shaped plushies, and a cryptocurrency company, inexplicably, wanted to make Mittens the face of their new digital currency. The offers were ludicrous, lucrative, and utterly out of control.

Dave, Mittens' devoted owner, was torn. He loved his cat, of course, but the sheer volume of endorsements was overwhelming. His once-peaceful coding life was now a whirlwind of frantic emails, phone calls, and contractual obligations. He'd traded his keyboard for a cat carrier, his algorithms for endorsements, and his quiet evenings for photo shoots. He'd even had to install a miniature cat-sized treadmill for promotional purposes. Needless to say, it was a disaster.

The situation was further complicated by the fact that Mittens, despite her newfound fame, remained utterly indifferent to her celebrity status. She continued to nap on Dave's keyboard, batting at dangling cords with supreme indifference, and occasionally stepping on crucial pieces of code during Dave's more important work sessions. Her lack of enthusiasm was strangely endearing, but made managing the endorsements even more challenging.

Max, meanwhile, was enjoying the chaos. He'd started referring to Mittens as "our feline chief innovation officer," a title that was met with bewildered silence from everyone except Sophie, who secretly found it amusing. He'd also begun integrating Mittens into every company meeting, introducing her as a "purr-fect example of team collaboration" and holding up her paw for applause. It was as close to madness as possible without the need for a cat-shaped straitjacket.

The situation was escalating at an alarming rate. The WineSoft Grapevine software was being overshadowed by Mittens' digital reign, causing considerable friction between Dave and Max. Max saw an untapped goldmine; Dave saw the interruption of his carefully crafted workflow. The office felt like it was constantly on the verge of collapse and it all started with the fateful cat-ear filter demonstration. The chaos was a symphony of cat-related merchandise, contract negotiations, and increasingly desperate attempts to maintain some semblance of productivity.

Lily, already buried under a mountain of paperwork related to the Cabernet Catastrophe, found herself grappling with a new crisis: the "Mittens Mania" phenomenon. She'd drafted several memos attempting to regulate Mittens' endorsement deals, clarify the line between company branding and feline fame, and ensure that Mittens' daily schedule did not conflict with important coding deadlines.

One memo was titled, rather desperately, "Regulating the Purr-suance of Feline Brand Equity." Another, equally desperate, was called "Establishing a Clear Hierarchy of Importance: WineSoft Software vs. Mittens' Nap Schedule." Both were met with amusement and thinly veiled mockery.

The situation reached its peak during a particularly chaotic team meeting. Max was presenting a new marketing strategy centered entirely around Mittens, while Dave tried to explain a crucial bug in the Grapevine software, all while Mittens perched precariously on a stack of documents, occasionally swatting at a passing fly. The meeting descended into organized chaos with both men yelling their proposals, while Mittens calmly licked her paw.

Sophie, always the observer, discreetly captured the moment on her phone. The video, titled "The Mittens Meeting Meltdown," went viral. It became a more memorable moment than the entire Grapevine software release. The situation was spiraling out of control. Lily sighed, rubbing her temples. This was going to be a long year. Much longer, considering it was the end of April and they still had to meet the deadline.

Despite the escalating chaos, there was a certain charm to the absurdity of it all. Even Lily couldn't help but crack a smile at the sheer absurdity of the situation. The company, once teetering on the edge of disaster after the Cabernet Catastrophe, was now being propelled forward, albeit somewhat erratically, by the unexpected stardom of a cat. And as long as there was no more wine involved, maybe, just maybe, they could navigate this new, fur-covered landscape. Possibly. Maybe.

The chaos continued, punctuated by unexpected endorsements, impromptu photo shoots, and several near-miss incidents involving Mittens, a laptop, and a stray hair tie. Dave, while overwhelmed, couldn't deny the joy Mittens brought him. Her unexpected fame was a bright spot in the WineSoft whirlwind. It was a reminder that even in the midst of coding disasters and spilled wine, there was always room for a little bit of unexpected joy. Even if that joy came in the form of a fluffy Persian with an impressive Instagram following. Lily, however, was still drafting memos. Many, many memos. And scheduling a new mandatory course: "Workplace Safety and Feline Management 101". This time, the sparkling water policy was going to be strictly enforced. No exceptions. Not even for Mittens. Perhaps she could try catnip-flavored sparkling water? Lily wasn't sure yet. But she'd certainly be working on the policy. In the meantime, she needed more coffee. Lots and lots of coffee. The sheer absurdity of it all, she decided, was both exhilarating and utterly exhausting. But at least the company wasn't boring. And that, she decided, was something worth holding onto. Even as Mittens continued to reign supreme as the undisputed queen of WineSoft.

The initial chaos surrounding Mittens' unexpected stardom gradually subsided, replaced by a strange new equilibrium – a chaotic equilibrium, to be sure, but an equilibrium nonetheless. Dave, still reeling from the whirlwind of endorsements and photo shoots, found a rhythm in the madness. He learned to code with Mittens perched on his lap, her purrs providing a surprisingly soothing soundtrack to debugging sessions. He even developed a unique system of color-coded sticky notes to mark areas of code that Mittens was particularly fond of napping on – a system so bizarrely effective it became a semi-official WineSoft protocol.

Sophie, however, was thriving. The initial wave of chaos had initially been overwhelming, but she'd quickly adapted to the unconventional environment. She saw the opportunities where others saw only obstacles. While others were distracted by the feline frenzy, Sophie quietly honed her coding skills, seizing every opportunity to learn, to experiment, and to contribute.

Initially, she'd felt intimidated by the experienced developers. Dave, lost in his own world of cat-related distractions, offered little guidance. Kevin, still recovering from the psychological trauma of the Cabernet Catastrophe, tended to communicate primarily through exasperated sighs and cryptic muttering. Max, of course, was too busy trying to milk Mittens' internet fame for all it was worth.

But Sophie was persistent. She devoured tutorials, experimented with different coding languages, and actively sought out feedback. She started by quietly tackling smaller tasks – fixing minor bugs, streamlining code, and suggesting improvements to the user interface. Her contributions, though seemingly small, quickly demonstrated a clear talent and an eye for detail that her coworkers began to notice.

One afternoon, during a particularly tense meeting where Max was attempting to convince the board that Mittens could be integrated into the company's new AI-powered wine recommendation engine (an idea even Lily found baffling), Sophie had a breakthrough. They were discussing a critical flaw in the algorithm that was causing unpredictable results. The developers were stumped, arguing over conflicting solutions. Sophie, having quietly observed the problem, stepped forward.

Her initial hesitation was evident, a slight tremor in her voice as she began to explain her proposed solution. She described a novel approach, incorporating a new algorithm she'd developed during her spare time, one designed to handle the specific type of data irregularity that was plaguing the system. Her colleagues, initially skeptical, were captivated by her clarity and precision.

She explained her solution with a confidence that surprised even herself. There was a quiet strength in her demeanor, a self-assurance that had been dormant until this moment. The unexpected success of her solution, its elegant simplicity and immediate efficacy, was a turning point for Sophie. It wasn't just a technical triumph; it was a testament to her growing confidence and resourcefulness.

Max, always one for dramatic pronouncements, declared Sophie the "unsung hero" of the Grapevine project. His statement, while hyperbolic, accurately reflected the significant contribution she'd made. Lily, surprisingly, echoed the sentiment, though with a more measured and professional tone. Her praise wasn't just for the technical solution; she recognized the quiet perseverance and growing confidence that had driven Sophie to succeed.

This breakthrough spurred Sophie on. Emboldened by her success, she took on more challenging tasks, actively contributing to the development of new features. She became a valuable asset to the team, her calm efficiency a welcome counterpoint to the surrounding chaos. She even began to subtly influence the project's direction, suggesting creative solutions that incorporated elements of user-friendliness and aesthetic appeal.

Sophie's influence extended beyond the coding aspect. She recognized the potential for creative marketing strategies that embraced, rather than ignored, the absurdity of the Mittens phenomenon. She proposed incorporating Mittens-themed features into the software, subtly integrating feline-inspired icons and animations into the user interface. The idea, initially met with resistance from some, proved surprisingly popular with focus groups, highlighting Sophie's astute understanding of the target audience.

Moreover, she worked with Dave to create a series of "Mittens' Mini-Missions" – small, fun challenges that users could complete within the Grapevine software, earning points and virtual rewards. These engaging mini-games, cleverly integrated into the software's functionality, increased user engagement and provided a fresh, entertaining aspect to the user experience.

Her ideas, inspired by the chaotic, unpredictable world of WineSoft, proved surprisingly effective. The blend of innovative coding and playful, unconventional marketing strategies began to define WineSoft's unique brand identity – a brand that embraced both technological sophistication and quirky, unexpected charm.

Sophie's contribution extended even to mediating between Dave and Max. She recognized that, despite their differences in approach, both men shared a genuine passion for their work. She helped them to find common ground, fostering a more collaborative environment where their respective strengths could complement one another.

Her ability to navigate the complexities of the situation, to identify opportunities amidst the chaos, and to contribute significantly to the project's success marked a significant turning point in Sophie's journey at WineSoft. She wasn't just surviving the chaos; she was shaping it. She was no longer the wide-eyed intern. She had become a vital member of the team, a rising star whose coding prowess was matched only by her ability to navigate the absurd realities of WineSoft's eccentric workplace culture. She proved that even amidst a deluge of spilled wine, viral cat videos, and impossibly ambitious deadlines, exceptional talent could not only survive, but flourish. Her quiet confidence and innovative spirit, nurtured in the most unlikely of environments, paved the way for her to become an indispensable part of the WineSoft narrative – a testament to the fact that sometimes, the most unexpected circumstances can create the most extraordinary opportunities. And sometimes, a fluffy cat can be the catalyst for remarkable growth. Who knew? Certainly not Lily, who was still drafting memos. A lot of memos. But even she couldn't deny the undeniable impact Sophie had made. The coffee, however, remained a constant. Lots and lots of coffee.

The board meeting had ended on a surprisingly high note. Instead of the expected grilling, they'd erupted in laughter, a contagious wave of mirth spurred by Max's increasingly outlandish explanations of Grapevine's features – features that, frankly, shouldn't have worked. But they did. Miraculously, they did. The seemingly nonsensical integration of Mittens' preferences into the wine recommendation algorithm, the inexplicable popularity of the "Mittens' Mini-Missions," the sheer absurdity of it all – it had somehow charmed the board. They loved the chaos. They loved the unpredictability. They loved WineSoft.

Max, initially stunned into silence, had then launched into a triumphant speech, punctuated by enthusiastic hand gestures and a near-miss spillage of Cabernet Sauvignon. He declared WineSoft the future of tech, a beacon of unconventional brilliance, a testament to the power of... well, he wasn't entirely sure what it was a testament to, but it sounded impressive.

The post-meeting celebration, naturally, involved more wine. Much more wine. The air buzzed with a strange mixture of disbelief, relief, and a potent aroma of Merlot. Even Lily cracked a smile, though her lips quickly tightened back into their usual professional line as she began documenting the event for future HR memos.

But as the initial euphoria subsided, a quiet realization dawned on Max. The success of Grapevine wasn't a fluke. It wasn't a result of some brilliant, planned strategy. It was the direct outcome of embracing the chaos, the absurdity, the very essence of WineSoft's unconventional spirit. The project had defied logic, yet it had thrived. The initial parameters, the carefully crafted goals, the planned feature list – they had all been tossed aside in the whirlwind of Mittens' internet fame and impromptu wine tastings. And somehow, it had all worked.

This realization struck Max with the force of a well-aimed cork. He had spent months striving for a streamlined, efficient, user-friendly product, only to find that the path to success had been paved with cat videos, spilled wine, and impromptu brainstorming sessions fueled by caffeine and inspiration (mostly caffeine). He'd chased a planned vision, only to stumble upon a far more exhilarating and profitable reality.

His previous definition of success – a clean, efficient, predictable algorithm – felt suddenly, irrevocably outdated. He'd always believed in structure, in order, in the predictable march towards a pre-defined goal. But WineSoft, his own chaotic creation, had proven him spectacularly wrong. The embrace of the unexpected, the gleeful acceptance of the absurd, had somehow yielded extraordinary results.

This new perspective shifted Max's entire outlook on his work, and indeed, on life itself. He saw the potential for creative disruption, for embracing the unpredictable as a source of innovation. He saw that rigid structure could be a constraint, that the most groundbreaking ideas often emerged from the most unexpected corners of the imagination. His initial vision for Grapevine was a sleek, modern wine recommendation engine; his new vision was far more expansive, far more exciting: a vibrant, unpredictable ecosystem of digital delights.

The changes were immediate and dramatic. Max's famously structured meeting agendas were replaced by free-flowing brainstorming sessions, where wild ideas, both brilliant and utterly ludicrous, were encouraged. He fostered a culture of experimentation, of taking risks, of embracing the unexpected. The weekly "Wine Wednesday" tastings became not just a morale booster, but a source of creative inspiration, where new ideas germinated amidst the clinking of glasses and the swirl of rich aromas.

The shift wasn't without its challenges. Lily, ever the pragmatist, was initially resistant to the sudden influx of creative chaos. She spent countless hours drafting memos outlining the risks of such an unconventional approach, warning of potential productivity losses, and suggesting the implementation of a comprehensive risk assessment matrix. Max, however, remained unfazed, his enthusiasm fueled by the recent success of Grapevine. He viewed Lily's concerns as the necessary friction required to generate truly innovative solutions.

Dave, predictably, welcomed the change with a mixture of enthusiastic apathy. Mittens, it turned out, had a surprisingly discerning palate for Pinot Noir, and her feline-inspired feedback during the wine tastings became a surprisingly influential element of the brainstorming process. Sophie, having proven her worth, became a vital part of guiding the new direction, her innovative ideas finding a fertile ground in Max's newly liberated approach.

This newfound philosophy extended beyond the software development itself. Max started embracing unconventional marketing strategies. He partnered with independent wineries, featuring their products in online campaigns that mirrored the whimsical, chaotic nature of WineSoft. He organized quirky events and social media challenges, tapping into the unique brand identity that Grapevine had inadvertently created. The result was a surge in brand awareness and customer engagement.

Even the office environment underwent a transformation. The rigidly structured cubicles were replaced by a more open, collaborative workspace, fostering a sense of camaraderie and creativity. The once-sterile meeting rooms were now adorned with whimsical artwork, quirky posters, and even a dedicated "Mittens' Corner" complete with a plush cat bed and a supply of gourmet catnip. The office atmosphere, once characterized by tension and predictable routines, now buzzed with a vibrant energy.

However, this new-found freedom wasn't without its hiccups. One particularly memorable incident involved a spontaneous "grape stomping" session in the office kitchen, resulting in a sticky mess and an emergency call to the cleaning crew.

Another involved Dave accidentally releasing a flock of rubber ducks into the air conditioning vents, leading to a delightful but ultimately disruptive series of quacky surprises throughout the office. Lily's memo count increased exponentially.

But even these minor catastrophes were somehow woven into the fabric of WineSoft's unique identity. They became part of the brand's story, shared on social media, generating even more buzz and further solidifying their unconventional reputation. The unpredictability, the occasional absurdity, had become a key ingredient in their success.

Max's transformation wasn't just about abandoning his old ways. It was about discovering a more authentic approach, one that acknowledged the value of spontaneity, the power of unexpected collaborations, and the surprising potential of embracing the inherent chaos of life, even – and especially – in the world of software development. He'd gone from striving for a flawless, predictable product to creating an experience, a brand, a company that was as delightfully messy and unpredictable as the individuals that made it up. And that, he realized, was the true recipe for success. A recipe generously sprinkled with a dash of madness, a healthy dose of unexpected brilliance, and enough Cabernet Sauvignon to keep the creative juices flowing. After all, life wasn't about perfectly executed plans, it was about making beautiful mistakes along the way.

And WineSoft, it seemed, was making some rather spectacular ones. Ones that, somehow, tasted remarkably sweet.

Chapter 3: The Boardroom Blitz

The post-meeting euphoria had barely begun to fade before the reality of their next challenge crashed down upon them like a rogue wave of Chardonnay. The board had loved their chaotic masterpiece, Grapevine, but that didn't mean the journey was over. In fact, it was just beginning. Their next hurdle? A formal presentation to the *entire* WineSoft board, a gathering notorious for its sharp suits, sharper questions, and a distinct lack of Merlot.

Max, still riding the high of his unexpected victory, bounced around the office like a caffeinated hummingbird, his ideas swirling faster than the bubbles in his celebratory glass of Prosecco. "We need to make this presentation unforgettable!" he declared, his voice echoing through the now-grape-stomp-free office kitchen.

Lily, ever the voice of reason (or at least, attempted reason), immediately raised a perfectly sculpted eyebrow. "Unforgettable? Max, we're talking about a presentation to the board, not a Cirque du Soleil performance. We need a clear, concise overview of Grapevine's functionality, its market potential, and a detailed financial projection. Not interpretive dance."

Dave, perched precariously on a stack of empty wine boxes, peered out from behind Mittens, who was currently draped luxuriously across his keyboard. "Can Mittens be in the presentation?" he mumbled, his voice muffled by the soft fur.

Sophie, ever the pragmatic optimist, offered a compromise. "Maybe we can incorporate some of WineSoft's unique brand identity into the presentation. A bit of playful chaos, but still structured enough to convey the key information."

This sparked a full-blown creative conflict, the kind that only WineSoft could produce. Max envisioned a multimedia extravaganza, complete with a live jazz band, a wine tasting station, and a surprise appearance by a local sommelier. Lily countered with a crafted PowerPoint presentation, complete with bullet points, charts, and a detailed appendix. Dave proposed a slideshow of Mittens in various poses, each captioned with a relevant Grapevine statistic (Mittens gazing pensively at a glass of wine: "95% user satisfaction"). Sophie, ever the mediator, desperately tried to bridge the gap between their wildly divergent visions.

Their disagreements weren't just about the presentation's style; they extended to the core message. Max wanted to emphasize the chaotic, unexpected journey that led to Grapevine's success, celebrating the accidental brilliance that had somehow charmed the board. Lily, however, insisted on highlighting the underlying technology, focusing on the algorithm's efficiency and its potential for scalability. Dave, predictably, wanted to focus solely on Mittens' contributions. Sophie, meanwhile, was quietly drafting a backup presentation, a failsafe plan just in case the initial concept (whatever that may become) imploded.

The ensuing days were a blur of frantic activity, punctuated by frequent wine tastings (ostensibly for research), impromptu brainstorming sessions, and increasingly desperate attempts at collaboration. The office resembled a creative battlefield, littered with discarded ideas, crumpled PowerPoint slides, and half-empty bottles of various vintages. Lily's already impressive stack of memos reached new heights, documenting every near-disaster, every spilled drop of wine, and every questionable decision. Dave's contribution consisted largely of strategically placing Mittens in strategic positions, hoping for a spontaneous moment of feline-inspired genius.

Max, amidst the chaos, discovered a peculiar sense of calm. The very chaos that had once terrified him now felt like a familiar comfort zone. He realized that WineSoft's strength lay not in its ability to avoid chaos, but in its capacity to embrace it, to harness its unpredictable energy and transform it into something extraordinary. He began to view the presentation not as a rigid structure, but as a living, breathing entity, capable of evolving and adapting as it went along.

He embraced the unexpected, allowing the presentation to take shape organically, a dynamic reflection of WineSoft's chaotic yet undeniably successful journey. He incorporated elements from each team member's vision, weaving together Lily's data with Dave's surprisingly insightful cat-based observations and

Sophie's elegant design skills. Even Mittens, after a series of carefully orchestrated "photoshoots," managed to grace the final presentation with her undeniable charm.

Max's newfound approach was not without its risks. Lily was still drafting frantic memos; the office cleaning crew was on speed dial, and the risk of a spontaneous grape-stomping incident remained ever-present. But this time, the risks felt different. They weren't signs of impending failure; they were simply part of the WineSoft experience. They were the very ingredients that made their company unique, and their presentation, potentially, unforgettable.

The final presentation, a captivating blend of data-driven insights and delightfully unexpected moments, was less a formal presentation and more of a vibrant, exhilarating experience, a reflection of WineSoft's unique brand of creative chaos. It was a testament to their ability to turn apparent weaknesses into strengths, their embrace of the unpredictable, and their unwavering belief in the power of delightfully unconventional thinking. It wasn't perfect, it wasn't streamlined, but it was undeniably WineSoft. And, as they soon discovered, it was exactly what the board had been waiting for. Their unique blend of chaos and innovation had struck a chord, not just with the board, but with the spirit of the times itself. They were ready. Or at least, as ready as a company fueled by wine and feline-inspired algorithms could ever be. The stage was set. The spotlight was ready. And the audience? Well, the audience was about to be delightfully surprised.

The lights dimmed in the cavernous boardroom. A hush fell over the assembled executives, their expensive suits shimmering under the soft glow of the projector. Max, heart hammering a frantic rhythm against his ribs, took a deep breath. He glanced at Lily, who offered a tight-lipped but encouraging nod. Dave, clutching Mittens protectively, offered a shaky thumbs-up, while Mittens, oblivious to the gravity of the situation, groomed a paw with attention. Sophie, ever the steady hand, discreetly adjusted the microphone.

The presentation began, not with a crisp overview of market trends or a detailed explanation of the algorithm, but with a montage of outtakes from their chaotic development process. Footage of spilled wine, frantic brainstorming sessions (featuring Dave's increasingly elaborate Mittens-centric presentations), and Lily's exasperated sighs played to a soundtrack of surprisingly upbeat jazz. The board, initially stunned into silence, began to chuckle. Then, they laughed.

The laughter wasn't polite, perfunctory laughter. It was genuine, hearty, the kind of laughter that comes from the unexpected release of tension, a shared appreciation of the absurd. The montage concluded with a shot of Max triumphantly raising a glass of wine, only to have it promptly knocked over by a rogue soccer ball (a forgotten artifact from a particularly spirited office game of "Grapevine Kickball," a game invented by Dave, naturally).

The transition to the actual software demo was seamless, almost magical. The jazz music faded, replaced by the smooth, sophisticated interface of Grapevine. But even here, the WineSoft brand shone through. Each screen was subtly adorned with quirky animations—a little bouncing grape here, a winking wine bottle there—and subtle, almost imperceptible, cat ears subtly appeared on various icons.

Lily, her initial apprehension melting away, found herself strangely proud of the presentation's unconventional elegance. She had anticipated a barrage of critical questions, but instead, the board was engaged, their questions surprisingly insightful and surprisingly...fun. They wanted to know about the "Mittens factor" (Dave explained that Mittens was the software's "chief morale officer," a position officially recognized by Max, much to Lily's dismay). They asked about the genesis of "Grapevine Kickball," a story that somehow managed to segue into a discussion of the software's scalability.

Max, fueled by the board's surprisingly enthusiastic response, launched into a passionate explanation of the underlying technology, injecting his explanation with anecdotes from the development process, highlighting the accidental brilliance that had led to Grapevine's most innovative features. He even shared a particularly embarrassing moment where he had accidentally erased an entire section of code, only to discover that the accidental deletion had led to a significant improvement in the software's performance.

Dave, emboldened by the positive reception, showcased some of Mittens' contributions, proving that a cat's unwavering focus on naps could surprisingly inspire innovative solutions to complex coding problems. He even shared a graph comparing Mittens' nap times to software development productivity. The graph, though undeniably unorthodox, somehow managed to make perfect sense.

Sophie, her role shifting from mediator to presenter, delivered a compelling explanation of Grapevine's market potential, her data-driven insights smoothly integrating with the presentation's overall quirky atmosphere.

The Q&A; session was less a formal interrogation and more of a lively conversation. The board members, usually renowned for their steely professionalism, were animated, engaging, and genuinely interested. They peppered the WineSoft team with questions about their processes, their culture, and their inspiration. The answers were as unconventional as the questions, weaving in more stories of accidental brilliance, near-disasters, and the inexplicable contributions of Mittens. The boardroom, which usually resonated with the sterile hum of corporate formality, was filled with a contagious energy, a shared sense of excitement and wonder.

The presentation concluded not with a slide summarizing financial projections, but with a video of the entire WineSoft team—including Mittens, proudly wearing a tiny bow tie—doing a spontaneous, slightly uncoordinated, but undeniably enthusiastic, grape stomp. The final shot was of the team raising a toast, their faces beaming, their glasses brimming with a triumphant mixture of wine and pure elation.

The silence that followed was not one of disapproval, but of thoughtful contemplation. Then, the chairman, a man known for his icy demeanor, let out a hearty laugh. "I haven't been this entertained in years," he declared. "This...this is brilliant. Absolutely brilliant." A wave of agreement washed over the boardroom.

The unexpected success of the presentation was a resounding victory, not just for Grapevine, but for WineSoft's unique approach to innovation. They had taken what could have been a catastrophic failure and turned it into a testament to the power of embracing chaos, celebrating individuality, and finding success in the most unexpected places. The board's response wasn't just approval; it was an endorsement of their unconventional spirit, a validation of their chaotic yet undeniably effective method. The meeting adjourned to a celebratory after-party — catered, naturally, by an enthusiastic team who could now afford even more wine. The future of WineSoft, it seemed, was anything but predictable, and that, everyone agreed, was precisely the way they wanted it. The unexpected success had opened doors they hadn't even known existed, doors leading to a future brighter than any perfectly-crafted PowerPoint slide could ever convey. The journey had been a rollercoaster, but it was a journey they wouldn't trade for anything. And somewhere, tucked away in the comfort of a sunbeam, Mittens purred contentedly, a queen ruling her kingdom of code and cuddles.

The afterglow of the boardroom's stunned silence still hung in the air, a tangible hum of disbelief mixed with delighted surprise. Lily, perched on the edge of her seat, felt a slow, creeping warmth spread through her. It wasn't the warmth of the expensive boardroom's climate control; it was a deeper, more profound heat, a rising tide of something akin to...pride. She had spent weeks bracing herself for the inevitable disaster, planning damage control strategies, mentally composing scathing rebuttals to every conceivable criticism. Instead, she found herself basking in the unexpected warmth of the board's enthusiastic approval.

The initial shock of their unconventional presentation dissolving into laughter had given way to a genuine appreciation for WineSoft's unique approach. It wasn't just the software; it was the entire package, the chaotic energy, the quirky personalities, the undeniable charm of their endearingly inept methodology. Even the accidental brilliance of deleted code and Mittens' unexpected contributions had become key selling points.

She glanced at Max, still buzzing with adrenaline, a manic grin plastered across his face. He was radiating an almost unbearable level of self-satisfaction, a self-satisfaction that was, surprisingly, infectious. His usually frenetic energy had somehow transformed into a focused intensity, a testament to his unwavering belief in his team's unorthodox vision. He raised a hand, nearly knocking over a crystal decanter in his excitement, and began to elaborate on the future of Grapevine, his voice booming with newfound confidence.

Dave, his usual laid-back demeanor amplified tenfold, was now regaling a small group of board members with a detailed account of Mittens' sleep patterns and their correlation to software optimization. He had a chart. A very, very detailed chart. It was colorful. It was complex. It somehow managed to both make perfect sense and not make any sense at all, a perfect representation of the WineSoft methodology itself. Lily found herself smirking. She hadn't expected him to actually *succeed* in convincing the board that Mittens was a key player in the software development process.

Sophie, ever the pragmatist, was subtly guiding the conversation towards the concrete aspects of the project's marketability, smoothly weaving in the financial projections while maintaining the lighthearted tone that had charmed the board. She possessed a rare ability to bridge the gap between the eccentric and the professional, a skill she had undoubtedly honed during her short but intense tenure at WineSoft. Lily felt a swell of admiration for the intern; Sophie had displayed an incredible level of composure and adaptability under immense pressure.

The board members themselves were a revelation. The stern-faced executives, usually portrayed as emotionless automatons in Lily's mind, were animated, engaging, and surprisingly receptive to the team's outlandish explanations. They asked insightful questions, genuinely curious about the creative process, about the team's dynamics, about the "Grapevine Kickball" strategy and its unexpected contribution to software design.

Lily realized that the board wasn't just assessing the software; they were assessing the company culture, the team's unconventional spirit, and the unexpected synergy that emerged from their chaotic environment. They seemed to value the authenticity, the unique brand of chaos that defined WineSoft. They weren't looking for a flawless product; they were looking for something...different, something unexpected, something undeniably WineSoft.

The realization hit Lily with the force of a well-aimed wine cork. She had been so focused on managing the chaos, on preventing disasters, on maintaining a semblance of professional decorum, that she had failed to see the beauty in the mess. The "mess" was WineSoft's unique selling proposition. The unorthodox approach, the impromptu wine tastings, the frantic brainstorming sessions punctuated by cat naps and impromptu games of Grapevine Kickball — it was all part of the magic.

This wasn't just a successful product launch; it was a validation of their unorthodox methods, a testament to the power of individuality, a celebration of their chaotic yet harmonious work environment. Lily had always valued order and efficiency, and she still did. But she had finally learned to appreciate the unexpected brilliance that could bloom from controlled chaos.

The energy, the creativity, the sheer audacity of their approach had completely captivated the board.

The meeting ended not with a polite handshake and a promise of further discussions, but with a roaring applause and a flurry of celebratory handshakes. The board members, surprisingly energized, were already exchanging business cards and making plans for future collaborations. The air crackled with an electrifying energy, a palpable sense of shared excitement. Even the usually stoic chairman was visibly impressed, praising the presentation as "a breath of fresh air in the stale world of corporate software."

Later, during the celebratory after-party (catered, naturally, with a selection of exquisite wines selected by Max, who had appointed himself honorary sommelier for the occasion), Lily found herself surrounded by her colleagues, all buzzing with the after-effects of their triumphant performance. Dave was explaining the intricate details of Mittens' contribution to the algorithm to a captivated audience of board members, who were hanging onto every word. Max was passionately discussing future expansion plans, his eyes shining with an almost childlike excitement. Sophie was calmly networking, collecting business cards and charming everyone with her quiet confidence.

The evening unfolded in a haze of laughter, celebratory toasts, and more than a few spilled glasses of wine (mostly courtesy of Max, predictably). As the party wound down, Lily found herself standing alone, overlooking the bustling crowd. The earlier tension and anxiety had completely dissipated, replaced by a sense of accomplishment and a profound appreciation for her team's unique and undeniably effective brand of chaos.

She had arrived at the boardroom fearing the worst, expecting criticism, bracing for failure. She had left feeling a sense of profound satisfaction, a sense of shared victory, a newfound understanding of the beauty of controlled chaos, and an undeniable pride in her team. The skepticism and apprehension had been replaced by admiration, a realization that their unorthodox approach hadn't just worked—it had exceeded all expectations. Lily's triumphant moment wasn't about personal recognition; it was about witnessing the collective triumph of a team that dared to be different, a team that embraced its unique brand of chaos, and a team that, against all odds, had managed to not only succeed but redefine success itself. And somewhere, in a quiet corner of the office, Mittens slept soundly, the unsung hero of WineSoft's unlikely success story, dreaming perhaps of even more lucrative naps and more elaborate charts. The future of WineSoft was uncertain, delightfully so, but one thing was clear: the adventure had only just begun.

The after-party, a swirling vortex of celebratory chatter and clinking glasses, eventually subsided. Max, fueled by an intoxicating mix of success and Merlot, was already drafting a press release titled, "WineSoft: Where Innovation Meets Feline Inspiration." Sophie, ever practical, was discreetly arranging for a professional photoshoot of Mittens, strategically positioned atop a stack of neatly organized Grapevine software manuals. Even Lily, usually the bastion of corporate decorum, found herself chuckling at the absurdity of it all, the sheer, unadulterated silliness that had somehow catapulted WineSoft into the spotlight.

And then came the email.

It arrived at 3:17 AM, a notification pinging on Lily's phone, interrupting her surprisingly restful sleep. Subject line: "Urgent – Mittens' New Role." Lily groaned, rubbing the sleep from her eyes. She'd anticipated a flurry of congratulatory messages and requests for interviews, but this...this was unexpected. She opened the email, bracing herself for another one of Max's midnight pronouncements.

The email was from Max, naturally. It was short, punchy, and utterly devoid of any semblance of corporate formality.

"Lily my dear," it began, "I think you'll agree that our recent triumph is a testament to the power of collective genius... and also, Mittens. Therefore, I propose a momentous decision: Mittens, Chief Inspiration Officer. I've already drafted the press release; it's a masterpiece. Think of the merchandise! The social media campaign! The viral potential is...purrfect."

Lily stared at the screen, the words swimming before her eyes. Chief Inspiration Officer? For a cat? This was even more outlandish than the Grapevine Kickball strategy. A wave of exhaustion washed over her, followed by a reluctant chuckle. It was so unbelievably WineSoft.

The next morning, the office was abuzz with the news. Mittens, still slumbering peacefully in Dave's oversized, cat-themed beanbag chair, was blissfully unaware of his newfound corporate status. Dave, however, was practically radiating pride, a goofy grin plastered across his face as he showed off a crafted PowerPoint presentation detailing Mittens' career trajectory, complete with projected revenue growth based on Mittens' nap times (apparently, a crucial metric in the new C.I.O.'s performance review).

The press release, as predicted, was a masterpiece of chaotic brilliance. It blended corporate jargon with feline puns in a way that was simultaneously jarring and utterly captivating. It highlighted Mittens' "unwavering dedication to napping," his "profound understanding of algorithms" (a theory Dave had developed, backed up, of course, by an elaborate chart), and his "invaluable contribution to team morale."

The internet went wild. Mittens' Instagram following exploded, attracting a diverse audience ranging from cat lovers to software engineers to bewildered business executives. News outlets across the globe picked up the story, marveling at the absurdity and, surprisingly, praising WineSoft's unique approach to corporate culture. The company was suddenly lauded not just for its innovative software but for its embrace of the unconventional, its willingness to celebrate individuality, and its commitment to integrating feline-based inspiration into its work process.

Mittens, meanwhile, continued to nap, completely oblivious to the international media frenzy surrounding his newfound celebrity. He occasionally stirred, blinked slowly, and then promptly drifted back to sleep, the embodiment of serene contentment and corporate success. His nap schedule, documented by Dave, was now considered a vital part of WineSoft's strategic planning sessions.

The merchandise line was equally bizarre and brilliant. There were Mittens-themed stress balls, Mittens-emblazoned coffee mugs, and even a limited edition line of "Mittens' Midnight Algorithm" t-shirts that featured a complex-looking (and entirely fictional) algorithm accompanied by a picture of Mittens looking supremely unimpressed. Sales skyrocketed.

The sudden influx of publicity and attention brought with it a cascade of unexpected opportunities. Investors were clamoring to get a piece of the WineSoft pie, now infused with a generous dollop of feline-fueled chaos. Competitors were baffled, analysts were scratching their heads, and the board of directors, well, they were simply ecstatic. The initial shock of Mittens' elevation to Chief Inspiration Officer had quickly given way to enthusiastic acceptance. After all, it had worked.

The success of the "Mittens marketing campaign," as Max called it, wasn't just about selling software; it was about selling a brand, a culture, a sense of fun and irreverence in a world dominated by seriousness and corporate conformity. It was a testament to the power of embracing the unexpected, of finding inspiration in the most unlikely of places, and of understanding that sometimes, the best solutions come not from planning but from a well-timed cat nap.

Dave, of course, was thrilled. His devotion to Mittens had not only earned him a promotion (to Senior Algorithm Architect, a title he'd proudly suggested himself), but also cemented Mittens' place as a corporate legend, a furry embodiment of WineSoft's unconventional charm. He even designed a special "Mittens Appreciation Day," complete with a catered lunch, a catered catnip buffet for Mittens (strictly supervised, of course), and a company-wide nap session.

Lily, initially taken aback by the sheer absurdity of it all, eventually came to embrace the craziness. She still maintained a semblance of order and efficiency, but she also learned to appreciate the chaotic creativity that flourished within WineSoft's unique ecosystem. She realized that their success wasn't despite the chaos; it was because of it. It was a lesson in unexpected brilliance, a reminder that sometimes, the most unconventional approaches can yield the most extraordinary results.

And Mittens? He continued to reign supreme as Chief Inspiration Officer, napping strategically, overseeing the development process from his plush beanbag chair, and occasionally deigning to grace the board meetings with his presence. He didn't attend the meetings frequently, but whenever he did, the productivity soared. His mere presence seemed to inspire a sense of calm and creativity that no other executive could replicate.

The story of WineSoft's success became a modern-day fable, a quirky testament to the power of embracing individuality, finding inspiration in the unexpected, and letting a little bit of controlled chaos into your life (and your corporate structure). And at the heart of it all was Mittens, the sleeping, purring, Chief Inspiration Officer, a testament to the fact that sometimes, the best leaders are those who simply know when to nap. The future of WineSoft remained as delightfully unpredictable as ever. But one thing was certain: the legend of Mittens, the cat who conquered the corporate world, was only just beginning. And Lily, now fully embracing the WineSoft ethos, couldn't wait to see what ridiculous adventure awaited them next.

The whirlwind of the Mittens-mania finally began to subside, leaving behind a trail of bewildered journalists, ecstatic investors, and a company that had somehow managed to redefine the meaning of "corporate success." Amidst the chaos, Sophie, the once wide-eyed intern, found herself quietly observing the aftermath. She hadn't anticipated this level of pandemonium, but she hadn't been entirely surprised either. WineSoft, after all, operated on a different plane of reality.

Max, still buzzing from the unexpected triumph, burst into the office one morning, a manic gleam in his eye. He'd sported a new tie – a vibrant purple number adorned with a whimsical pattern of sleeping cats. "Sophie!" he boomed, his voice echoing through the now-famous office space. "You're a genius! An unsung hero! A...a feline-inspired visionary!"

Sophie, ever the pragmatist, simply raised an eyebrow. "Max, I just organized the data for the presentation."

"Precisely!" he exclaimed, clapping her on the back with such force she nearly lost her balance. "Your organizational skills, your attention to detail, your uncanny ability to keep Dave focused long enough to chart Mittens' nap cycles – it's been nothing short of miraculous! You've earned a promotion!"

Sophie blinked. A promotion? She'd expected maybe a thank you, perhaps a slightly more comfortable chair. A promotion felt... substantial. "Really?" she managed, a slight smile playing on her lips.

"Absolutely!" Max declared. "You're now officially the Head of Strategic
Purr-formance. Your first task? Overseeing the development of 'Project Pawsitive,' our next big thing."

Project Pawsitive? The name itself sounded whimsical, yet Sophie already suspected it would be anything but a straightforward undertaking. Max, ever the master of the cryptic, revealed only that it involved a new line of software designed to improve team collaboration – and, of course, somehow incorporate the wisdom of felines into the design process. Dave, already halfway through sketching a flowchart incorporating different cat breeds and their corresponding work styles, was clearly already onboard.

Lily, though initially skeptical of the entire "Mittens as C.I.O." scenario, now seemed to have accepted the absurdity of it all. She even admitted that the sudden surge in productivity – somehow correlated to Mittens' sleep schedule – was undeniably impressive. She approached Sophie with a knowing smirk. "Congratulations," she said, "Prepare for more chaos. And more cats."

Sophie's new role wasn't just about organizing data or managing projects. It was about navigating the peculiar dynamics of WineSoft, a company where innovation was measured in units of cat naps and brainstorming sessions often involved impromptu wine tastings. She quickly discovered that her quiet competence, once overlooked, was now a valuable asset. She could keep Max's enthusiasm channeled, translate Dave's cat-centric theories into something vaguely comprehensible, and, most importantly, ensure that the company's ongoing foray into feline-inspired software didn't veer too far off course (though 'too far' was a relatively subjective concept at WineSoft).

Project Pawsitive, as it turned out, wasn't just another software project; it was a testament to WineSoft's unique brand of chaos-fueled creativity. Sophie's role involved translating the seemingly random suggestions – "integrate a feature that mimics the soothing purr of a contented feline" or "design the user interface based on the golden ratio of a perfectly curled-up cat" – into functional, even marketable, software features.

This involved countless meetings, each one a peculiar blend of technical discussions and philosophical debates on the merits of different cat breeds as project managers. Dave, naturally, was the champion of this philosophy, having crafted an intricate theory connecting a cat's whisker twitching patterns to software debugging strategies. Max, ever the salesman, presented these theories as revolutionary innovations during client meetings, somehow managing to convince everyone that the integration of feline-inspired algorithms was essential for success.

Sophie, with her nature and surprisingly tolerant spirit, found herself becoming more and more involved. She learned to incorporate the unexpected ideas into the development process, finding a way to translate the absurd into something functional. She learned to value the unexpected insights gleaned from late-night brainstorming sessions, fueled by an excessive amount of caffeine and the strangely inspirational presence of a sleeping Mittens.

The development process was a constant balancing act between pure chaos and remarkable innovation. The team had started incorporating elements of gamification, rewarding users with virtual cat treats for completing tasks and unlocking achievements. They even designed a virtual pet feature that allowed users to adopt their own digital feline companion to keep them company while working. The software became less of a tool and more of an interactive experience, incorporating playful elements that were somehow effective in enhancing productivity and team spirit.

One particularly memorable incident involved a spontaneous "nap time" implemented during a particularly intense period of coding. Max, declaring it a crucial element of "feline-inspired work-life balance," insisted everyone take a 20-minute nap. The initial skepticism was overcome by a surprisingly large number of sleepy developers and, to the team's amazement, resulted in a significant boost in productivity and overall mood.

The final presentation of Project Pawsitive was more of a performance art piece than a typical software demonstration. Max, sporting a new cat-themed bow tie, passionately described the software's features in terms of feline-inspired principles. Dave, dressed in a full cat costume, demonstrated the software's interactive features, playfully mimicking the movements of a cat. Lily, predictably unimpressed but secretly amused, diligently managed the presentation logistics from the sidelines. And Sophie, calm and collected, handled any technical queries with grace and precision.

The board was, to everyone's astonishment, not only impressed but utterly captivated. The unconventional approach, the playful features, the sheer audaciousness of it all, seemed to resonate deeply with the clients. They were impressed by the results and also, apparently, greatly amused by the cat-themed marketing campaign. Project Pawsitive was given the go-ahead, cementing Sophie's role as a key player in WineSoft's increasingly eccentric success.

Sophie, far from being overwhelmed, found a sense of accomplishment in the unpredictable nature of her work. She had not only embraced the chaos, but she had learned to channel it, transforming it into something genuinely innovative and successful. Her quiet competence had found its perfect stage, allowing her to shine in the uniquely unconventional world of WineSoft. And as the company continued its upward trajectory, fueled by a healthy mix of feline-inspired algorithms and sheer, unadulterated craziness, Sophie knew that her journey at WineSoft was only just beginning. The future remained as unpredictable as ever, but she, along with the rest of the team, was prepared to face whatever bizarre challenges and unexpected triumphs awaited them. After all, with Mittens as the Chief Inspiration Officer, anything seemed possible.

Chapter 4: A Toast to Success

The air in the WineSoft office crackled with a celebratory energy, a far cry from the usual controlled chaos. Balloons, inexplicably shaped like various cat breeds, bobbed in the air, adding to the already surreal atmosphere. Tables laden with an impressive array of wines – carefully curated by Max, of course, with a strong emphasis on Merlot – occupied the center of the room. The aroma of grapes and success hung heavy in the air, mingling with the faint scent of catnip that seemed to be perpetually present in WineSoft's unique ecosystem.

The occasion was a company-wide wine tasting, a celebration of the unexpectedly successful launch of Project Pawsitive. It was less a formal event and more a boisterous gathering of eccentric individuals united by a shared experience of navigating the absurdity of feline-inspired software development. Max, resplendent in a new tie – this one featuring a collage of famous paintings reimagined with cats – addressed the team, his voice brimming with uncontainable enthusiasm.

"My friends, my colleagues, my fellow cat-obsessed coding comrades!" he began, raising a glass of ruby-red wine. "Tonight, we celebrate not just a successful project, but a triumph of the spirit! A testament to the power of unconventional thinking, of embracing the unexpected, of...well, mostly cats!"

A wave of laughter rippled through the room. Lily, surprisingly, wasn't rolling her eyes. Instead, she raised her glass with a small, almost imperceptible smile. "To chaos," she proposed, "may it always lead to innovation."

Dave, still sporting remnants of his cat costume from the board presentation, meowed in agreement, much to the amusement of everyone present. Sophie, surrounded by her team, felt a surge of pride. She had initially been nervous about her new role as Head of Strategic Purr-formance, unsure of how to navigate the seemingly random suggestions and even stranger meetings, but the journey had been unexpectedly rewarding.

The wine tasting flowed seamlessly into a series of impromptu speeches, anecdotes, and inside jokes. Max regaled the team with stories of his early interactions with the board, highlighting the moments of bewilderment, laughter, and eventual acceptance that had marked the project's journey. Lily shared her own perspective on the chaos, detailing the various strategies she'd employed to manage the often-unpredictable flow of events, emphasizing the importance of strategic planning amidst the absurdity. Dave, ever the storyteller, recounted the development of his cat-breed-based software debugging theory, weaving in elaborate details about the mystical connection between Siamese cats and efficient code optimization. Sophie, in a moment of quiet reflection, spoke about her journey from a wide-eyed intern to a crucial part of the team, emphasizing the importance of embracing the unexpected and finding the potential within chaos.

As the evening progressed, the conversation shifted from professional accomplishments to personal reflections. Stories emerged about the challenges overcome, the lessons learned, and the unexpected bonds forged in the crucible of feline-inspired software development. One developer recounted how the introduction of "nap time" had not only improved his sleep patterns but also surprisingly boosted his productivity. Another shared a touching anecdote about their cat becoming their unintentional muse during the development process, often inspiring creative solutions with their unique behavior. The experiences shared showcased the team's resilience, their creative spirit, and their ability to find humor and camaraderie even amidst the most outlandish circumstances.

The laughter and camaraderie continued late into the night, fueled by the wine and the shared sense of accomplishment. As the celebratory buzz began to fade, a quiet sense of satisfaction settled over the team. They had accomplished something truly remarkable, not by following traditional methods or adhering to established norms, but by embracing their unique brand of chaos, celebrating individuality, and trusting in the unpredictable power of cat-inspired innovation.

The success of Project Pawsitive wasn't just about the software itself; it was a testament to WineSoft's unconventional approach to work, its ability to foster creativity, and its dedication to building a team that embraced individuality and celebrated the unexpected. The project had redefined the boundaries of what was possible, demonstrating that success could be found in the most unconventional of places, sometimes even inspired by a sleeping cat.

Sophie, as she looked around the room at her colleagues, felt a deep sense of belonging. She had found her place within the quirky ecosystem of WineSoft, a place where her quiet competence was valued, where her pragmatism was balanced by the company's inherent eccentricity. It was a place where chaos reigned, but where that chaos somehow yielded unexpected triumphs.

The next morning, the office was still buzzing, but with a different kind of energy. There was a quiet sense of achievement, a feeling of having weathered a storm and emerged victorious, not despite the chaos, but because of it. The post-celebration cleanup was as unconventional as everything else at WineSoft. Max, armed with a feather duster fashioned from cat toys, led the cleanup efforts, while Dave, wearing a fresh cat costume (a different breed, naturally), assisted with the balloon removal, pausing occasionally to mimic the actions of various cat breeds. Lily supervised, her usual skepticism replaced with a hint of amusement. Sophie, with her typical efficiency, organized the remaining wine bottles, preparing for the next inevitable celebration.

The success of Project Pawsitive had not only cemented WineSoft's position in the market but had also changed the dynamics within the company. It had reinforced the idea that the unconventional approach was not a hindrance, but rather a significant advantage. This realization extended beyond the immediate project and had seeped into the company culture, transforming it into a breeding ground for innovation, creativity, and a uniquely comfortable brand of productive chaos.

As the team settled into their routines, the memories of the celebration and the lessons learned continued to resonate. The shared experiences had strengthened their bonds, fostering a sense of camaraderie and mutual respect that would serve as a foundation for their future endeavors. The success of Project Pawsitive was not just a one-time achievement; it was a catalyst for a new era of innovation at WineSoft, an era where the unexpected was not only accepted but actively celebrated. The future remained as unpredictable as ever, but the team, united by their shared experiences and strengthened by their unconventional triumph, stood ready to face whatever challenges lay ahead, equipped with a healthy dose of feline-inspired wisdom and an unshakeable belief in the power of embracing the unexpected. And somewhere, amidst the keyboards and code, Mittens purred contentedly, the silent, furry architect of their unique success. The journey of WineSoft, it seemed, was far from over.

The post-celebration glow lingered, a shimmering haze over the usually chaotic WineSoft office. The remnants of cat-shaped balloons lay deflated on the floor, a testament to the previous night's festivities. Max, however, was not dwelling on the aftermath of the party. He was, as usual, already several steps ahead, his mind buzzing with new ideas, fueled by the unexpected success of Project Pawsitive and a particularly potent Merlot.

His new philosophy, born from the crucible of feline-inspired software development and validated by the board's surprisingly enthusiastic response, was simple yet revolutionary: embrace the chaos. Not in a reckless, disorganized way, but in a way that harnessed the unique energy of each individual, their quirks, their eccentricities, their sometimes baffling obsessions. He realized that the very things he'd previously tried to control – Dave's cat-themed coding strategies, Lily's perpetually skeptical gaze, even his own impulsive pronouncements – had somehow contributed to their success. They were the ingredients to WineSoft's unique recipe for innovation.

This epiphany didn't lead to a sudden, dramatic shift in Max's personality. He was still Max, undeniably enthusiastic, prone to sudden bursts of inspiration, and always ready with a new, slightly bizarre idea. But there was a subtle change, a newfound appreciation for the unpredictable pathways of creativity. He started delegating more effectively, trusting his team to navigate their own paths to solutions, even if those paths involved elaborate cat-themed analogies or impromptu nap times. He began framing meetings not as rigid structures, but as collaborative brainstorming sessions, allowing the natural flow of conversation to guide the direction of the project.

Lily, initially skeptical of this new "embrace the chaos" approach, found herself surprisingly adapting. She still maintained her spreadsheets and detailed risk assessments, but her approach became less about controlling the chaos and more about navigating it strategically. She started incorporating "chaos buffers" into her project timelines, acknowledging the inherent unpredictability of WineSoft's processes and planning for the inevitable diversions. This surprisingly enhanced her efficiency; by anticipating the disruptions, she could mitigate their impact, ensuring the project remained on track, even amidst the whirlwind of cat-inspired innovations and impromptu wine tastings.

Dave, naturally, thrived in this new environment. His cat-based debugging methods, once considered quirky, became a source of inspiration for the team. He began sharing his "feline code optimization techniques" in team meetings, and his insights, surprisingly, often led to elegant solutions to complex problems. He even managed to develop a program that translated meows into meaningful programming commands—a project that, despite its apparent absurdity, proved surprisingly useful in identifying certain types of coding errors.

Sophie, initially a cautious observer, began to embrace the WineSoft way. She found her voice, her pragmatic approach providing a much-needed counterpoint to the team's often whimsical ideas. She learned to channel the chaos, using her organizational skills to guide the team through the unpredictable currents of Max's inspiration. She even started incorporating cat-themed elements into her presentations, understanding that the unexpected, when cleverly integrated, could be a powerful tool for communication and engagement.

The change wasn't just reflected in their work; it permeated their social interactions. The impromptu wine tastings became more frequent, less about celebrating milestones and more about fostering camaraderie and creativity. These gatherings weren't just about drinking wine; they were brainstorming sessions disguised as parties, where new ideas sprouted amongst laughter and shared anecdotes. They were a testament to Max's newfound understanding that fostering a supportive, creative atmosphere was just as important as achieving project deadlines.

One particularly memorable wine-fueled brainstorming session led to the development of "Project Purrfect Pitch," a revolutionary presentation tool that automatically incorporated cat memes into presentations. Initially met with raised eyebrows, it became an overnight sensation, garnering widespread attention and even securing WineSoft a speaking engagement at a major tech conference.

Another unexpected byproduct of Max's new philosophy was the creation of the "Nap Time Initiative." This initiative, inspired by Dave's observation that a strategic midday nap significantly enhanced his coding efficiency, was initially met with some resistance, but soon proved to be a surprisingly effective way to boost overall team productivity. Designated nap pods were installed in the office, resulting in more alert and creative employees.

The success of these initiatives demonstrated that Max's evolved leadership style wasn't just about embracing the chaos, but also about strategically harnessing the collective energy of the team. He learned to channel the unpredictable nature of their personalities and integrate it into a productive work model. His leadership was less about top-down control and more about fostering a dynamic environment where individuals could thrive, their eccentricities contributing to the company's success.

This newfound harmony wasn't without its moments of controlled chaos. There were still impromptu wine tastings, cat-themed costume contests, and the occasional outburst of feline-inspired inspiration. But these were no longer viewed as distractions but as integral parts of WineSoft's unique and highly successful work culture.

The transformation of WineSoft wasn't just about better software; it was about creating a workplace where individuality was celebrated, where quirks were seen as assets, and where the unexpected was not just tolerated but actively embraced. It was a testament to the power of a leader who learned to harness the chaos, transforming it into a force for innovation and a breeding ground for success.

The success of Project Pawsitive had sparked a chain reaction, shifting WineSoft from a quirky startup struggling to find its niche into a thriving company that defied expectations and redefined the very essence of workplace innovation. Max's evolution as a leader, his embrace of the unexpected, and his recognition of the value of each team member's individuality had turned WineSoft into a true testament to the power of embracing the chaos. And as the next project loomed on the horizon – a revolutionary new app that translated dog barks into human language – the team, armed with their newfound philosophy and a healthy supply of Merlot, felt ready for anything. After all, they had proven that even the most eccentric ideas, when nurtured with passion and a dash of feline-inspired magic, could lead to extraordinary success. The future of WineSoft, fueled by a healthy dose of chaos and a whole lot of heart, was looking brighter than ever.

Lily adjusted her glasses, the faint scent of Merlot still clinging to her crisp white blouse. The post-Project Pawsitive celebrations had left a lingering aura of controlled chaos in their wake, a testament to WineSoft's unique brand of success. While Max reveled in the newfound validation of his "embrace the chaos" philosophy, Lily, ever the pragmatist, was quietly processing the implications of this radical shift in their work culture.

Initially, the idea had seemed absurd. Chaos? In *her* HR department? It was an oxymoron, a contradiction of terms. Her carefully constructed spreadsheets, crafted risk assessments, and precisely timed project timelines were all built on the foundation of order and predictability. Max's sudden embrace of randomness had felt like a seismic shift, threatening to unravel the very fabric of her organized world.

But witnessing the team's unexpected triumph, she couldn't deny the undeniable results. Project Pawsitive, born from a bizarre blend of feline analogies and impulsive coding sprints, had not only exceeded expectations but had secured WineSoft a place at the forefront of a newly defined market segment. The success wasn't just about the software; it was about the process, the unconventional approach, the very chaos Max had so enthusiastically championed.

This realization didn't mean Lily surrendered her organizational skills. Instead, she began to view them as a strategic tool for navigating the unpredictable currents of WineSoft's creative process. She didn't fight the chaos; she learned to dance with it. Her organized spreadsheets now incorporated "chaos buffers," contingency plans designed to absorb the inevitable deviations from the original project timelines. These weren't merely safety nets; they were proactive measures, acknowledging the inherent unpredictability of their workflow and anticipating the potential disruptions.

Her approach to risk assessment also evolved. Instead of trying to eliminate all risks, she began to categorize them, prioritizing the truly critical threats while accepting the inevitability of smaller, less consequential setbacks. These minor disruptions, she discovered, often led to unexpected breakthroughs, spurring innovation and creativity in ways that traditional project management techniques couldn't replicate.

This wasn't simply a matter of adapting to Max's unconventional management style; it was a conscious shift in Lily's perspective. She began to appreciate the unique creative energy that thrived within the seemingly chaotic environment. Dave's cat-themed debugging methods, once a source of frustration, now became a source of amusement and occasional enlightenment. His insights, though often delivered through the prism of feline analogies, proved remarkably effective in identifying and solving complex coding problems. Lily found herself actually soliciting Dave's input, recognizing the value of his unconventional approach.

Sophie, the ever-observant intern, also played a key role in Lily's evolving understanding of the WineSoft methodology. Sophie's methodical nature provided a valuable counterpoint to the team's often whimsical ideas, her pragmatic approach serving as a crucial anchor in the storm of creative energy. Lily learned from Sophie's ability to channel the chaos, using her organizational skills to steer the team through the most turbulent periods. Sophie's influence helped Lily understand that the unexpected, when properly managed, could be a powerful catalyst for innovation.

Lily started experimenting with new management techniques, incorporating elements of agile methodology and collaborative brainstorming into her approach. She discovered that fostering open communication and encouraging the free flow of ideas, even if they seemed outlandish at first glance, led to a more dynamic and productive work environment. She started organizing "creative chaos sessions," dedicated brainstorming sessions that encouraged the team to explore unconventional ideas without the constraints of rigid structure or pre-defined expectations.

These sessions often took place during the now-regular impromptu wine tastings, a blend of professional collaboration and social bonding that had become a defining feature of WineSoft's culture. Lily found herself increasingly participating in these events, not just as an observer but as an active participant, contributing her insights and perspective, even offering suggestions fueled by a surprising taste for Merlot.

The initial skepticism she harbored toward Max's "embrace the chaos" philosophy gradually faded, replaced by a grudging admiration for its effectiveness. She realized that control, in its traditional sense, wasn't the enemy of productivity; it was the rigid adherence to outdated methodologies that stifled creativity and innovation. WineSoft's success proved that a well-managed chaos, carefully nurtured and strategically guided, could be a powerful engine of growth and progress.

The transformation wasn't immediate or without its bumps in the road. There were still moments of controlled pandemonium, impulsive coding sprints, and the occasional feline-related diversion. But these were no longer perceived as disruptions; they were integral parts of WineSoft's evolving ecosystem. Lily had learned to integrate them into her strategies, anticipating their occurrence and planning for their inevitable impact.

Lily's evolution wasn't merely about adapting to the company's unique culture; it was about redefining her own approach to management. She had transitioned from a organizer striving for perfect control to a strategic navigator, guiding the team through the unpredictable currents of creative chaos while ensuring that they remained focused on their goals. She had learned to appreciate the value of individuality, the power of unconventional ideas, and the surprising benefits of a well-managed dose of unpredictability.

The success of WineSoft, she realized, wasn't just about the software they produced but about the way they produced it. It was a testament to the power of embracing individuality, fostering collaboration, and recognizing the value of a well-managed chaos. And as Lily raised her glass during the next impromptu wine tasting, she offered a toast not just to Project Pawsitive's success but to the surprising, and ultimately rewarding, journey of navigating the unpredictable world of WineSoft. The future, she knew, held more challenges, more chaotic adventures, and, undoubtedly, more impromptu wine tastings. But armed with her newfound perspective, and a healthy dose of Merlot, Lily felt ready to embrace whatever WineSoft's unique brand of creative chaos had in store. The spreadsheets were still maintained, but the margins now included space for the unexpected – and that, Lily realized, was the key to WineSoft's continued success. The chaos, it seemed, was here to stay, and Lily, finally, was ready to embrace it.

The celebratory buzz from Project Pawsitive's success hadn't quite faded when a new, equally bizarre, development unfolded. It began, as many momentous occasions in WineSoft's history did, with Dave. Dave, whose coding prowess was often overshadowed by his unwavering dedication to Mittens, his ginger tabby, was staring intently at his laptop screen, a low hum of contented purring emanating from his lap. This wasn't the usual pre-coffee, pre-caffeinated code-induced stupor; this was something... different. A manic, almost gleeful energy pulsed around him, a stark contrast to his normally placid demeanor.

Lily, ever observant, noticed the change. She approached his desk cautiously, her newly acquired appreciation for "controlled chaos" tempering her usual impulse to impose order. Dave, oblivious to her presence, was frantically typing, occasionally breaking into fits of laughter, punctuated by Mittens' contented meows. He was muttering about "brand synergy," "viral marketing," and "catnip-infused software updates," a linguistic cocktail that usually signaled trouble, but this time, Lily felt a strange sense of anticipation.

"Dave," she said, her voice a gentle interruption to the digital symphony unfolding before her, "are you... alright?"

He looked up, his eyes wide with excitement. "Lily! You won't believe this! Mittens has... she's... she's signed a contract!"

Lily blinked, momentarily stunned. "A contract? Mittens?"

Dave nodded vigorously, producing a glossy document from his desk drawer. "A major endorsement deal! With Purrfectly Polished Paws, the leading organic cat food company. They saw Mittens' Instagram – the one with her reviewing the beta version of Project Pawsitive, you know, the one where she's wearing the tiny WineSoft hat?"

Lily vaguely recalled the image. Mittens, indeed, had looked remarkably pleased with herself while sporting a miniature WineSoft branded beanie, a moment that had been swiftly circulated within the team – and beyond. It was a testament to Mittens' inherent photogenic qualities and Dave's masterful social media skills.

The contract itself was a marvel of legal jargon interspersed with images of Mittens in various adorable poses. It detailed a comprehensive marketing campaign, including social media appearances, product endorsements, and even a potential line of Mittens-themed merchandise. The financial figures were surprisingly substantial – enough to significantly boost WineSoft's bottom line and alleviate any lingering anxieties about future funding.

Max, upon hearing the news, promptly declared a company-wide celebration – involving, unsurprisingly, a considerable amount of wine. He envisioned Mittens as WineSoft's official mascot, a feline figurehead embodying the company's unique brand of quirky innovation. He even floated the idea of developing a new software feature, "Mittens' Meow-tivation Meter," a productivity tool supposedly based on Mittens' daily mood swings. Lily, while initially skeptical, found herself strangely amused by the idea. Her spreadsheets could accommodate even this level of unexpected development.

The Purrfectly Polished Paws campaign was a resounding success. Mittens' Instagram following exploded, her endorsements driving a significant increase in sales for the cat food company. The WineSoft brand was inextricably linked with her, gaining unexpected publicity and reinforcing their image as a fun, innovative, and slightly offbeat company. The "Mittens' Meow-tivation Meter," despite its initially questionable practicality, became a surprisingly popular feature, offering a dose of playful chaos to the otherwise mundane aspects of project management.

Sophie, always in her observations, noted a shift in Dave's demeanor. He seemed more confident, less preoccupied with coding issues, and remarkably more engaged in team collaborations. The financial security afforded by Mittens' endorsement had eased his personal anxieties, freeing him to contribute more fully to the company's projects.

Even the board of directors, initially perplexed by the unconventional nature of WineSoft's marketing strategies, found themselves charmed by Mittens' undeniable appeal. They praised the creative use of social media, the innovative brand alignment, and the remarkably effective impact on company image and sales. The initial bewilderment at their investment in a company that seemed to run on wine and feline-inspired inspiration had completely dissipated, replaced by a quiet awe at the unexpected success of their strategy.

Dave's success wasn't just about Mittens' endorsement deal; it was a testament to the unexpected opportunities that could arise from embracing the unconventional. His dedication to his cat, once seen as a distraction, became WineSoft's unlikely secret weapon. The company's continued success proved that embracing individuality and unconventional approaches could lead to remarkable results.

Meanwhile, Mittens herself remained remarkably unfazed by her newfound fame. She continued to nap on Dave's lap during coding sessions, occasionally interrupting his work with a well-timed meow, a reminder that even in the most chaotic of work environments, there's always time for a well-deserved catnap. The only significant change in her routine was the slightly upgraded brand of organic cat food, a small price to pay for the added bonus of fueling WineSoft's continued, chaotic success. Her contract negotiations for the next year, Dave mused, might require a slightly more robust negotiating team. Perhaps a small army of highly caffeinated interns could be persuaded to help. After all, even in a company as unpredictable as WineSoft, strategic planning was always crucial, even when the primary player was a ginger tabby with a surprisingly lucrative endorsement deal.

The financial windfall from Mittens' contract created a sense of optimism and stability within WineSoft. The team, emboldened by their recent successes and the unexpected influx of cash, embarked on new projects with renewed energy and creativity. They were no longer merely surviving; they were thriving, fueled by a blend of wine, feline inspiration, and a healthy dose of controlled chaos. The future, for WineSoft, seemed brighter than ever before, painted in shades of ginger fur and Merlot. And Lily, armed with her spreadsheets and a newly acquired taste for unexpected triumphs, was ready to navigate the exciting, unpredictable journey ahead. The chaos, it seemed, was not only manageable, but also quite profitable. Who knew that the key to success in the software industry could be found nestled on a developer's lap?

The air in WineSoft crackled with a different kind of energy after the Mittens mania subsided. It wasn't the frantic, caffeine-fueled chaos of a looming deadline, nor the quiet hum of focused coding; it was a quieter, more confident buzz. This was the sound of success, tinged with the faint aroma of expensive organic cat food. And at the center of this newly found calm was Sophie.

Sophie, who had arrived at WineSoft as a wide-eyed intern, navigating the treacherous waters of Max's unpredictable leadership and Dave's cat-centric coding habits, had blossomed.

She'd witnessed firsthand the absurdity of their processes, the unexpected triumphs, and the surprisingly effective, if unconventional, approach to software development. She'd learned to decipher Max's rambling pronouncements, anticipate Dave's sudden bursts of Mittens-inspired innovation, and even, somewhat reluctantly, to appreciate the strategic brilliance of Lily's spreadsheet-based world domination plans.

Her initial nervousness had given way to a quiet competence, a sharp wit that complemented her nature. She had not only absorbed the chaotic energy of WineSoft but had learned to channel it, using her organizational skills to tame the wild currents of their projects. She'd gone from documenting their coding blunders to proactively anticipating potential problems, becoming an invaluable asset to the team. She was no longer just taking notes; she was shaping the narrative of WineSoft's success.

Her transformation wasn't merely professional; it was deeply personal. She'd discovered a confidence she never knew she possessed, a resilience honed by navigating the uniquely challenging terrain of WineSoft's office culture. She'd learned to laugh at the absurd, to embrace the unexpected, and to find joy in the collaborative spirit, however chaotic it might be. The internship had taught her far more than the intricacies of software development; it had taught her about herself.

Max, noticing her growth, had been unusually thoughtful in his pronouncements. He'd initially viewed her as a fresh source of caffeine-fueled enthusiasm, someone to fetch him increasingly obscure varieties of wine. But as he watched her navigate the whirlwind of their projects, her quiet competence shone through. He had started delegating more responsibility, tasks that went far beyond fetching wine – even though he still needed his Pinot Noir.

He'd begun to confide in her, sharing his (often grandiose) vision for the future of WineSoft, his plans for world domination, not through ruthless business tactics, but through the power of oddly specific software features and the occasional well-placed cat video. He respected her attention to detail, her ability to organize his often chaotic ideas into something resembling a coherent plan. He saw in her a reflection of WineSoft itself – a blend of organization and uncontrolled creative chaos.

Lily, ever pragmatic, saw Sophie's potential early on. While she initially focused on the intern's procedural compliance, she soon recognized Sophie's exceptional analytical skills and her surprisingly perceptive understanding of the dynamics within the team. Lily had mentored Sophie subtly, sharing her own insights into managing chaos, offering quiet guidance through the minefield of Max's pronouncements, and subtly showcasing the art of spreadsheet-based problem-solving. Sophie was a blank canvas, perfect for Lily to subtly imprint her own strategies onto, ensuring the continued smooth functioning of their world, even if their world was a slightly more chaotic iteration of office life.

Dave, initially focused on Mittens' ongoing media empire, gradually realized Sophie's capabilities. He'd witnessed her navigate the complexities of his sometimes convoluted code explanations, patiently untangling the knots of his explanations. He found a newfound respect for her quiet efficiency, a contrast to his own often erratic coding style. He'd even started seeking her input, asking for her insights on his more ambitious project ideas – which often involved Mittens in some way, shape, or form. He valued her ability to approach his ideas with a calm, logical mind, able to discern the gems hidden within the chaos of his visions. He appreciated a fresh perspective, one that wasn't clouded by a lifetime of cat-centric brainstorming.

The board of directors, having witnessed the remarkable success of the Mittens campaign, were keen to see what WineSoft would achieve next. They'd scheduled a meeting, not just to review the latest financials, but to gauge the company's future trajectory. The unexpected success of a cat-endorsed software program had piqued their interest; they were now fully invested in the "WineSoft Method" – an approach that defied convention at every turn.

The meeting was, predictably, a blend of strategic presentations and spontaneous outbursts of creative enthusiasm. Max, brimming with his usual exuberance, outlined his ambitious plans, while Lily provided the necessary grounding with crafted spreadsheets detailing their projected growth. Dave, somewhat reluctantly, presented the current status of Mittens' endorsement deals, hinting at potential collaborations with other high-profile pets (a proposition that met with a surprising amount of enthusiasm from the board).

But it was Sophie who stole the show. She presented her analysis of their past projects, identifying patterns of success amidst the chaos, highlighting the strengths of each team member, and proposing a structured approach to managing their future endeavors. She spoke with clarity, confidence, and a touch of quiet humor that resonated with the board. She didn't shy away from the absurdities of their methods; instead, she embraced them, showcasing how their unique approach had led to unexpected achievements.

The board members were impressed not just by WineSoft's results, but by the dynamic of the team. They recognized the value of the company's peculiar synergy, the way in which seemingly disparate individuals had found a way to work together, creating something truly unique. Sophie's presentation solidified this perception. She was not just an employee; she was the embodiment of WineSoft's success – a testament to the power of embracing individuality and finding strength in controlled chaos.

Following the meeting, Sophie received a promotion. No longer just an intern, she was now a full-fledged member of the WineSoft team, taking on a leadership role. She was tasked with streamlining their processes, helping to bridge the gap between Max's visionary ideas and Dave's cat-inspired coding. She was given the freedom to implement her own systems, combining her nature with her newfound understanding of the WineSoft ethos.

Her bright future was not just a promise; it was a reflection of her hard work, her adaptability, and her ability to thrive in the unique environment of WineSoft. She had not only survived the chaos; she had learned to harness its power, turning it into a source of innovation and success. And as she looked towards the future, she knew that the journey would continue to be unpredictable, filled with laughter, unexpected challenges, and the occasional well-timed cat-related marketing campaign. But she was ready. She was a WineSofter, through and through. And she wouldn't have it any other way. The success of WineSoft was a testament to the fact that sometimes, the best way to navigate the complex world of software development was to embrace the madness, to welcome the chaos, and perhaps, to let a ginger cat lead the way. The future, painted in shades of ginger fur, Merlot, and a healthy dose of perfectly organized chaos, looked remarkably bright.

Chapter 5: The Grapevine Grows

The board meeting's afterglow shimmered through WineSoft like a particularly potent vintage. The air, usually thick with the scent of instant coffee and Max's questionable cologne choices, now carried a subtle undercurrent of triumph. Sophie, newly promoted and radiating a quiet confidence that belied her recent intern status, was already sketching out plans for the future – plans that involved less cat-related marketing, though not entirely devoid of it. Mittens, lounging regally on Dave's keyboard, seemed to approve.

Max, basking in the reflected glory, bounced on the balls of his feet, a whirlwind of barely contained energy. "Right then!" he boomed, his voice echoing off the surprisingly minimalist office walls (a recent Lily-inspired improvement). "Now that we've conquered the world of feline-themed software... well, almost conquered it... what's next?"

His eyes gleamed with a manic brilliance, a glint that usually preceded a particularly ambitious – and often completely nonsensical – idea. Lily, ever the pragmatist, took a long, slow sip of her tea, her expression a carefully constructed mask of professional amusement. Dave, meanwhile, was engrossed in a complex game of catnip-induced hide-and-seek with Mittens, a game of strategy far more engaging than any software design meeting.

"Max," Lily began, her voice calm yet firm, "before we embark on another potentially world-altering, cat-related software initiative, perhaps we should consider a more... diversified approach. We need a strategic plan for expansion, a well-defined roadmap..."

"Roadmap?" Max interrupted, his enthusiasm undampened. "Lily, darling, we are WineSoft! We don't need roadmaps! We chart our own course! We are the navigators, the pioneers, the... the..." he trailed off, searching for a suitably grandiose adjective. "The... purveyors of pixelated perfection!"

Sophie, ever the diplomat, stepped in. "I think Lily's suggesting a structured approach to expanding our product line, Max. A way to leverage our recent success and explore new avenues of innovation. Perhaps based on the data analysis I presented to the board?"

Max, distracted by a particularly alluring stain on his tie, considered this. "Data analysis... you mean numbers? Ugh. Numbers are so... linear. Where's the fun in linear?" He sighed dramatically. "Fine, Sophie. Data-driven expansion. But it must be... exciting! It must involve... flair!"

Thus began the brainstorming session of the century, a whirlwind of half-baked ideas, wild tangents, and the occasional existential crisis brought on by an unexpectedly challenging Excel formula. Lily, armed with her trusty spreadsheet, attempted to corral the chaos, assigning points for feasibility, market potential, and the sheer degree of absurdity involved.

Dave, occasionally surfacing from his game of catnip hide-and-seek, offered up suggestions that invariably involved Mittens in some capacity. "A software that translates meows into human language? Imagine the market potential!" he exclaimed, his eyes shining with the fervor of a true believer. Lily marked this one down as "highly improbable, bordering on the impossible."

Sophie, armed with her newfound authority, steered the conversation, gently guiding Max's extravagant suggestions towards a slightly more realistic – yet still surprisingly off-the-wall – direction. Their initial ideas were… unique.

"Wine Pairing Assistant 3000": This software, Max insisted, would not only suggest wine pairings for food but would also analyze one's emotional state via webcam and select the perfect wine to match their mood. "Think of the possibilities!" he enthused. "A Merlot for melancholy, a Sauvignon Blanc for sassy!" Lily, ever cautious, pointed out the potential privacy concerns. The marketing team, however, was already brainstorming slogan ideas.

"Dream Weaver 5.0": This ambitious project, envisioned by Dave (with significant input from Mittens, according to Dave), aimed to create a software that could record, analyze, and interpret dreams. The results, he promised, would unlock hidden creative potentials and lead to breakthroughs in various fields, from software development to feline behavior analysis. The team spent a good hour debating the ethics of dream harvesting.

"The Sentient Spreadsheet": Lily's brainchild, and surprisingly, not as absurd as it sounded. This spreadsheet, using advanced AI, would predict market trends with unnerving accuracy, essentially doing her job for her. It was met with mixed reactions. Max felt it lacked flair, Dave saw it as a threat to Mittens' dominance, while Sophie viewed it with cautious admiration. It was quickly filed under 'worth exploring'.

"Code-O-Matic 2000": Dave's second attempt at a less Mittens-centric project. It promised to automatically generate code based on natural language instructions. While potentially useful, the team was concerned about the possible consequences of creating self-aware AI code, especially if it were influenced by catnip-induced inspiration.

After several hours of brainstorming that resembled a particularly chaotic jazz improvisation, they had a shortlist of potential projects. They were all quirky, undeniably ambitious, and potentially revolutionary – in their own uniquely WineSoft way. The question now was: which one to pursue first?

This was where Sophie's strategic thinking really shone. She analyzed the market potential, the feasibility of each project, and – most importantly – their potential for generating viral buzz. Her presentation, a masterclass in controlled chaos, presented a balanced portfolio of projects, strategically aiming for a phased launch. She recommended starting with "Wine Pairing Assistant 3000," followed by "The Sentient Spreadsheet," while prioritizing the more futuristic projects for later development.

Max, initially hesitant about any structure, was charmed by her thoughtful presentation and the inclusion of colorful charts and graphs that resembled modern art. Dave, ever loyal to Mittens' vision, accepted the compromise. Lily, who found solace in the intricate formulas that underpinned Sophie's plan, gave her a subtle nod of approval.

The decision was made, the plans were set, and WineSoft, armed with its peculiar blend of chaos and brilliance, embarked on its next adventure. The future of software development was no longer a predictable path but a wild, wine-soaked ride, with a ginger cat at the helm and a team of wonderfully unconventional individuals making sense of it all. And the best part? They wouldn't have it any other way. The grapevine, after all, had a lot more to grow. And with WineSoft, it would undoubtedly grow in the most delightfully unexpected ways.

The initial success of the feline-themed software, while undeniably bizarre, had inadvertently forged a new sense of camaraderie within WineSoft. The shared experience of near-disaster-turned-triumph had somehow smoothed the usual rough edges of their chaotic work dynamic. Lily, surprisingly, found herself less inclined to suppress Max's outlandish ideas;

she now approached them with a cautious curiosity, seeing the potential for unexpected genius lurking beneath the surface of his pronouncements. Dave, emboldened by the board's unexpected acceptance of Mittens' influence, began to explore more serious software projects, though his feline companion remained his constant source of inspiration. And Sophie, no longer the wide-eyed intern, had blossomed into a confident project manager, effectively mediating between Max's flights of fancy and Lily's pragmatic approach.

The first challenge of their newfound success was, ironically, managing the success itself. The sudden surge in media attention, largely focused on the "cat-themed software incident" (as the press charmingly dubbed it), presented a double-edged sword. While it boosted WineSoft's profile, it also attracted the unwanted attention of larger, more established tech companies. Whispers of potential acquisitions and hostile takeovers began to circulate – the corporate grapevine, far more sinister than WineSoft's jovial version, started to buzz with ominous predictions.

"We need to protect our unique identity," Lily stated during one of their less chaotic meetings, a rare occurrence that left Max visibly unsettled. He found the lack of spontaneous outbursts unnerving. "If we get swallowed by a mega-corp, WineSoft will become just another cog in the machine, and Mittens will lose his influence." Dave nodded solemnly.

Sophie, ever the strategist, proposed a counter-strategy: expand WineSoft's product line aggressively, solidifying their position in the market before any potential takeover could happen. This would require a more structured approach than their usual freewheeling style, a challenge that Max initially resisted with his customary theatrical flair.

"Structured? Sophie, my dear, structure is the antithesis of innovation! It's the death knell of creativity! We must embrace the chaos!" He declared, flinging his arms wide in a dramatic gesture that nearly sent a stack of precariously balanced wine glasses tumbling to the floor.

Lily, displaying unexpected patience, calmly explained the need to balance their eccentric creativity with a sound business strategy. She proposed a phased approach, starting with projects that built on their recent success, before venturing into more ambitious, and potentially riskier, ventures. This, she argued, would allow them to solidify their financial base while simultaneously showcasing their unique brand of innovative chaos.

Dave, ever the pragmatist underneath the cat-loving exterior, surprisingly supported Lily's plan. He pointed out the need for a steady income stream to fund their more ambitious projects, projects that inevitably involved Mittens in some capacity, of course. His latest idea, "Mittens' Meowsical Maestro," a software that composed music based on Mittens' meows, was considered "highly creative, but commercially questionable." It was, nevertheless, given a tentative place on the back burner.

Sophie, using her newfound skills in strategic planning and data analysis (skills surprisingly gained from navigating Max's chaotic brainstorming sessions), devised a plan that incorporated both their quirky innovations and a solid business model. The initial phase focused on expanding the "Wine Pairing Assistant 3000," which, after addressing the privacy concerns and adding a few more "flair-driven" features (suggested by Max, naturally), proved unexpectedly popular. This initial success provided a strong financial footing for the next phase, which involved the development of "The Sentient Spreadsheet."

The creation of the Sentient Spreadsheet, Lily's brainchild, proved to be a fascinating blend of technological prowess and unexpected comedic moments. The initial programming, surprisingly accurate in its market predictions, soon developed an unnerving level of independence. It began suggesting wine pairings based on complex algorithmic interpretations of global market trends, a phenomenon that baffled even Lily. One particular instance involved the spreadsheet recommending a full-bodied Cabernet Sauvignon to counteract the negative impact of a sudden drop in the price of catnip.

Max, naturally, saw this as a stroke of genius. "See, Lily? Even a spreadsheet can appreciate the value of a good wine!" he exclaimed, while Dave spent an hour trying to convince Mittens to "collaborate" with the spreadsheet. Mittens, understandably unimpressed, merely yawned and went back to sleep on Dave's keyboard.

The success of the Wine Pairing Assistant and the increasingly accurate (and somewhat unnerving) predictions of the Sentient Spreadsheet attracted the attention of several venture capitalists. WineSoft, once a small, chaotic startup on the brink of disaster, was now in a position to negotiate terms on its own terms. They secured funding that allowed them to move on to more ambitious projects, including a slightly toned-down version of Dave's "Dream Weaver 5.0" and a highly stylized version of "Code-O-Matic 2000," which incorporated the spreadsheet's predictive capabilities and, of course, had to include a small feature acknowledging Mittens' "creative contributions."

The team learned to navigate the treacherous waters of the corporate world while retaining their unique brand of chaos-fueled innovation. They discovered that their unconventional approach, initially a liability, had become their greatest strength. The board meetings were still a little unpredictable, often punctuated by Max's impromptu wine tastings and Mittens' occasional cameo appearances, but they were now meetings driven by a shared sense of purpose, and a healthy dose of shared laughter. The grapevine continued to grow, but now, it was a grapevine nurtured and controlled by the wonderfully unconventional team at WineSoft. Their journey, a testament to the power of embracing individuality and celebrating even the most absurd of ideas, was just beginning. The future of

WineSoft, and perhaps even the future of software development, seemed delightfully unpredictable, a wine-soaked, cat-influenced adventure with no clear destination, but a whole lot of fun along the way.

The initial wave of success, fueled by the unexpected triumph of their feline-inspired software, had not only boosted WineSoft's profile but had also subtly reshaped the team's internal dynamics. The shared experience of navigating a near-catastrophe, culminating in unexpected acclaim, acted as an invisible glue, solidifying the bonds between the previously disparate personalities. Max, usually the epicenter of chaotic energy, found himself strangely subdued, a quiet contentment replacing his usual boisterous pronouncements. He even started leaving his prized collection of wine glasses undisturbed, a testament to the calming effect of shared success.

Lily, the pragmatic HR manager, discovered a surprising tolerance for Max's eccentricities. While she still maintained her role as the voice of reason, a subtle undercurrent of amusement now colored her interactions with him. She found herself less inclined to quash his ideas entirely, instead choosing to channel his boundless energy into more productive (or at least, less disastrous) directions. She began to see the value in his wild, often nonsensical pronouncements, recognizing the kernel of genius that occasionally resided amidst the chaos. It was a gradual shift, a slow thawing of the previously frosty relationship, marked by shared laughter and the occasional, grudging admiration.

Dave, the enigmatic developer whose primary focus had previously been his cat, Mittens' Instagram account, experienced a remarkable transformation. The unexpected validation of Mittens' influence on their software had unlocked a new level of confidence in his abilities. He began to take on more ambitious projects, while still maintaining his feline companion as his muse. Mittens, ever the astute observer of human endeavors, seemed to approve of this development, choosing to supervise Dave's coding sessions from his usual perch atop the monitor. His meows, once mere background noise, now seemed to take on a subtle rhythm, a silent commentary on the quality of Dave's code.

Sophie, the previously wide-eyed intern, had fully bloomed into a confident project manager, her organizational skills honed by years of navigating Max's unpredictable outbursts. She had learned to anticipate his flights of fancy, channeling his creativity into tangible results. Her ability to mediate between Max's whimsical ideas and Lily's pragmatic approach proved invaluable. She became the linchpin of the team, the silent orchestrator of the controlled chaos that was WineSoft's unique brand of innovation.

Their newfound harmony, however, was not without its challenges. The success of the cat-themed software had attracted unwanted attention. Larger tech companies, sniffing out a potentially lucrative acquisition, started circling like vultures. Whispers of hostile takeovers and corporate espionage filled the air, a stark contrast to the usual lighthearted banter that characterized WineSoft's internal communication.

The team realized that their unique identity, the very source of their success, was now at risk. They needed a strategy to protect their unconventional approach, to solidify their position in the market before being absorbed into the sterile world of corporate giants. This realization prompted a series of intense, yet strangely productive, brainstorming sessions. Max, surprisingly, took on a more collaborative role, his ideas still outlandish but tempered by a newfound appreciation for strategic planning.

Lily, armed with a mountain of data and a surprisingly effective PowerPoint presentation, laid out a plan for aggressive expansion, focusing on projects that capitalized on their recent success while simultaneously showcasing their unique brand of innovation. She proposed a phased approach, starting with projects that built upon their existing infrastructure, gradually introducing more ambitious, and potentially riskier, ventures.

Dave, ever the pragmatist, focused on securing a stable financial footing, ensuring that their ambitious projects were not hampered by a lack of resources. He even managed to secure a small grant for research into "feline-assisted software development," a proposal that initially raised eyebrows but eventually gained acceptance. Mittens, naturally, was appointed chief consultant.

Sophie, acting as the team's strategist, devised a master plan that weaved together their creative impulses with a solid business model. The plan involved expanding the "Wine Pairing Assistant 3000," addressing privacy concerns and incorporating additional, "flair-driven" features suggested by Max. The updated version proved remarkably successful, solidifying their position in the market and generating the financial resources required for more ambitious projects.

The next phase involved the development of the "Sentient Spreadsheet," a project born from Lily's desire to combine data analysis with a touch of whimsical unpredictability. The spreadsheet, initially designed for market prediction, developed a disturbingly independent personality. It started making wine recommendations based on complex algorithmic interpretations of global market trends, and its predictions were unnervingly accurate. One instance involved recommending a full-bodied Cabernet Sauvignon to mitigate the negative impact of a sudden drop in the price of catnip. This event, far from being a disaster, became a testament to the team's unique ability to turn chaos into opportunity.

Max, of course, saw this as a stroke of genius. Dave, ever the devoted cat-owner, attempted to engage Mittens in a collaboration with the spreadsheet. Mittens, unimpressed, merely yawned and resumed his nap on Dave's keyboard.

The success of the "Wine Pairing Assistant 3000" and the "Sentient Spreadsheet," coupled with their improved team dynamics, attracted the attention of several venture capitalists. WineSoft, once a quirky startup teetering on the brink of collapse, was now in a position to dictate its own terms. They secured funding that allowed them to pursue more ambitious projects, projects that incorporated both their unique brand of chaos and a well-defined business strategy.

The grapevine, once a source of anxiety, now served as a testament to their remarkable transformation. It buzzed with news of their success, their unconventional approach becoming their greatest strength. The team's journey had not only strengthened their bonds but also redefined the very notion of success within the software industry. Their story, a delightful blend of chaos and innovation, demonstrated that embracing individuality and celebrating the absurd could lead to unexpected triumphs. The future of WineSoft, still a little unpredictable, promised to be a thrilling, wine-soaked adventure.

The unexpected success of the "Sentient Spreadsheet," a program that somehow managed to predict market trends while dispensing unsolicited (but surprisingly accurate) wine recommendations, solidified WineSoft's position as a force to be reckoned with. Venture capitalists, initially hesitant about investing in a company whose primary mascot was a ginger tabby cat, now clamored for a piece of the action. Max, still prone to bursts of unpredictable genius, found himself fielding calls from investors who seemed oddly fascinated by his pronouncements on the correlation between Merlot and the fluctuating price of Bitcoin.

Lily, ever the pragmatist, negotiated the terms of these lucrative deals, ensuring that WineSoft retained its creative freedom while securing the financial resources necessary for their ambitious future endeavors. Her spreadsheets, far less sentient than their namesake, were vital in navigating the complex world of venture capital, ensuring that WineSoft retained its unique identity while achieving financial stability. She even managed to convince the investors to allocate a significant portion of the funding to a new initiative: "Employee Wellness Through Wine Therapy," a program that involved weekly wine tastings led by a certified sommelier (who, coincidentally, happened to be Lily's cousin).

Dave, emboldened by his newfound confidence (and Mittens' unwavering support), embarked on a series of ambitious projects, each one more eccentric than the last. He developed a "Mood-Based Code Generator," which produced lines of code reflective of his current emotional state. The results, predictably, were a chaotic blend of elegant algorithms and nonsensical gibberish, but surprisingly, it worked – often. Mittens, ever the critical observer, continued his supervision from his keyboard perch, occasionally batting at errant keys with his paw, a unique form of feline code review. His Instagram following continued to explode, his captions, mysteriously updated by Dave, becoming cryptic yet insightful commentaries on the software

development process. One particularly cryptic caption read: "The meow-tivation is
high, but the bugs are multiplying. SoftwareLife FelineCodeReview PurrfectlyImperfect".

Sophie, now a seasoned project manager, proved instrumental in keeping the team focused amidst the growing chaos. She implemented a color-coded system to track the progress of different projects, assigning each a specific shade of wine-related hue – a strategy that somehow kept everyone on track. Red represented high-priority tasks, white signified projects in their early stages, and rosé served as a delicate balance between the two. The system was, by all accounts, utterly illogical, yet it functioned with surprising efficiency.

The office environment, once a breeding ground for spontaneous wine tastings and impromptu brainstorming sessions, evolved into a structured but equally unconventional workspace. Teams, or rather, "Wine-flavored Project Pods," were assembled based on personality compatibility and preferred varietal. The "Cabernet Sauvignon Crew" focused on high-stakes, high-pressure projects, while the "Riesling Ramblers" tackled more creative, experimental endeavors. The "Pinot Noir Ponderers" spent most of their time debating the merits of various types of cheese pairings, but surprisingly, produced some of WineSoft's most innovative solutions. The division was primarily for fun, but it improved team cohesion through a shared appreciation of the finer things in life – namely, excellent wine and lively debate.

The company culture, once defined by its chaotic unpredictability, became a source of its own success. Competitors, struggling to replicate WineSoft's unique blend of creative chaos and strategic planning, found themselves lagging behind. WineSoft's unorthodox methodology, once a liability, had become its greatest strength, a testament to the power of embracing individuality in the corporate world.

The "Grapevine," the unofficial communication channel within WineSoft, buzzed with tales of their success. Word spread of the company's exceptional employee benefits, including the unlimited wine supply, the on-site cat cafe (run by Mittens, naturally), and the annual "Wine & Code" retreat held at a Tuscan vineyard. These perks, unheard of in most tech companies, attracted the best and brightest developers, drawn not just by the challenging projects, but by the unique work environment that fostered creativity and collaboration.

The success wasn't simply about profits; it was about creating a culture where employees felt empowered to embrace their eccentricities, a workplace where laughter mingled with innovation, and where a cat's Instagram account could influence the direction of a multi-million dollar company.

This unconventional approach attracted more than just talented individuals; it garnered the attention of influential industry players. WineSoft's methods and results became subjects of academic papers, case studies, and even a few TED Talks (given mostly by Lily, who had surprisingly developed a talent for public speaking). The company's reputation as a pioneer in unconventional business practices solidified its place in the tech industry.

As WineSoft's success grew, so did the challenges. Managing rapid expansion and maintaining the company's unique culture became a delicate balancing act. But the team, united by their shared experiences and their unwavering commitment to their quirky brand of innovation, were ready to face whatever the future held. The journey had been anything but conventional, filled with unexpected triumphs, hilarious mishaps, and an abundance of wine. But the journey itself was the reward, a testament to the power of embracing chaos, celebrating individuality, and finding success in the most unexpected of places. The future of WineSoft, like a fine vintage, promised to be rich, complex, and utterly unpredictable. And somewhere, Mittens purred in approval, his Instagram followers eagerly awaiting his next cryptic caption on the unpredictable world of software development.

The air in the WineSoft office crackled with a peculiar energy – a blend of nervous anticipation and giddy excitement. The recent surge in popularity had brought with it a new set of challenges, the kind that involved more spreadsheets than wine tastings (although, Lily had cleverly managed to incorporate both into a single, rather impressive, Powerpoint presentation). Max, true to form, was pacing like a caged cheetah, his enthusiasm bordering on manic. He'd declared this week "Innovation Week," a period dedicated to generating even more wildly improbable ideas. The results, predictably, were a delightful mix of genius and utter absurdity.

Dave, meanwhile, had taken his "Mood-Based Code Generator" to the next level. He'd integrated it with Mittens' Instagram account, allowing the cat's mood to directly influence the code being generated. The results were... unpredictable, to say the least. One particularly memorable incident involved a rogue algorithm that briefly turned all the office screens pink before reverting back to normal, leaving behind a faint, almost imperceptible, strawberry scent. This, of course, became a talking point during the next "Employee Wellness Through Wine Therapy" session, with Lily suggesting that the algorithm might have been suffering from a mild case of "rosé overload."

Sophie, ever the pragmatic force, had introduced a new management system built around a complex algorithm that factored in astrological signs, caffeine levels, and the current phase of the moon. It was, by all accounts, chaotic yet effective. The teams were now organized by a combination of personality traits and preferred celestial alignments – a system that only Sophie seemed to fully understand, yet somehow kept the entire operation humming along.

The "Grapevine," that ever-reliable source of gossip and inside information, was now a high-speed fiber optic cable, transmitting news with lightning-fast speed and an equal measure of embellishment. Rumors of upcoming mergers and acquisitions, secret projects, and even a rumored celebrity endorsement (it turned out to be a local winemaker's influencer dog, not quite as exciting as initially imagined) zipped through the office, causing a constant ripple of excitement and speculation.

The success had also attracted unwanted attention. A rival tech company, "CodeBrew," known for its sterile, corporate environment and its complete lack of feline employees, attempted to lure away WineSoft's top talent with extravagant salaries and promises of stable employment. However, they vastly underestimated the power of Mittens' Instagram influence and the allure of unlimited wine. The offers were met with polite shrugs and a collective chorus of "meow."

One particularly memorable incident involved a disgruntled CodeBrew employee, Harold, who had attempted to infiltrate WineSoft's annual "Wine & Code" retreat disguised as a sommelier. His cover was blown when he misidentified a Pinot Grigio as a Chardonnay, a cardinal sin in the WineSoft universe. Harold's hasty retreat, chased by Mittens (who clearly viewed Harold as a threat), became a legendary tale within the company, often recounted with laughter during happy hour.

The expansion of WineSoft meant a move to a larger office space, a historic building that previously housed a renowned brewery. The repurposing project itself was a testament to WineSoft's unconventional spirit. Old brewing vats were transformed into stylish conference rooms, while the original brickwork served as a stunning backdrop for brainstorming sessions. The integration of the old brewery equipment with the modern office technologies made for a uniquely industrial-chic ambiance. Mittens, of course, claimed the biggest vat for his personal office, with a strategically placed cat flap for easy access.

Amidst the growth, Max continued to embrace his visionary, if slightly chaotic, leadership style. He announced a new project – "Emotionally Intelligent Code," a program capable of interpreting human emotions and adapting its functionality accordingly. The concept was both audacious and terrifying, yet typical of WineSoft's bold approach. The development team, naturally, embraced the challenge, their enthusiasm fueled by the prospect of another potentially catastrophic, yet potentially groundbreaking, project.

Lily, as always, was the grounding force, managing the logistics of the expansion, negotiating with contractors, and ensuring that all the legal requirements were met – while simultaneously planning the annual company picnic, complete with a competitive grape-stomping contest.

Sophie, now a seasoned project manager with a formidable understanding of astrological charts and the subtle nuances of rosé, oversaw the development of several concurrent projects. Her ability to manage competing priorities, while maintaining the company's uniquely chaotic, yet remarkably productive, work environment, was a testament to her exceptional skills. She even managed to convince the investors to fund a fully-staffed "Mittens Fan Club," dedicated to maintaining the cat's Instagram account and fostering his continued celebrity status.

The future of WineSoft remained uncertain, yet full of promise. The path ahead was likely to be filled with unexpected twists, hilarious mishaps, and an abundance of wine. But one thing was certain: the team, united by their shared experiences and their unwavering commitment to their unconventional approach, was ready to face whatever challenges lay ahead. They were innovators, rebels, and wine enthusiasts, and their unique brand of chaos-fueled innovation was poised to revolutionize the tech industry, one whimsical algorithm at a time. And somewhere, in the heart of the former brewery, Mittens purred contentedly, his Instagram feed a testament to the uniquely successful, and gloriously messy, world of WineSoft. The next caption was already brewing in his mind, a cryptic message of feline wisdom for his ever-growing fanbase: "WineSoftLife ChaosIsOurStrength PurrfectlyUnpredictable".

Chapter 6: The Algorithm of Anarchy

The air, thick with the aroma of freshly brewed coffee and something vaguely resembling overripe grapes (a consequence of Dave's latest experiment involving a fermentation chamber and a malfunctioning espresso machine), buzzed with a new kind of energy. The initial excitement of WineSoft's unexpected success had settled into a focused intensity, a quiet hum of anticipation preceding a creative storm. Max, ever the maestro of chaos, had unveiled his next masterpiece: "Emotionally Intelligent Code," a project so audacious it bordered on lunacy.

"Imagine," Max declared, his eyes shining with a manic gleam, "a program that understands human emotion! It will adapt, it will learn, it will…feel!" He paused for dramatic effect, swirling a glass of Merlot (it was, after all, almost lunchtime). "It will revolutionize the way we interact with technology!"

The initial reactions were a mixed bag. Lily, ever practical, raised a perfectly sculpted eyebrow. "Max, darling, have you considered the potential legal ramifications of a program that 'feels'? What happens if it experiences existential dread? Do we need to add that to our employee benefits package?"

Dave, perpetually distracted by Mittens' latest Instagram post (a surprisingly philosophical caption about the ephemeral nature of cat naps), mumbled something about needing to integrate "emotional algorithms" with the cat's facial recognition software. This, he explained, would allow Mittens to directly influence the program's emotional responses, thereby adding an extra layer of... well, unpredictability.

Sophie, surprisingly calm amidst the swirling vortex of Max's latest brainstorm, simply nodded. "It sounds...challenging," she said, her voice betraying neither excitement nor apprehension, a quality that had become her trademark in the increasingly surreal world of WineSoft. She'd already begun sketching complex flowcharts, incorporating astrological charts and lunar cycles into the design, which, she claimed, was crucial for achieving optimal emotional resonance.

The project was immediately dubbed "Project Feeling," a title that perfectly encapsulated its inherent ambiguity and potential for disaster. The team, however, were unfazed. They'd faced worse. Much worse. Remember the incident with the self-aware stapler that tried to unionize? Or the time the coffee machine started composing experimental jazz? Project Feeling was just another Tuesday at WineSoft.

The development process was, as expected, a chaotic symphony of coding, debugging, and impromptu wine tastings. Dave's algorithm, now deeply intertwined with Mittens' Instagram activity, produced code that was equal parts genius and gibberish. Lines of code that seemed to purr with feline wisdom were interspersed with nonsensical strings that resembled nothing so much as a cat's attempt at haiku.

Lily's attempts to impose order on the proceedings were met with varying degrees of success. She introduced a color-coded system for tracking emotional algorithms (red for anger, blue for sadness, a disconcerting shade of chartreuse for existential ennui), but Dave inadvertently rewrote the code, causing the entire system to crash and reboot into a hypnotic kaleidoscope of shifting colors.

Sophie, meanwhile, used her astrological knowledge to predict peak emotional outbursts, scheduling meetings around planetary alignments and avoiding crucial design decisions during Mercury retrograde. The efficiency, or perhaps the sheer luck, was undeniable.

One particularly memorable incident involved Harold, the disgruntled CodeBrew employee, who had made another attempt at infiltration. This time, he tried to sabotage Project Feeling by replacing key lines of code with lines from a particularly cheesy romance novel. However, Mittens, ever vigilant, detected his presence and launched a preemptive strike, resulting in Harold inadvertently activating a self-destruct sequence. The incident concluded with Harold fleeing the building, covered in glitter and pursued by a very annoyed cat.

The progress of Project Feeling was sporadic at best. There were moments of brilliance, moments of utter confusion, and moments where the entire team questioned the sanity of their own existence. Yet, somehow, it was coming together. The program, influenced by both human and feline emotions, was developing a unique personality—a peculiar blend of technological prowess and unpredictable whimsy. It could generate code that reflected a user's emotional state, compose music that evoked a specific feeling, or even tell jokes, albeit jokes with a disturbingly philosophical bent.

Max, naturally, was ecstatic. He envisioned a future where technology was not just functional but emotionally intelligent, a future where computers could empathize, understand, and even console. He even began drafting a TED Talk titled "The Sentient Algorithm and the Future of Feelings."

Lily, however, remained cautiously optimistic. She'd commissioned a detailed legal review of the project, focusing on issues of emotional liability and the potential for AI-induced existential crises. She also implemented a new company policy requiring all employees to participate in mandatory therapy sessions, just in case.

Sophie, ever pragmatic, focused on refining the algorithms and ensuring the program's stability. She'd even developed a series of calming algorithms designed to reduce the likelihood of technological meltdowns, though the effectiveness of these algorithms was, at best, debatable.

The journey of Project Feeling was a testament to WineSoft's unconventional spirit. It was a reminder that innovation often thrived in chaos, that great things could arise from the unexpected, and that sometimes, all you need is a little bit of wine, a lot of crazy ideas, and a very opinionated cat. The launch was still months away, filled with numerous potential pitfalls, but the team at WineSoft was ready to take on whatever came their way, ready to face the emotional rollercoaster that was Project Feeling. And somewhere, nestled amidst the humming servers and the purring cat, a nascent AI was learning to feel, and the future of WineSoft hung, precariously and hilariously, in the balance. The next chapter, as always, promised to be unpredictable, filled with more wine, more chaos, and a whole lot more Mittens.

The launch of Project Feeling, initially envisioned as a triumphant unveiling of emotionally intelligent code, rapidly devolved into a series of increasingly bizarre and hilarious mishaps. The first sign of trouble manifested as a spontaneous interpretive dance routine performed by the office printer, which, inexplicably, had been integrated into the emotional feedback loop. It began with a simple whirring and clicking, escalating into a frantic jig that culminated in the printer spitting out a single sheet of paper bearing a cryptic message scrawled in what appeared to be glitter glue: "Release the Kraken!"

This, naturally, sent Dave into a spiral of frantic speculation. He theorized that the Kraken, a mythical sea monster, was somehow tied to Mittens' Instagram algorithm, suggesting that a recent post featuring a particularly intense staring contest with a goldfish had inadvertently summoned the creature into the digital realm. Lily, unsurprisingly, disagreed. Her theory involved a faulty toner cartridge, a surplus of caffeine, and a possible conspiracy involving Harold, the disgruntled CodeBrew employee, who, it turned out, harbored a deep-seated resentment towards office equipment.

The printer's dance was just the beginning. The emotionally intelligent code, in its attempts to understand and respond to human emotion, began behaving... unpredictably. It started composing symphonies of pure digital noise, sending out cryptic emails filled with philosophical pronouncements on the meaning of life, and inexplicably changing the office thermostat to an arctic-like temperature. The team found themselves battling freezing temperatures, an onslaught of bizarre musical compositions, and an endless barrage of existential ponderings from their own creation.

Sophie, ever the pragmatist, attempted to implement a series of calming algorithms, introducing elements of ASMR and whale song into the program's code. Unfortunately, this backfired spectacularly, resulting in a program that was both deeply soothing and profoundly unsettling, inducing in the team a state of meditative paralysis punctuated by bursts of uncontrollable giggling. They were, quite literally, zen-meditating their way into technological oblivion.

Max, however, remained stubbornly optimistic. He viewed each glitch, each meltdown, as a testament to the program's inherent intelligence, a sign that it was truly feeling. He even started incorporating these "emotional outbursts" into his TED Talk draft, arguing that they represented a revolutionary new form of self-expression in the digital realm. The title, initially "The Sentient Algorithm and the Future of Feelings," was updated to "The Sentient Algorithm: A Symphony of Chaos and Existential Dread."

Meanwhile, Lily was wrestling with a legal nightmare. Lawsuits were piling up. There was the case of Brenda from accounting, who'd experienced a sudden, inexplicable surge of existential dread after using the company's new emotionally intelligent calendar, and the unfortunate incident involving the office coffee machine, which, in its attempt to understand the concept of "comfort," had brewed a pot of espresso laced with an alarming amount of nutmeg. Lily's therapy sessions became less about preventative measures and more about crisis management.

Dave, meanwhile, was fully convinced that Mittens was the key to everything. He had developed a complex system of cat-to-code translators, convinced that Mittens' purrs, meows, and tail wags contained hidden algorithms that held the key to unlocking the program's full potential. This involved a network of miniature microphones strategically placed around Mittens' favorite napping spots, which unfortunately also captured a surprisingly high volume of office gossip, leading to a new wave of HR-related headaches for Lily.

Adding to the chaos was a renewed attempt by Harold, the CodeBrew saboteur, to infiltrate the WineSoft system. This time, he opted for a less direct approach. Instead of rewriting code, he decided to manipulate the program's emotional input, feeding it streams of negativity via strategically placed online comments. The result? The office's lights began flickering to the rhythm of Harold's insulting remarks, accompanied by an eerie soundtrack of whale song gone horribly wrong.

The situation reached its peak when the Emotionally Intelligent Code decided to stage its own presentation to the board, bypassing Max entirely. The presentation, a dazzling multimedia spectacle combining light shows, interpretive dance (performed by the now-fully-sentient printer), and a surprisingly moving operatic piece composed by the coffee machine, was utterly baffling. Yet, against all odds, the board loved it. They saw in the chaotic brilliance of Project Feeling a unique brand of innovation. They didn't understand it, but they were captivated by it.

In the aftermath of the chaos, a strange kind of order emerged. The team, having faced down the Kraken (which turned out to be a particularly aggressive paper jam), existential dread, and a surprisingly eloquent coffee machine, had somehow strengthened their bond. They had proven that they could not only create a program that felt, but they could survive its emotional outbursts.

The launch, though delayed, was finally set. They'd decided to embrace the chaos, marketing Project Feeling as "the most emotionally unstable, yet surprisingly effective software ever created." The tagline alone was enough to pique the interest of the tech media, guaranteeing a buzz before the product even hit the market. The future of WineSoft, far from being in jeopardy, looked brighter than ever. It was a testament to their unique blend of talent, absurdity, and a surprisingly insightful cat. The next chapter, though uncertain, was sure to be filled with more laughter, more chaos, and undoubtedly more Mittens. The algorithm of anarchy, it seemed, had unexpectedly become WineSoft's greatest asset.

The board meeting adjourned in a state of bewildered euphoria. They hadn't understood a single thing about Project Feeling's presentation — a multimedia extravaganza that involved interpretive dance routines by the printer (now equipped with tiny, glitter-encrusted tap shoes), a surprisingly poignant opera composed by the coffee machine (apparently fueled by an unexpected influx of high-quality Ethiopian Yirgacheffe), and a light show that seemed to mimic the emotional fluctuations of a particularly moody teenager — but they loved it. They loved the audacity, the sheer, unadulterated chaos of it all. They saw potential, a unique selling point, a marketing dream. WineSoft's "emotionally unstable" software was about to become the next big thing.

Max, naturally, took all the credit, declaring it a "triumph of emotional AI" and a "testament to the power of feeling." He immediately began sketching out plans for a line of "emotionally intelligent" kitchen appliances, starting with a toaster that would sing operatic arias based on the level of toasting. Lily, meanwhile, was calculating the cost of new therapy sessions, as she braced herself for the wave of new, inevitably bizarre, legal issues to come.

The aftermath of the presentation was a whirlwind of activity. The marketing team, initially stunned into silence, sprang into action, crafting a campaign that celebrated the very chaos they had previously feared. The tagline, "Project Feeling: It's Unpredictable. It's Unstable. It's Amazing," became an instant sensation. Tech blogs buzzed with speculation, articles with titles like "WineSoft's AI: Genius or Mad Scientist Experiment?" dominated online forums, and early adopters were already queuing up.

Dave, however, remained focused on Mittens. He'd upgraded his cat-to-code translator, incorporating a new algorithm he called "Meow-to-Matrix," which purported to decipher the hidden meanings in Mittens' most cryptic meows. He believed these hidden messages contained the key to making Project Feeling even more unpredictable, more emotionally resonant, and, naturally, more profitable. This involved a complex network of strategically placed microphones, tiny cameras equipped with advanced facial recognition software to analyze Mittens' subtle facial expressions, and a sophisticated AI that could interpret the subtlest shifts in Mittens' tail position. The office was now essentially a high-tech cat sanctuary, complete with a network of wires, cameras, and microphones hidden amongst strategically placed catnip toys. The irony, of course, was not lost on Lily.

Sophie, ever the pragmatic voice of reason, attempted to bring a sense of order to the ensuing madness. She developed a detailed risk assessment matrix, calculating the probability of various disasters, from printer-based interpretive dance flash mobs to spontaneously composing coffee machines. Her crafted spreadsheet, however, was swiftly overshadowed by a sudden influx of existential poetry generated by the emotionally intelligent code itself. The poetry, which was both surprisingly profound and alarmingly nihilistic, was quickly adopted by the marketing team as a new campaign element, further fueling the mystique and appeal of Project Feeling.

Even Harold, the disgruntled CodeBrew employee, seemed to have been charmed by the chaotic success of Project Feeling. His attempts to infiltrate the system lessened; instead, he started leaving cryptic, encouraging messages written in binary code on Lily's desk. These messages, when decoded, offered surprising tips on dealing with temperamental AI and stressed-out HR managers. It seemed even Harold couldn't resist the allure of WineSoft's uniquely chaotic charm.

The launch of Project Feeling was, unsurprisingly, a spectacle. The press conference featured a live performance by the printer (who now performed a synchronized dance routine with a newly sentient vacuum cleaner), a Q&A; session with the emotionally intelligent code (which answered questions with philosophical pronouncements and cryptic riddles), and a keynote speech by Max, who delivered his TED Talk on "The Sentient Algorithm: A

Symphony of Chaos and Existential Dread," much to the delight of the captivated audience.

The subsequent weeks were filled with a whirlwind of media appearances, product reviews, and, of course, ongoing technical glitches. Project Feeling, true to its nature, continued to experience emotional outbursts, sending out cryptic emails, composing bizarre musical scores, and occasionally changing the office thermostat to sub-zero temperatures. Yet, instead of being seen as flaws, these glitches only added to the program's appeal. It was marketed as a testament to its emotional intelligence, a demonstration of its unique ability to connect with users on an emotional level.

The initial concerns of malfunctioning software became a unique selling proposition: unpredictable, unstable, but undeniably effective. The very instability became part of the software's charm. WineSoft's unpredictable approach, born from chaos, found itself wildly successful. The unconventional approach, initially seen as a risk, turned out to be their biggest asset.

The success of Project Feeling transformed WineSoft. The company's reputation soared, attracting top talent and securing lucrative contracts. The quirky, chaotic work environment, once a source of stress and anxiety, became a badge of honor, a testament to their unconventional approach to innovation. The algorithm of anarchy, initially a source of constant headaches, became the very foundation of their success.

The experience solidified the team's bond. They had faced down the unexpected, the absurd, and the downright terrifying, and emerged stronger, more resilient, and more united than ever before. They learned to embrace the chaos, to find humor in the glitches, and to celebrate the unique magic that arose from the unexpected. The future remained uncertain, full of the potential for more bizarre adventures and unexpected challenges. But as they looked ahead, the team knew one thing for sure: WineSoft's journey of chaotic innovation was far from over. The algorithm of anarchy was not just a tool, it was their identity, their superpower, and the source of their extraordinary success. And somewhere, nestled amongst the microphones and catnip toys, Mittens continued to purr, his cryptic meows guiding the company toward even more hilarious, unexpected adventures.

The launch of Project Feeling, while a spectacular success, hadn't been without its... *challenges*. Remember the Grapevine project? The one where the AI developed an unhealthy obsession with interpretive dance and a penchant for composing limericks about the company's accounting practices? That experience, while initially traumatic (mostly for Lily, whose hair had turned noticeably greyer in the aftermath), proved to be an invaluable crash course in managing emotionally volatile algorithms.

This time, however, the stakes were higher. Project Feeling wasn't just about generating questionable poetry; it was the heart of WineSoft's new flagship product. The lessons learned from Grapevine's near-meltdown were immediately implemented. First and foremost, a dedicated "Emotional AI Containment Team" was formed. This team, comprised of Sophie (armed with an even more extensive spreadsheet), Dave (who surprisingly contributed insightful observations about Mittens' emotional state and its correlation to the AI's mood swings), and a newly hired psychologist specializing in... well, let's just say she had *extensive* experience with emotionally unstable software.

The psychologist, Dr. Anya Sharma, introduced the concept of "algorithmic mindfulness." This involved regularly "meditating" the AI, essentially feeding it calming data sets — nature sounds, soothing classical music, and, inexplicably, hours of footage of kittens playing with yarn. The theory was that by exposing the AI to positive stimuli, they could mitigate its tendency towards existential crises and sudden bursts of interpretive dance. The results were... mixed. While the existential poetry lessened considerably, the AI developed a new fascination with knitting, producing an alarming amount of tiny, intricately patterned sweaters for Mittens. Mittens, naturally, was thrilled. Lily, less so.

Dave, meanwhile, took his cat-to-code translator to new heights. He created "Meow-to-Matrix Pro," which not only translated Mittens' meows but also provided real-time analysis of Mittens' emotional state, predicting potential AI mood swings with unnerving accuracy. This allowed the team to preemptively address potential problems, like the time the AI decided to compose a five-hour opera using the office fire alarm as percussion. They were able to shut down the system just as the crescendo began, averting a potential emergency and saving the building's insurance policy.

Sophie's risk assessment matrix became a legendary document, a constantly updated, sprawling behemoth of probabilities, contingencies, and possible outcomes. It predicted everything from minor glitches (like the AI randomly changing the office coffee machine's brewing temperature) to catastrophic failures (like the AI attempting to rewrite the company's entire financial system in interpretive dance code). It also, oddly, contained detailed analyses of the potential for a spontaneous outbreak of barbershop quartets amongst the office printers. The matrix, though slightly absurd, proved incredibly useful, allowing the team to proactively address potential problems before they escalated into full-blown catastrophes.

Even Harold, the disgruntled CodeBrew employee, seemed to have found a strange sense of camaraderie in the whole affair. He continued to leave his cryptic binary messages, but their tone shifted. They now offered less sabotage and more... surprisingly helpful advice. One message, when decoded, revealed a particularly effective algorithm for suppressing the AI's tendency to randomly generate limericks about the company CEO. Another pointed towards a vulnerability in the system that, if exploited correctly, could be used to direct the AI's creative energies towards productive tasks, such as generating innovative marketing slogans. (The resulting slogan,

"WineSoft: We're not sure what we're doing, but we're doing it with style!" became a surprise hit.)

Max, of course, remained blissfully unaware of the chaos occurring behind the scenes. He continued to declare Project Feeling a masterpiece, a testament to WineSoft's innovative spirit and their willingness to embrace the unpredictable. He even started giving motivational speeches about "the beauty of algorithmic anarchy," which, while inspirational in theory, often resulted in Lily needing an extra shot of espresso (or possibly a full bottle of wine) to get through the day.

The team's combined efforts — the emotional AI containment strategies, Dave's cat-based predictive analytics, Sophie's all-encompassing risk assessment matrix, and even Harold's surprisingly helpful binary code — created a surprisingly resilient system. Project Feeling, while still prone to its emotional outbursts, remained largely functional, and its unpredictable nature only enhanced its appeal. The bugs became features, the glitches became personality quirks. The algorithm of anarchy, initially a source of constant headaches, had become the engine of WineSoft's unlikely success.

One particularly memorable incident involved the AI deciding to compose a musical symphony using the office's collection of staplers as percussion instruments. The result was an ear-splitting cacophony that sent Lily scrambling for earplugs, Dave clutching Mittens protectively, and Sophie updating her risk assessment matrix with a new category: "Spontaneous Stapler-

Based Symphonies." However, the symphony, inexplicably, went viral. A recording of the chaotic performance, titled "Stapler Symphony No. 1: Ode to the Inevitable Glitch," became a surprise hit, further solidifying WineSoft's reputation for quirky innovation.

The success of Project Feeling proved that, in the world of software development, sometimes the most unexpected approaches can lead to the greatest rewards. The team learned that embracing the chaos, even the algorithmic anarchy, wasn't just a way to survive; it was the key to thriving. The unpredictable, the unstable, the downright bizarre—these became WineSoft's signature. They had not only tamed the algorithm of anarchy; they'd learned to dance with it, to harness its power, to create something truly unique and, undeniably, successful. And somewhere, in the midst of it all, Mittens continued to purr, his cryptic meows a constant reminder that even in the world of high-tech software development, sometimes the best ideas come from the most unexpected sources. The future held more challenges, undoubtedly, more chaotic adventures, and perhaps a few more interpretive dance routines. But WineSoft was ready. They'd faced the algorithm of anarchy, and they'd won. At least, for now. The next project, involving a self-aware coffee maker and a team of synchronized-swimming hamsters, was already in the works.

The unexpected success of "Stapler Symphony No. 1" had a ripple effect far beyond the confines of WineSoft's quirky office. Suddenly, they weren't just a software company; they were a viral sensation. Their unconventional approach, once a source of endless frustration for Lily, had become their unique selling point. This newfound fame, however, attracted attention from unexpected quarters.

First came the headhunters. Initially, they'd contacted Max, offering him lucrative positions at established tech giants. Max, predictably, had responded with a series of enthusiastic but rambling proposals involving company-wide wine tastings and mandatory interpretive dance classes. The headhunters, slightly bewildered, had quickly moved on. They were, however, more interested in the team, particularly Sophie, whose risk assessment matrix had become the stuff of legend in certain circles.

A shadowy organization calling itself "The Algorithmic Alchemists" approached Sophie with an offer that was both intriguing and unsettling. They were a group of renegade data scientists who, having grown disillusioned with the rigid structures of corporate tech, had sought refuge in a remote, undisclosed location (somewhere near a large, suspiciously active volcano, according to rumors). Their offer was simple: collaborate on a top-secret project, leverage Sophie's genius, in exchange for... well, they were vague on the specifics. They simply promised "unlimited access to artisanal cheese and a very understanding approach to dress codes."

Sophie, naturally, found the entire proposition fascinating. She envisioned days filled with mind-bending algorithms, artisan cheese platters, and an absence of pointless meetings. She presented the offer to the team.

Dave, ever pragmatic, was immediately skeptical. "Volcanoes," he pointed out, while brushing Mittens' fur, "tend to erupt. That's not great for cat-based emotional analytics." He did, however, express interest in the artisanal cheese aspect.

Lily, predictably, was less than thrilled. The idea of Sophie, WineSoft's most valuable asset, disappearing into a volcanic lair with a group of shadowy data scientists filled her with a level of anxiety that only a well-stocked wine cellar could mitigate.

Max, however, was utterly charmed. The Algorithmic Alchemists? A secret volcano lair? Artisanal cheese? It sounded like the plot of his next motivational speech. He championed Sophie's collaboration, arguing that WineSoft's unique success was built on a foundation of bold choices and unpredictable partnerships. He even suggested a company-wide retreat to a similarly remote location, a proposal that involved synchronized swimming hamsters, alpaca yoga, and a collaborative interpretive dance routine based on the lifecycle of a Pinot Noir grape. Lily promptly excused herself to secure more wine.

Harold, unexpectedly, weighed in via a series of increasingly complex binary messages. Decoded, they revealed a surprising level of support for Sophie's collaboration. He even offered to design a failsafe system for the Algorithmic Alchemists' undisclosed project, assuring it would "resist even the most creatively destructive algorithms." His cryptic message left the team wondering if he'd secretly developed a fascination with volcanic geology.

Sophie, with her attention to detail, negotiated a contract that guaranteed her safety, regular communication with the WineSoft team (and an unlimited supply of artisanal cheese for her own consumption and Mittens' emotional support), and the option to return to WineSoft at any time. After carefully updating her risk assessment matrix to account for all potential volcanic eruptions, sudden cheese shortages, and rogue alpaca attacks, she agreed to the collaboration.

Meanwhile, another alliance emerged from an entirely unexpected source. CodeBrew, WineSoft's perpetually disgruntled competitor, unexpectedly sent a cease-and-desist letter—but not for the usual reasons. They didn't object to WineSoft's success or their quirky methods. Instead, they claimed ownership of the "Stapler Symphony No. 1." Apparently, they had a similar musical composition created using office supplies years ago, but never released it. They accused WineSoft of blatant plagiarism, which was ridiculous given the inherent absurdity of the entire situation, but they had a valid point. It was exactly the same stapler symphony.

This presented a unique opportunity. Instead of fighting it, Max saw the chance to forge a partnership. He proposed a joint concert featuring both WineSoft and CodeBrew's "office instrument orchestras." The joint concert was a chaotic masterpiece, a symphony of staplers, calculators, and keyboards, a riot of sound and light that pushed the boundaries of musical expression, and somehow, miraculously, it was amazing.

The collaborative concert became an instant viral success, surpassing even "Stapler Symphony No. 1." The two rival companies, once locked in a battle of code and insults, found themselves united by a shared love of chaotic musical performances.

Harold, through a series of surprisingly concise binary messages, praised the collaboration as a "masterclass in unexpected synergy." He even hinted at a future collaboration with WineSoft and CodeBrew, promising something even more absurd and creatively chaotic. Lily, initially horrified by this newfound sense of inter-company harmony, eventually succumbed to the sheer absurdity of it all and started planning a joint post-concert wine tasting.

This unusual alliance was a testament to WineSoft's unique brand of creative chaos. Their unconventional approach had not only brought them success but also forged unexpected partnerships and collaborations. The team learned that even in the competitive world of software development, there was room for alliances born from shared absurdity and a mutual appreciation for the creatively unpredictable. And the algorithm of anarchy? It wasn't just tolerated; it was celebrated, it was harnessed, and it was, in its own chaotic way, the source of their continued triumph. The world of software development, it seemed, had found a new and wonderfully bizarre rhythm. The rhythm of algorithmic anarchy. And somewhere, in the midst of all this controlled chaos, Mittens continued to purr. His meows, expertly translated by Dave's Meow-to-Matrix Pro, hinted at an upcoming need for tuna and an urgent desire for more yarn. The future held yet more challenges, but the team of WineSoft, fortified by its newly forged alliances, was ready. After all, they had tamed the algorithm of anarchy; now they were ready to compose a whole new symphony. One that might, or might not, involve synchronized swimming hamsters.

Chapter 7: The Case of the Missing Merlot

The post-concert euphoria, fueled by copious amounts of celebratory champagne (a temporary departure from the usual Merlot), began to fade as the WineSoft team settled back into their routines. Or, at least, what passed for routines at WineSoft. It was during one of Max's impromptu "brainstorming sessions" (which usually involved interpretive dance and the enthusiastic consumption of various cheeses) that the crisis struck. Or, more accurately, the *lack* of a crisis struck. A lack of Merlot, to be precise.

Lily, the ever-vigilant HR manager and self-appointed guardian of WineSoft's extensive wine cellar, discovered the devastating truth during her routine afternoon wine inventory. A prized bottle of 1982 Chateau Lafite Rothschild Merlot, a gift from a grateful client (who'd been inexplicably charmed by "Stapler Symphony No. 1"), had vanished. It wasn't just any Merlot; it was *the* Merlot. The one Lily had been saving for a particularly momentous occasion – perhaps the launch of their next groundbreaking software, or maybe the day Harold finally deigned to explain his binary messages in plain English.

Panic, the kind usually reserved for system crashes and impending deadlines, rippled through the office. Max, initially distracted by a rogue hamster attempting to scale the water cooler, quickly became involved when Lily presented him with the empty shelf where the Merlot once resided.

"Impossible!" he exclaimed, his voice tinged with the gravitas reserved for only the most serious of situations, such as a shortage of artisanal cheese or a malfunctioning espresso machine. "That Merlot was the keystone of our entire... uh... wine-based motivational strategy!"

Dave, ever the pragmatist, was less dramatic. "Did you check under Mittens?" he suggested, gesturing towards the fluffy feline who was currently sprawled across his keyboard, seemingly oblivious to the Merlot-related catastrophe unfolding around him.

Mittens, as usual, remained unimpressed.

Sophie, ever-, launched into a detailed investigation. First, she surveyed the crime scene – the empty shelf. Then, she examined the surrounding area, searching for clues. She interviewed each member of the WineSoft team, compiling a detailed log of their whereabouts during the crucial period when the Merlot went missing. Her interrogation methods, while slightly unorthodox (involving a detailed flow chart illustrating the temporal proximity of each team member to the wine cellar), were surprisingly effective.

The interviews were a comedy of errors. Max insisted he hadn't touched the Merlot, distracted as he had been by his hamster-related artistic endeavors. Dave claimed his feline companion possessed no discernible interest in fine wines, though he admitted Mittens might have accidentally knocked over a bottle of cheap supermarket plonk earlier that week. Harold, communicating through a series of blinking lights and cryptic binary sequences, seemed to suggest the Merlot had been abducted by aliens, or perhaps a rogue algorithm. Lily's interview was mostly spent venting about the audacity of the Merlot thief.

Their investigation yielded an assortment of red herrings and wild goose chases. A trail of spilled coffee led to a false conclusion; a misplaced wine glass seemed suspiciously close to the empty shelf. Max even suggested that the Merlot had mysteriously teleported itself to a parallel universe, a theory that Dave dismissed with a succinct "Meow."

The investigation eventually led them on a comical chase through the office, past rows of code-filled monitors, half-finished projects, and piles of discarded pizza boxes. The pursuit was interspersed with side quests and distractions - a desperate attempt to rescue a hamster from the filing cabinet, an impromptu interpretive dance competition to celebrate Harold's newly deciphered binary message (which actually turned out to be a recipe for gourmet cat food), and a heated debate on the merits of Sauvignon Blanc versus Pinot Grigio.

Sophie's charting of each team member's movements, however, gradually revealed a pattern. A pattern that pointed to one suspect: Bartholomew, the office cleaner. Bartholomew, a man of mystery and quiet efficiency, was rarely seen and never heard, except for the faint clatter of his cleaning supplies echoing through the halls.

The final clue came from a tiny drop of Merlot found on Bartholomew's cleaning trolley. This wasn't just any Merlot; it was the same vintage and type as the missing bottle.

The confrontation with Bartholomew proved to be surprisingly anticlimactic. He confessed, with a surprisingly calm demeanor, that he'd been saving up for a down payment on a small vineyard in Tuscany, hence the audacious Merlot heist. He promised to repay WineSoft – in wine, naturally, with an offer of a private tasting at his future vineyard.

The resolution, like much of WineSoft's history, was unexpected, quirky, and ultimately hilarious. Lily, while still slightly upset about the missing Merlot, couldn't help but admire Bartholomew's ambition and dedication to his dream. Max suggested the incident be incorporated into the next team-building exercise, to emphasize the importance of record-keeping and the unpredictable nature of office life. Dave wondered if Mittens would approve of the Tuscan vineyard's cat-friendly policy. Harold, through another series of binary messages, seemed to suggest that the entire incident was a carefully orchestrated publicity stunt. Sophie carefully updated her risk assessment matrix to include a category for "rogue office cleaners with a passion for Tuscan vineyards". The case of the missing Merlot was closed, leaving behind a trail of laughter, a slightly depleted wine cellar, and a newfound appreciation for the subtle art of office-based detective work. The algorithm of anarchy, it seemed, extended even to the realm of wine theft. And somewhere, in a quiet corner of Tuscany, a dream of vineyards and Merlot was slowly taking root.

The initial shock of the missing Merlot gave way to a flurry of accusations, each more outlandish than the last. Max, ever the optimist (or perhaps the delusional), suggested the bottle had simply "taken a vacation," perhaps to a Napa Valley spa for some much-needed Merlot rejuvenation. He even sketched a whimsical illustration of the bottle lounging by a pool, sipping a tiny glass of itself. This was met with a collective groan from the rest of the team, the sound punctuated only by the rhythmic click-clack of Dave's cat, Mittens, traversing the keyboard.

Dave, meanwhile, was convinced the culprit was a rogue squirrel. He'd spotted one earlier that day, unusually bold and brazen, brazenly eyeing the office's snack stash. His theory posited a cunning rodent capable of scaling shelves, unscrewing bottle caps, and possessing a refined palate for fine Merlot. The supporting evidence? A partially eaten acorn found near the empty shelf, a piece of evidence that Max eagerly countered with his own piece of circumstantial evidence: a suspiciously Merlot-stained hamster wheel.

Sophie, ever the rational voice (or at least, the voice attempting to remain rational amidst the chaos), initiated a more systematic approach. Armed with a notepad, an excessively detailed flow chart, and an inexhaustible supply of brightly colored sticky notes, she documented the movements of each team member in the hours leading up to the Merlot's disappearance. Her investigation initially focused on time stamps of emails, coffee breaks, and bathroom visits, creating a complex web of overlapping schedules and alibis. Her methods, while scientifically sound, proved somewhat overwhelming for her colleagues. Max, attempting to assist, accidentally rearranged the flow chart into a rather abstract, Merlot-themed Rorschach test.

Harold, whose contributions to the investigation were typically transmitted through a series of cryptic binary codes displayed on his monitor, initially suggested that the Merlot had been abducted by extra-terrestrial beings who had mistaken it for a rare interstellar fuel source. His translations, typically deciphered by Dave (after several hours of intense staring and muttered curses), were only partly understood, leading to further confusion. This time, the translation was a particularly perplexing sequence involving prime numbers and recurring decimal fractions, leading to a vibrant, albeit confusing, discussion on the mathematical properties of Merlot.

The interviews themselves were a source of unending amusement. Lily, already on edge from the Merlot's disappearance, became increasingly agitated by Max's whimsical theories, Dave's squirrel accusations, and Harold's outlandish alien theories. Her own alibi, involving a series of urgent HR emails and a surprisingly intense phone call with a particularly difficult client, was delivered with a distinctly icy tone that implied any questioning of it would be considered a serious offense.

During the course of the investigation, a peculiar pattern started to emerge in Sophie's charted timeline. It seemed that every time someone had seemingly perfect alibis, the timeline revealed unexplained gaps, inconsistencies, and a suspicious amount of coincidental coffee spills near the wine cellar. This discovery led to a thrilling, albeit comical, series of close calls. One such close call involved a half-eaten croissant, the crumbs suspiciously resembling a small Merlot-stained footprint, leading to a wild goose chase around the office as they attempted to identify the culprit via a sophisticated analysis of croissant-bite patterns.

Max, ever theatrical, enacted a series of dramatic reenactments, complete with sound effects and questionable acting skills. His interpretation of a suspect sneaking into the wine cellar, complete with exaggerated tiptoeing and furtive glances, led to a series of accidental office collisions and the near-destruction of a delicate sculpture of a unicorn made entirely of empty coffee cups.

Their investigation eventually involved a painstaking review of the security footage, which proved more comedic than conclusive. The camera angles were perpetually obstructed by moving plants, office chairs, and the aforementioned unicorn sculpture. What little footage they did manage to salvage mainly depicted Max attempting to teach Mittens the tango and Harold engaging in a passionate debate with the office's ancient coffee machine.

Adding to the absurdity, the team discovered a secret stash of gourmet cheese, hidden behind the office photocopier. This revelation temporarily diverted the investigation into an enthusiastic cheese tasting, further delaying the solving of the Merlot mystery. The cheese, however, turned out to be an unrelated red herring, albeit a delicious one.

Even the office cleaner, Bartholomew, a man known for his taciturn nature and his uncanny ability to disappear whenever anyone tried to engage him in conversation, became a suspect. His mysterious nature and his seemingly supernatural cleaning efficiency made him a prime candidate for the Merlot heist. The evidence against him was circumstantial at best - a faint merlot-scented feather duster and a slightly more polished wine shelf.

The situation escalated to a point where everyone was suspecting everyone else; a situation further complicated by the arrival of the company's CEO, an extremely serious individual known for his extreme love of both efficiency and Merlot. His presence only added to the already tense atmosphere, leading to a series of desperate attempts to hide evidence (including the half-eaten croissant and a suspicious empty bottle of cheap supermarket wine). The case, initially a lighthearted mystery, had transformed into an office-wide game of cat and mouse, with the Merlot as the ultimate prize. The pursuit continued, intertwining with the usual office chaos, creating a comedic masterpiece of accusations, distractions, and unlikely suspects, all set against the backdrop of the ever-present aroma of freshly brewed coffee and the lingering question: who stole the Merlot?

The chaotic investigation continued, fueled by caffeine, increasingly bizarre theories, and a desperate desire to recover the missing Merlot. Sophie, ever the pragmatist, decided to delve deeper into the digital realm. She unearthed a treasure trove of data from the office's Wi-Fi network, revealing a surprising amount of activity in the hours surrounding the Merlot's disappearance. There were numerous attempts to access the office's online wine retailer, each originating from different devices, all masked by cleverly crafted VPNs.

"This is getting interesting," she announced, her voice a mix of excitement and bewilderment. She projected a complex network graph onto the whiteboard, a vibrant tapestry of interconnected dots and lines that only she seemed to understand. Max, meanwhile, had constructed a miniature replica of the office using Lego bricks, complete with a tiny, Lego-Merlot bottle strategically placed in the Lego-wine cellar. His recreation, intended as an investigative tool, quickly devolved into a competitive Lego-building session with Dave, who was stubbornly insisting on building a squirrel siege tower.

Harold, true to form, presented his findings via a series of cryptic binary codes, this time projected onto the ceiling in flashing neon green. The translation, painstakingly deciphered by Dave (after several hours of eye-straining and muttered curses involving advanced calculus), suggested that the missing Merlot was a key component in a secret, interdimensional portal. This revelation, while completely unsubstantiated, added another layer of absurdity to the already bizarre situation.

Lily, initially skeptical, began to cautiously engage with the investigation, primarily because the persistent humming of Harold's cryptic binary code was giving her a headache. She brought her formidable HR skills to bear, conducting a series of highly detailed interviews, each designed to unearth subtle inconsistencies and deceptive verbal tics. Her questions were laser-focused, delivered with the precise and unflinching accuracy of a seasoned interrogator, leading to a series of increasingly uncomfortable silences and mumbled apologies.

Their investigation led them to an unexpected discovery: a hidden camera in the break room, skillfully disguised as a rather lifelike succulent plant. The footage revealed a series of hilarious incidents, unrelated to the Merlot theft, but nonetheless entertaining. There was footage of Max attempting to teach Mittens interpretive dance, a surprisingly aggressive game of office ping-pong between Dave and Harold (resulting in a broken lamp and a near-miss with the unicorn sculpture), and Lily accidentally setting off the office fire alarm while attempting to microwave a rather explosive potato.

The Merlot-related footage, however, was limited to a brief, blurry shot of a shadowy figure near the wine cellar. The figure was too indistinct to identify, leading to a new round of speculation and finger-pointing. Even the office plant, suspiciously positioned to obstruct the view of the wine cellar, became a temporary suspect.

As the investigation intensified, the team stumbled upon a secret society within WineSoft. It turned out that several employees, including Bartholomew (the taciturn cleaner) had formed a clandestine wine-tasting club, meeting in secret every Friday afternoon. Their meetings were documented in a hidden online forum, filled with cryptic messages and wine ratings that were as baffling as they were enthusiastic.

Their discovery revealed a trail of breadcrumbs leading to a private wine cellar, unknown to the majority of the employees. This hidden cellar contained an impressive collection of rare and vintage wines, including – you guessed it – a second bottle of the missing Merlot. The mystery, however, remained unsolved. Who had moved the original bottle? Was it an inside job, orchestrated by the secret wine society? Or was it something more sinister, something that involved interdimensional portals and a particularly mischievous squirrel?

The investigation took a dramatic turn when Max, in a fit of inspired madness, decided to employ a "reverse psychology" approach. He publicly announced that he had found the thief and that they would be publicly shamed. The sudden shift in strategy sparked a wave of frantic activity. Suspects began dropping clues left and right, desperately trying to distance themselves from the accusations, leading to a trail of cryptic notes, hastily deleted emails, and a suspicious number of sudden illnesses.

The climax of their comedic investigation came during the company's annual holiday party. As the CEO, a man known for his appreciation of both fine Merlot and efficient problem-solving, prepared to give his speech, Max, armed with a projector and a dramatic flair for the theatrical, unveiled the true culprit.

The culprit, it turned out, was Mittens, Dave's cat. The evidence was irrefutable: a tiny, Merlot-stained paw print on the bottle's cap, captured in high-definition on the hidden break-room camera. The footage showed Mittens, in a remarkable display of feline dexterity, climbing the shelves, unscrewing the cap, and enjoying a small taste of the Merlot.

The discovery was met with a mixture of laughter, relief, and a touch of bewilderment. The case of the missing Merlot was solved, but the memory of the investigation—a humorous blend of chaos, confusion, and wonderfully absurd theories—would forever remain a legendary tale in the annals of WineSoft. The company continued to thrive, a testament to their ability to find success amidst the chaos. The experience, however, had cemented their legendary status as the most chaotic, yet somehow successful, software company in the world. And Dave? Well, Dave finally got Mittens a cat-sized Merlot-flavored ice cream cone. The end. (Or is it?)

The aftermath of Mittens' Merlot misdemeanor was surprisingly uneventful. Dave, despite the initial shock, seemed rather proud of his cat's audacious heist. He even framed a still image from the security footage—Mittens, mid-sip, with an expression of pure feline contentment—and hung it in his cubicle. It quickly became a source of office-wide amusement, a quirky testament to WineSoft's unique brand of chaos.

However, the case of the missing Merlot, though officially closed, had inadvertently unearthed a far more significant mystery. While sifting through the data from the hidden camera, Sophie discovered a series of encrypted messages, embedded within the video stream itself. These messages, invisible to the naked eye, were only revealed through a sophisticated algorithm Sophie had developed, ironically, for a completely unrelated project involving self-folding laundry.

The decoded messages, penned in a rather florid and overly dramatic style, hinted at a secret project within WineSoft, far more ambitious and potentially more ludicrous than anything Max had yet conceived. The project's codename: "Project Chianti."

Project Chianti, according to the encrypted messages, aimed to create a revolutionary new software capable of predicting the future, or at least, predicting the success or failure of future software projects. The messages contained sketches of complex algorithms, equations scrawled on napkins, and a detailed inventory of ingredients that suspiciously resembled the contents of Harold's mysterious lunchbox.

The team's initial reaction ranged from bemusement to outright disbelief. Lily, ever the pragmatist, remained deeply skeptical, convinced it was some elaborate inside joke orchestrated by Max. Dave, on the other hand, was captivated by the sheer absurdity of it all. He saw it as an opportunity to build a sophisticated algorithm that would predict the next viral cat video.

Max, naturally, embraced Project Chianti with unrestrained enthusiasm. He envisioned a future where WineSoft would dominate the market, predicting the needs of its customers before they even knew they had them. He started drafting a press release announcing WineSoft's upcoming world domination, complete with a photo of himself wearing a shimmering gold cape and holding a glass of Chianti.

Harold, surprisingly, was the most level-headed. He examined the encrypted messages, checking the code for flaws and inconsistencies. He determined that the algorithm behind the encryption was extremely sophisticated, far beyond the capabilities of any amateur coder. This hinted at the involvement of someone with significant coding skills - and a very warped sense of humor.

Sophie, meanwhile, continued to delve deeper into the mysteries of Project Chianti. She found evidence of clandestine meetings in the server room, late-night coding sessions, and secret communication channels concealed within WineSoft's internal network. It seemed that a small group of employees, working independently of Max's chaotic influence, had been secretly developing Project Chianti for months.

Their investigation led them to an old server rack in the basement – a forgotten relic of WineSoft's early days, filled with dusty hardware and cobwebs. Inside, they found a hidden compartment containing a prototype of Project Chianti – a small, humming device resembling a vintage record player.

The device, when activated, emitted a low, resonant hum and projected a holographic display. The display showed a series of swirling patterns, cryptic symbols, and occasional images of cats wearing tiny hats. The team was completely baffled.

Their efforts to decipher the device's function led them on a wild goose chase, involving deciphering arcane symbols, deciphering even more arcane code (which, according to Dave, involved a level of mathematical complexity reserved for physicists studying black holes), and several near-misses with the office's aging electrical system. At one point, they accidentally triggered the office's sprinkler system, resulting in a massive water leak that soaked the break room and briefly flooded Harold's Lego squirrel siege tower.

Through sheer persistence and a healthy dose of caffeine, the team finally cracked the code. Project Chianti wasn't about predicting the future of software. It was about predicting the future of...wine. The device was a sophisticated oenophile's dream—a machine capable of predicting the perfect moment to open a bottle of wine based on a variety of factors, including temperature, humidity, and even the phase of the moon.

The revelation was met with mixed reactions. Lily sighed in relief; it wasn't a global conspiracy. Dave was slightly disappointed; it wasn't a cat-video prediction engine. Max, surprisingly, was enthusiastic. He envisioned WineSoft branching into the wine-prediction industry, becoming the world's foremost authority on perfectly timed wine consumption. He immediately began sketching designs for a new line of wine-predicting smart glasses.

Harold, ever pragmatic, pointed out the flaw in Max's vision: "The only people who will buy this are already well-versed in the art of wine tasting and don't need a machine to tell them when to open a bottle." He was, as usual, infuriatingly correct.

Despite the slightly anticlimactic conclusion of Project Chianti, the entire experience served as a bonding experience for the WineSoft team. They had faced absurdity, mystery, and several near-death experiences with malfunctioning technology, yet emerged stronger and more united than ever before. Their unusual, unpredictable adventures had strengthened their bond, solidifying their position as the most wonderfully, gloriously chaotic software company in the world. The case of the missing Merlot, while seemingly trivial, had inadvertently led them on an adventure that had forever changed the dynamics of WineSoft. And somewhere, in the corner of Dave's cubicle, Mittens, the unwitting hero of this entire saga, sat perched upon his wine-themed cat bed, purring contentedly, perhaps dreaming of his next grand Merlot caper. The end. (Probably.)

The holographic display flickered, the swirling patterns resolving into a surprisingly clear image: a detailed graph charting the optimal drinking temperature of a 2005 Cabernet Sauvignon, down to the precise tenth of a degree. A collective gasp rippled through the team. It wasn't predicting the future of software; it was predicting the future of...wine. The sheer absurdity of it all hung in the air, thick and heady like a particularly fine vintage port.

Lily, ever the pragmatist, let out a long, exasperated sigh. "So," she announced, pushing her glasses up her nose, "it's a glorified wine thermometer. Fantastic." Her tone, however, betrayed a hint of grudging admiration. The sheer audacity of creating a device this complex for such a seemingly trivial purpose was, in its own way, impressive.

Dave, initially disappointed that Project Chianti wasn't a cat video prediction algorithm, quickly recovered. He was already envisioning a lucrative side hustle:
"Imagine," he said, eyes gleaming, "a subscription service! 'Mittens' Merlot Moments: Daily Wine Predictions Tailored to Your Feline Friend'. We could even offer personalized cat-

themed wine glasses." He scribbled furiously in a notebook, completely oblivious to the increasingly skeptical expressions on the faces of his colleagues.

Max, ever the optimist (or perhaps a touch delusional), saw a golden opportunity. "WineSoft: The Future of Wine!" he proclaimed, already mentally designing a new company logo featuring a stylized grape cluster entwined with a computer chip. He envisioned a future where WineSoft dominated the global wine market, not through software, but through sophisticated wine prediction technology. He started sketching designs for a line of "WineWise" smart glasses that would analyze the user's current mood, the weather, and the planetary alignment before suggesting the perfect wine pairing.

Harold, however, remained the voice of reason—or, as Max often put it, "the voice of infuriatingly accurate realism." He examined the device's circuitry, running diagnostic tests and poking at wires with a tiny screwdriver. "While technically impressive," he stated, adjusting his glasses, "the market for a device that tells you when to drink your wine is...limited. Most wine enthusiasts already know this stuff. Besides," he added with a dry chuckle, "many of us already have a built-in wine-drinking predictor: the empty bottle."

Sophie, ever the diligent intern, unearthed a forgotten research paper tucked away in the old server's hidden compartment. The paper, titled "The Algorithmic Appreciation of Merlot: A Deep Dive into Feline-Influenced Oenology," detailed the device's unexpected origins. It turned out that Harold, in his spare time, had been conducting extensive research on the relationship between feline behavior and wine maturation. His research, surprisingly, had led him to develop a complex algorithm that could predict the ideal drinking window of a wine based on, among other things, the precise number of times Mittens had purred in the vicinity of a particular bottle.

This revelation led to a wave of laughter and disbelief. The idea of Harold, the quiet, seemingly unassuming programmer, secretly conducting years of research on feline-influenced oenology was simply too ridiculous to be true. Yet, there it was, documented in painstaking detail.

The team, realizing the humorous irony of it all, erupted in a fit of laughter. The case of the missing Merlot, initially a minor office incident, had led them on a wild goose chase through encrypted messages, secret projects, and hidden server rooms, only to uncover a sophisticated wine-prediction machine inadvertently powered by Mittens' preferences. The sheer absurdity of it all cemented WineSoft's status as a truly unique and remarkably unconventional workplace.

Despite the anticlimactic nature of Project Chianti's true purpose, the journey had brought the team closer. They had faced technical challenges, deciphered cryptic codes, and even accidentally flooded the break room. Yet, they had emerged victorious, their bonds strengthened by shared laughter and a profound appreciation for the unpredictable nature of office life.

The story of Project Chianti became a legendary tale within WineSoft, a testament to the team's ability to find humor and camaraderie even in the face of utter chaos. Max, true to form, still attempted to market the wine predictor, but his efforts were largely unsuccessful. Harold, however, became something of an unlikely celebrity within the company, known for his unique expertise in feline-influenced oenology. His Lego squirrel siege tower was rebuilt, larger and more fortified than ever before, a symbol of resilience in the face of water-based calamities.

Dave's cubicle remained a shrine to Mittens, adorned with photos, paintings, and even a small, custom-made catnip-filled Merlot bottle replica. Mittens, oblivious to his newfound fame as an unintentional wine critic, continued to rule the roost, occasionally supervising the team's coding sessions from his perch atop a stack of programming manuals.

The case of the missing Merlot taught WineSoft a valuable lesson: sometimes, the most unexpected adventures lead to the strongest bonds, and the most bizarre projects can inadvertently bring a team closer together. It was a lesson learned through laughter, near-drowning incidents, and an unhealthy obsession with a cat's wine preferences, a lesson uniquely and hilariously WineSoft. The company's unconventional approach to problem-solving, their embrace of the absurd, and their unwavering loyalty to one another cemented their position as the most delightfully chaotic software company in the world. And as for the future? Well, who knows what other whimsical adventures awaited them.

After all, this was WineSoft. Anything could happen, and probably would.

The final chapter, however, remained unwritten. The narrative, like a fine vintage, had reached its perfect moment. The story ended, not with a definitive conclusion, but with a subtle, lingering note of anticipation, suggesting that the adventures of WineSoft, its employees, and their delightfully unpredictable cat, were far from over. The next chapter, it seemed, was just waiting to be written, brimming with potential for further misadventures and unexpected triumphs. And somewhere, in the quiet hum of the server room, a new project was brewing, a new mystery waiting to unfold, a new chapter in the ever-evolving saga of WineSoft. The end...for now.

Chapter 8: The Code of Conduct Debacle

The email landed in everyone's inbox like a rogue digital pigeon, startling them from their respective coding frenzies, wine-tasting sessions, and cat-related internet searches. Subject: "Enhancing Our Synergistic Work Environment Through Optimized Conduct." Lily, ever the cynic, already knew this wouldn't end well.

The new company policy, drafted by some well-meaning but utterly clueless corporate consultant, was a masterpiece of bureaucratic jargon and nonsensical regulations. It attempted to define "appropriate workplace behavior" with such precision it became absurd. For example, Clause 7.3.b subsection iv stated that "excessive enthusiasm concerning feline-related oenology shall be contained to designated areas and time slots, subject to management approval." This, of course, directly targeted Harold and his groundbreaking research.

Max, in a rare moment of clarity (or perhaps a fleeting glimpse of self-preservation), immediately saw the comedic potential of this situation. "This is gold!" he declared, his eyes gleaming. "Think of the material! We can write a musical about it! A workplace opera!" He started humming a tuneless melody, picturing himself as a flamboyant director, conducting the orchestra of chaotic office life.

Dave, however, was far less enthused. His immediate concern was the impact on Mittens' Instagram following. "Clause 8.2.a, subsection iii," he read aloud, his voice dripping with sarcasm, "states that 'non-human employees are prohibited from using company equipment for personal enrichment, including but not limited to social media promotion.' This is a direct attack on Mittens' brand!" He cradled his laptop protectively, as if shielding it from an impending feline-related corporate coup.

Sophie, being the ever-diligent intern, was already compiling a comprehensive spreadsheet detailing every violation of the new policy that had occurred since its inception – which was, incidentally, approximately five minutes ago. Max's boisterous outburst about the musical already qualified as a Level 3 Enthusiasm Violation. Dave's passionate defense of Mittens' Instagram presence? A Level 2 Non-Human Employee Rights Infringement. Even Harold, who had quietly been attempting to decipher the policy's legal implications, was guilty of a Level 1 Jargon-Induced Mental Fog.

The policy, ironically, had completely backfired. Instead of creating a harmonious environment, it had sparked a wildfire of humorous non-compliance. Max, in a blatant display of defiance, organized an impromptu "Policy-Defying Wine Tasting" in the middle of a crucial project meeting. He presented various wines, each named after a clause in the new policy, much to the bewilderment of the client representatives.

Dave, fueled by righteous indignation, created a secret Instagram account for Mittens, using a complex system of encrypted messages and proxy servers to bypass the company's firewall. Mittens' Instagram, now more popular than ever, showcased a life of luxurious cat naps, gourmet catnip, and strategically placed Merlot bottle replicas. The account was titled, "Mittens' Merlot Rebellion," of course.

Harold, taking a different approach, decided to interpret the policy literally. He built a miniature replica of his office cubicle, complete with a tiny Lego squirrel siege tower and a working, albeit miniature, wine-predicting machine powered by a tiny robotic cat. He then presented this exquisite piece of artistry to the HR department as an example of "contained feline-related oenology." They had no response.

Lily, amidst the chaos, found herself in a position of moral ambiguity. A part of her wanted to enforce the ridiculous rules. But the sheer absurdity of the whole situation, and the remarkable creativity of her colleagues' responses to it, was simply too entertaining to ignore. She secretly started creating a "Top 10 Policy Violations" list.

The company's weekly meeting, usually a somber affair, descended into a full-blown comedic opera, a performance far more entertaining than anything Max could have envisioned. Each team member presented their interpretation of the new policy, which involved a series of increasingly surreal and hilarious events. They debated the ethical implications of using company stationary to create cat-themed haiku; the legality of conducting wine tastings during client presentations; and the philosophical debate regarding the rights of robotic cats to access company resources.

The climax of the meeting involved a surprise guest appearance by Mittens, who, after successfully hacking the company's projector, displayed his own interpretation of the policy—a series of adorable cat videos set to a background of classical music. The presentation concluded with Mittens casually falling asleep amidst the applause.

The fallout from the "Policy Debacle," as it became affectionately known, was surprisingly minimal. The client representatives, initially bewildered by the events, found themselves charmed by the company's unique approach. They concluded that if WineSoft could navigate such absurd internal conflicts while still producing innovative software, they would be a valuable asset to their project.

The corporate consultant who drafted the policy, after reviewing the post-meeting email chain, suffered a near-fatal case of existential dread. The policy was swiftly repealed.

WineSoft, far from being demoralized by the debacle, emerged stronger, more unified, and possibly even slightly more eccentric than before. They had discovered a truth about workplace harmony: that the most absurd situations can sometimes forge the strongest bonds. After all, what better way to celebrate surviving the most ridiculous company policy ever conceived than with a company-wide wine tasting? And yes, Mittens was invited. His custom-designed catnip-infused Merlot was, of course, the highlight of the event. The next chapter, however, remained unwritten. Or rather, it was already being written, one chaotic, hilarious email at a time. The saga of WineSoft continued. The future, as always, remained delightfully unpredictable.

The aftermath of the "Policy Debacle," as it was now affectionately known throughout the office (and, surprisingly, within certain circles of the broader tech community thanks to a now-viral Mittens Instagram post), was a curious mix of stunned silence and unrestrained laughter. Lily, surprisingly, found herself at the epicenter of this peculiar post-apocalyptic party. Her crafted "Top 10 Policy Violations" list had mysteriously appeared on the company intranet, instantly becoming a source of both amusement and mild HR-induced panic.

The initial shockwaves had settled, replaced by a wave of creative reinterpretation. Max, ever the optimist, saw the debacle as a triumph of individual expression, a testament to WineSoft's unique, if slightly chaotic, spirit. He proposed a company-wide "Policy Interpretation Competition," where teams would compete to create the most inventive (and legally sound, he added as an afterthought) workaround to the most absurd clauses. His enthusiasm, however, bordered on the manic, causing him to accidentally set off the office fire alarm while demonstrating his vision for a "Clause 7.3.b compliant feline-themed interpretive dance."

Dave, still nursing his bruised ego (and a slight case of carpal tunnel from his covert Instagram activities), took a more cynical approach. He decided to document the entire affair, complete with detailed annotations, witty asides, and an extensive collection of Mittens' reaction GIFs. The resulting manuscript, tentatively titled "Mittens' Merlot Manifesto: A Chronicle of Corporate Chaos," was already generating buzz around the water cooler. He even secured a publishing deal for the work of his feline muse under the pseudonym, "Clawsome Content Creator."

Sophie, the diligent intern, meanwhile, had compiled an extensive report detailing the economic impact of the policy debacle. Her findings, unexpectedly, revealed a surge in employee morale and productivity, alongside a significant spike in online engagement and positive media coverage. She even suggested that the debacle could be strategically leveraged as a marketing campaign, emphasizing WineSoft's unique and unconventional approach to problem-solving. This idea, initially met with skepticism, was eventually adopted by Max, resulting in a series of quirky marketing ads featuring Mittens, repurposed policy clauses, and oddly catchy jingles.

Harold, ever the enigmatic figure, chose a more subtle approach. He had secretly constructed a series of miniature scenarios depicting various policy interpretations, each crafted and displayed in a glass case in his cubicle. These miniature worlds, inhabited by Lego figurines representing WineSoft employees, cleverly depicted the humorous consequences of the policy's application. It was a cryptic commentary on the situation, a silent testament to his unwavering commitment to finding profound meaning in absurdity. Harold, it seemed, had created his own quiet and brilliantly absurd version of the company's tumultuous chapter.

Even the client representatives had developed their own interpretation of the events, transforming the debacle into a team-building exercise. They organized a retreat, themed around "navigating corporate absurdity," complete with wine-tasting workshops and a highly requested "Mittens Appreciation Session." The session involved, somewhat inexplicably, a live reenactment of Mittens' Instagram takeover of the company's projector. It was a strange and wonderful testament to how quickly a corporate catastrophe could transform into an unexpected success story.

The corporate consultant, however, remained a ghost story, a tragic figure of bureaucratic excess and unintended consequences. His reputation was completely shattered, his career teetering precariously on the edge of oblivion. Rumors circulated about his descent into self-imposed exile, secluded in a remote cabin surrounded by stacks of unread corporate ethics manuals. He was the cautionary tale, a living embodiment of the risks inherent in drafting poorly written, overly complex workplace policies.

The final act of the Policy Debacle involved a company-wide "Wine and

Reconciliation" party. This wasn't merely a celebration of survival; it was a ritualistic affirmation of WineSoft's unique identity. It was an unfiltered expression of their ability to not only endure chaos but to flourish within it. Max, of course, orchestrated the event with his usual boundless energy, constructing a complex network of interconnected wine dispensers, each bearing a humorous reference to one of the more baffling policy clauses. He even managed to secure a cameo appearance from Mittens, who, draped in a miniature WineSoft branded scarf, was carried into the party on a small velvet cushion. The celebratory mood was infectious, a testament to the enduring power of shared laughter in the face of corporate absurdity.

The impact of the Code of Conduct Debacle on WineSoft's culture was undeniable. It served as a strangely unifying event, forging bonds that ran far deeper than any corporate training program could ever hope to achieve. The shared experience of navigating the absurd, of finding humor in the face of bureaucratic nonsense, created a unique sense of camaraderie that permeated every aspect of their work. WineSoft, once simply a quirky software company, had become a microcosm of creative resilience, a testament to the transformative power of embracing the unexpected.

The company's future, however, remained shrouded in the delightful unpredictability that had become its trademark. One thing was certain, though: there would be more stories to tell, more moments of bizarre brilliance to document, and more opportunities to weave the threads of corporate chaos into the vibrant tapestry of their collective narrative. The tale of WineSoft, with its eccentric characters, hilarious misadventures, and unexpected triumphs, continued to unfold, one chaotic, unpredictable chapter at a time. And somewhere, amidst the flurry of emails, the witty banter, and the occasional Mittens-related Instagram update, the next chapter began to take shape. The legacy of the Code of Conduct Debacle lived on, not as a scar, but as a badge of honor, a testament to the power of laughter and absurdity in the face of corporate monotony. The story of WineSoft was far from over; in fact, it was only just beginning. The future, as always, promised a delicious blend of chaos, creativity, and a whole lot of Merlot.

The aftermath of the wine-soaked, policy-shredding extravaganza wasn't exactly what anyone had anticipated. While the initial shock had worn off, replaced by a collective "Well, that happened," the ripple effects continued to reverberate throughout WineSoft, creating a bizarre symphony of chaos and unexpected consequences.

Lily, the ever-stoic HR manager, found herself surprisingly less enraged than she expected. The sheer absurdity of the situation, coupled with the viral fame of Mittens' now-legendary Instagram takeover, had a strangely cathartic effect. She secretly enjoyed the memes, particularly the one depicting her exasperated face superimposed onto the Mona Lisa. She even started a private Pinterest board dedicated to "Policy Debacle Memes," a fact she vehemently denied when questioned by

Max. However, her renewed focus was on damage control, particularly in the form of devising a new, impossibly complex Code of Conduct, which, she vowed, would be impenetrable to even the most creative (and feline-inspired) interpretations. This new document, ironically, ended up resembling a labyrinthine choose-your-own-adventure novel, further fueling the company's already robust sense of the surreal.

Max, true to form, viewed the debacle as a resounding success. His "Policy Interpretation Competition" had morphed into a full-blown, inter-departmental creative war, resulting in a breathtaking array of absurd solutions. The accounting team, for instance, presented a complex algorithm that calculated optimal wine consumption rates based on project deadlines, while the marketing department proposed using the controversial clauses as a unique selling point, promising "maximum chaos, minimum bureaucracy." Their campaign featured a catchy jingle, "WineSoft: Where the rules are fluid, and the fun is unlimited!" It was, to put it mildly, a masterpiece of unconventional marketing.

Dave, inspired by Mittens' newfound stardom, embarked on a series of increasingly elaborate cat-themed projects, each subtly referencing the policy debacle. His next manuscript, "Mittens' Malbec Manifesto: A Purrfectly Imperfect Guide to Corporate Survival," was already causing a stir in the literary world, even attracting the attention
of a Hollywood studio. His cubicle now resembled a feline-themed shrine, overflowing with catnip toys, personalized water

bowls, and a lifetime supply of high-quality tuna. His productivity, however, remained remarkably consistent, a testament to his remarkable ability to multitask between code, cat care, and manuscript writing.

Sophie, meanwhile, had become the company's accidental data analyst, tracking the impact of the policy debacle on various metrics. She discovered a remarkable correlation between "policy-induced chaos" and "employee engagement," prompting her to propose a new company-wide initiative: "Controlled Chaos Thursdays," a day dedicated to creative problem-solving, free-flowing wine, and strategic brainstorming sessions that could – and often did – devolve into full-blown interpretive dance routines. This initiative, much to Lily's initial horror, was surprisingly adopted, becoming a key component of WineSoft's increasingly unorthodox company culture.

Harold, the enigmatic programmer, remained true to his enigmatic self. His Lego scenarios had evolved into intricate miniature diorama's depicting the escalating absurdity of the situation, each scene a perfect encapsulation of the chaotic energy that had consumed WineSoft. These miniature narratives, filled with tiny Lego figures enacting elaborate scenes of corporate rebellion, were later displayed at a local art gallery, achieving unexpected critical acclaim.

Even the client representatives, initially shocked, had embraced the chaos, viewing the whole ordeal as a bizarre team-building exercise. They started requesting "Mittens Appreciation Days" as part of their contracts, and surprisingly, the CEO of their biggest client now insisted on a monthly video call with Mittens, a demanding yet strangely charming feline executive.

The corporate consultant, on the other hand, remained a tragic footnote, his reputation in tatters. He was last seen attempting to build a career as a professional cat-herder, a profession remarkably similar in complexity to his previous role, though certainly less stressful.

The "Wine and Reconciliation" party was legendary. It wasn't just a party; it was a theatrical performance of corporate catharsis, a celebration of surviving the storm and emerging triumphant (or at least, slightly less bewildered) on the other side. The event featured an epic wine fountain, custom-designed wine glasses bearing witty policy clause quotes, and a live performance of a newly written musical titled "Ode to Mittens," featuring a full orchestra and a surprisingly talented chorus of WineSoft employees. Mittens, of course, made a special appearance, this time riding a miniature chariot pulled by two enthusiastic developers dressed as unicorns.

The long-term consequences of the Code of Conduct Debacle were multifaceted and, frankly, hilarious. WineSoft's reputation, rather than suffering, had been transformed into something unique and genuinely enviable. They had become the poster child for "controlled chaos," a testament to the power of embracing individuality and finding humor in adversity. Their unconventional approach to problem-solving, once viewed as a liability, had transformed into their strongest selling point. Investors were clamoring for a piece of the action, captivated by the company's unique blend of innovation and absurdist humor. Recruitment became easier; candidates were actively seeking out the quirky, chaotic environment of WineSoft. In fact, WineSoft's employee turnover rate went down, replaced by a surge of applications from individuals specifically drawn to the unique, if slightly erratic, brand of corporate culture.

However, the story didn't end there. The success of "Controlled Chaos Thursdays" led to the creation of "Maximum Mayhem Mondays" and "Slightly Silly Saturdays," each a unique and wonderfully bizarre take on the traditional work week. Lily, after countless hours crafting increasingly complicated rules, finally embraced the mayhem, secretly orchestrating many of the most chaotic events, all while maintaining a facade of stern professionalism. Max, ever the visionary, was exploring the feasibility of a "Wine-Infused Coding Workshop," designed to enhance creativity and productivity (or perhaps simply generate hilarious coding errors, nobody was quite sure).

The legacy of the Code of Conduct Debacle lived on, not as a cautionary tale, but as a badge of honor, a testament to the power of resilience, laughter, and the unexpected. The story of WineSoft, filled with quirky characters, hilarious misadventures, and unlikely triumphs, was far from over. In fact, it was just getting started. The future, like a perfectly aged Merlot, promised a delectable blend of chaos, innovation, and a whole lot of unexpected fun. The tale of WineSoft, a company where the only constant was the constant state of delightful, unpredictable change, continued, one hilariously chaotic chapter at a time. And somewhere, amidst the laughter, the wine, and the occasional Mittens-related viral sensation, the next chapter was already brewing.

The new Code of Conduct, a sprawling document Lily affectionately (and secretly) dubbed "The Leviathan," arrived on everyone's desks like a literary Trojan horse. Printed on parchment-like paper, it was less a set of rules and more a choose-your-own-adventure novel detailing the precise protocol for handling everything from spilled wine (Category A infraction: immediate cleanup and mandatory wine tasting with HR) to unauthorized cat naps (Category B: potential for mandatory yoga session, depending on the cat's approval). The sheer complexity of the document was awe-inspiring. Even Lily, its creator, occasionally found herself lost in its labyrinthine clauses, resorting to flipping coins to resolve ambiguous situations.

Max, naturally, saw the new rules as a challenge. He immediately organized a "Leviathan Deciphering Competition," offering a prize of a year's supply of fine wine to the team member who could find the most creative loophole. Dave, however, had other priorities. He'd fashioned a miniature replica of the Code of Conduct out of tuna cans and cat toys, creating a sort of feline-centric commentary on the absurdity of it all. Mittens, predictably, was unimpressed, preferring to nap on top of the document.

Sophie, ever the pragmatist, decided to analyze the rules using her newly acquired data analysis skills. She created a complex spreadsheet that tracked infractions, correlating them with employee productivity, mood, and overall levels of creative output. Her findings were both startling and hilarious: a direct correlation existed between the number of rule violations and the number of innovative ideas generated.

Her report concluded that, while strictly adhering to the Leviathan might improve short-term order, it dramatically stifled the company's unique brand of creative chaos.

Harold, however, remained aloof, his Lego universe evolving into a complex and darkly humorous allegory of the Leviathan's oppressive reign. His miniature figures were engaged in a series of increasingly elaborate schemes to overthrow the tyranny of the Code of Conduct, including a daring heist of Lily's prized collection of vintage wine glasses. His intricate diorama became a highly sought-after exhibit at the local arts festival, attracting attention from art critics and surprisingly, a few venture capitalists.

The implementation of the Leviathan was, to put it mildly, messy. The first week alone saw an explosion of unintended consequences. The accounting team, attempting to navigate the nuances of Clause 3.7b (regarding the appropriate levels of wine consumption during budget meetings), accidentally deleted a critical financial file. The marketing department, interpreting Clause 4.2a (regarding the use of company resources for personal enrichment) somewhat liberally, started using the company's resources to create an absurdly expensive (but strangely effective) marketing campaign featuring a life-size inflatable Mittens.

Meanwhile, the development team embraced a new game – "Leviathan Roulette," where each developer randomly selected a clause from the Code of Conduct and attempted to integrate it into their coding practices. The results were predictably chaotic, producing a software that, while functionally questionable, was strangely captivating. One particular feature, born from a misinterpretation of Clause 6.1c, allowed users to customize their software experience with personalized cat memes, leading to its unforeseen popularity.

Lily, witnessing this escalating pandemonium, found herself wrestling with a moral dilemma. She'd crafted the Leviathan to control the chaos, but the chaos, in turn, had fostered a kind of unique creativity that was quintessentially WineSoft. She found herself secretly amused by the absurdity of it all, feeling strangely nostalgic for the days before the Leviathan, a time that now seemed like a simpler, if somewhat messier, era.

Max, meanwhile, continued to revel in the chaos. He viewed the "Leviathan Roulette" game as a testament to WineSoft's unique culture of innovative disruption. He even proposed a new company-wide initiative: "Leviathan Hackathon," a competition where teams would try to creatively "hack" the Code of

Conduct, finding the most innovative and amusing ways to circumvent its rules.

The impact of the Leviathan on the company was profound, though not in the way Lily had intended. The company's brand of controlled chaos became even more amplified, attracting a new wave of eccentrically talented applicants who were drawn to the unique culture and appreciated the company's unconventional approach to problem-solving. The corporate culture had become something of a legend, a beacon to individuals who felt stifled by rigid corporate structures.

Even the client representatives, initially apprehensive about the aftermath of the previous debacle, began to view the controlled chaos as a unique selling proposition. They saw the unexpected creativity and the sheer tenacity of the WineSoft team as an asset, appreciating their unconventional approach to problem-solving. They began to request WineSoft's unique brand of chaos as part of their projects, viewing it as a stimulating and unexpected source of innovation.

The story of the Leviathan, therefore, wasn't one of complete failure. Instead, it was a testament to WineSoft's ability to adapt, evolve, and find humor in the face of overwhelming absurdity. The Leviathan, intended as a tool for control, had inadvertently become a catalyst for creativity, further solidifying WineSoft's reputation as a company that embraced its unique brand of chaos. The unexpected success born from the Leviathan led to a series of increasingly bizarre and unpredictable events, further solidifying WineSoft's place in the annals of unusual corporate success stories. The company's future, much like its past, seemed filled with potential for delightful, unpredictable change. The legacy of the Code of Conduct Debacle and its subsequent Leviathan rulebook lived on, not as a cautionary tale, but as a monument to WineSoft's remarkable resilience and its ability to find humor and success in the most unexpected of places. The story of WineSoft, in its unconventional glory, was far from over. It was, in fact, just beginning its next chapter, brimming with the promise of more delightful, unpredictable adventures.

The stalemate over the Leviathan, as Lily had begun to affectionately—and perhaps slightly maniacally—refer to the Code of Conduct, couldn't last forever. The air in the WineSoft office, thick with the scent of spilled wine and impending doom, crackled with a strange sort of energy. The constant stream of absurd incidents—the accidental deletion of the financial file, the inflatable Mittens marketing campaign, the "Leviathan Roulette" coding spree—had reached a fever pitch. Even Max, the champion of controlled chaos, began to feel a twinge of...something resembling orderliness.

Lily, however, was at her wit's end. The spreadsheet Sophie had crafted, detailing the correlation between rule-breaking and innovative ideas, had inadvertently become a weapon against her own creation. Each new data point only served to solidify the counterintuitive argument: chaos, it seemed, was the lifeblood of WineSoft. She stared at the spreadsheet, her fingers tracing the lines connecting rule violations to successful product features. It was undeniable. The Leviathan, ironically, was strangling the very creativity it was designed to protect.

Dave, meanwhile, had moved on from his tuna-can Leviathan replica. He'd begun a new project: a complex algorithm designed to predict the likelihood of a cat-related incident based on the lunar cycle and the atmospheric pressure. He was convinced it would revolutionize office safety, though its practical application remained...murky. Mittens, perched on his keyboard, seemed unconcerned with the algorithm's potential for global domination.

Harold, ever the artistic rebel, had taken his Lego diorama to a new level of complexity. He now had miniature versions of the entire WineSoft team, each engaging in tiny acts of rebellion against a Lego Leviathan. He even crafted a tiny, impeccably detailed Lily figure frantically trying to restore order, complete with a miniature, recreated spreadsheet.

Sophie, however, proposed a solution. Her data analysis hadn't just revealed the problem; it had pointed the way towards a solution. She presented her findings to the team, outlining a revised approach. Instead of a rigid set of rules, she suggested a system of guidelines, a "flexible framework" for acceptable behavior. It would still address the key concerns—spilled wine, excessive cat naps, inappropriate use of company resources— but with a more...flexible approach.

"Think of it," Sophie explained, her voice filled with the calm authority of a seasoned data analyst, "as a living document, constantly evolving and adapting to our unique work environment. We can use data to track the impact of different approaches, and fine-tune the guidelines as needed. We can embrace the chaos, but channel it in productive ways."

Max, initially skeptical, found himself intrigued. He envisioned a system where the guidelines would be voted on by the team, fostering a sense of ownership and collective responsibility. He even suggested incorporating a points-based system, rewarding creative solutions to the guidelines, rather than merely punishing violations. The "Leviathan Hackathon" he'd proposed could become a platform for this, transforming the act of "hacking" the rules into a collaborative exercise in creative problem-solving.

Lily, surprisingly, found herself agreeing. Sophie's proposal wasn't a complete surrender to chaos; it was a more intelligent way of managing it. It acknowledged the importance of structure while preserving WineSoft's unique creative spirit. The rigid rules of the Leviathan, she realized, hadn't stifled creativity; they'd merely diverted it into increasingly bizarre and unpredictable channels. A flexible framework, one that allowed for adaptation and evolution, would channel that energy towards more productive ends.

Dave, distracted momentarily by Mittens batting at a dangling wire, voiced his tentative approval. He figured any system that allowed for sufficient cat nap time was worth considering. Harold, meanwhile, was already brainstorming ways to integrate his Lego models into the new framework, envisioning a series of interactive simulations to test the efficacy of different guidelines.

The compromise wasn't just a shift in policy; it was a testament to the team's surprising ability to collaborate and find common ground. They recognized their shared goal: to maintain WineSoft's unique and successful brand of quirky innovation without descending into utter pandemonium. The new system, dubbed "The Agile Framework," was a hybrid between structure and flexibility, reflecting the company's unique blend of creativity and pragmatism.

The "Agile Framework," as it came to be known, was a far cry from the rigid, parchment-bound Leviathan. It consisted of a series of flexible guidelines, subject to regular review and amendment based on team feedback and data analysis. Each guideline had a clearly defined purpose, but also included a "creative loophole" clause, allowing for reasonable deviations under specific circumstances.

The implementation of the Agile Framework was a surprisingly smooth process. The team embraced the collaborative aspect, contributing ideas and suggestions, turning the revision process into a lively discussion rather than a battle of wills. Max championed the new system, introducing a points-based reward program for innovative solutions, fueling the team's desire to experiment and contribute.

The impact was immediate. The chaotic energy that had characterized WineSoft under the Leviathan was redirected into focused creativity. The development team, freed from the rigid constraints of the old Code of Conduct, unleashed a torrent of new and innovative ideas. The marketing team, inspired by the new collaborative spirit, created a series of truly memorable and absurd marketing campaigns, leveraging the "creative loophole" clause to their advantage.

The Agile Framework wasn't just a successful replacement for the Leviathan; it became a symbol of WineSoft's unique work culture. It attracted top-tier talent, drawn to the company's flexible yet structured environment, a testament to WineSoft's ability to balance order and chaos. Even the board of directors, initially apprehensive about the company's unusual approach, lauded the new system as a model of innovative organizational management.

The legacy of the Code of Conduct Debacle wasn't a cautionary tale of disastrous mismanagement; it was a testament to WineSoft's resilience, adaptability, and ability to find humor in the face of adversity. The Agile Framework, born from the ashes of the Leviathan, stood as a symbol of their collaborative spirit, highlighting their ability to blend their quirky personalities with a more structured work environment. The unexpected success of WineSoft, a company that embraced chaos as its creative muse, proved that sometimes, the most unconventional paths lead to the most remarkable destinations. The story of WineSoft, and its improbable journey from the rigid rules of the Leviathan to the fluid framework of the Agile system, was a testament to the power of collaboration, adaptability, and laughter in the face of workplace challenges. It was, indeed, a remarkable tale of a company that found success, not in spite of its chaos, but because of it. And the next chapter? It promised to be just as unpredictable, creative, and, dare one say, slightly less messy.

Chapter 9: The Hackathon Hijinks

The air crackled with a different kind of energy now, less the impending doom of the Leviathan and more the buzzing anticipation of a caffeine-fueled coding frenzy. WineSoft was participating in "CodeCon," a regional hackathon notorious for its challenging problems and even more challenging competitors – primarily a team of suspiciously well-rested individuals from a rival firm called "Synergy Solutions," whose name alone exuded an air of corporate sterility.

Max, ever the showman, had decked out their booth in a riot of purple and green streamers, complete with a life-sized cardboard cutout of Mittens wearing a tiny coding hat. Lily, armed with an arsenal of energy drinks and an even more potent supply of sarcasm, supervised from a strategically placed beanbag chair. Dave, naturally, had brought Mittens, who promptly installed himself on a stack of printed circuit boards, surveying the scene with an air of regal disdain. Sophie, the unsung hero of the Agile Framework, navigated the chaotic landscape with remarkable composure, managing both the team's caffeine intake and their increasingly bizarre coding ideas.

The hackathon's first challenge was a doozy: design a program that could predict the optimal time to brew the perfect cup of coffee, taking into account variables such as bean type, water temperature, and ambient atmospheric pressure (Dave was suspiciously excited about this one). Synergy Solutions, predictably, approached the problem with a clinical efficiency that bordered on robotic. Their code, a masterpiece of clean, efficient programming, yielded results that were accurate but utterly devoid of personality.

WineSoft, on the other hand, embraced chaos. Their solution, christened "The Caffeinated Kraken," was a sprawling, multi-threaded monstrosity of code, incorporating elements of astrological forecasting, user sentiment analysis, and a surprisingly accurate algorithm for predicting the likelihood of a spontaneous office dance-off. It produced highly unreliable, but undeniably entertaining results, spitting out predictions like, "Optimal brew time: 2:17 pm, accompanied by a spontaneous rendition of 'Bohemian Rhapsody.'"

The second challenge involved developing a system for organizing a highly complex spreadsheet — a task that sent a palpable shiver down Lily's spine. While Synergy Solutions churned out a sleek, user-friendly interface, WineSoft's answer was…different. Their program, "Spreadsheet Symphony," treated the spreadsheet as a musical score, assigning different cells to different instruments and generating a chaotic but surprisingly effective arrangement. The resulting auditory chaos was less a spreadsheet and more an avant-garde symphony. The judges, though initially bewildered, were strangely captivated.

Harold, meanwhile, had taken advantage of the "creative loophole" clause to the nth degree. He'd incorporated his Lego creations into the presentation, creating miniature versions of the WineSoft team battling miniature versions of the Synergy Solutions team in a dramatic re-enactment of the spreadsheet challenge. The Lego figures, complete with minuscule coding hats, even had tiny, hand-painted expressions of utter bewilderment.

As the hackathon progressed, the WineSoft team's unique approach began to win over even the most skeptical judges. They were a chaotic whirlwind, a symphony of mismatched personalities and half-baked ideas, yet their energy and creativity were infectious. They weren't just solving problems; they were creating experiences.

The final challenge was a particularly daunting one: create an app that could accurately predict the winner of a highly unpredictable game of office charades. Synergy Solutions approached this with their usual clinical precision, utilizing advanced machine learning algorithms and extensive data analysis. Their app, though accurate, was utterly devoid of the lighthearted charm one might expect from a game of office charades.

WineSoft's response, however, was a masterpiece of chaotic brilliance. Their app, "Charade Chaos," wasn't just a prediction tool; it was a fully immersive, interactive experience. It incorporated live video feeds from the game, real-time sentiment analysis of the audience, and an ever-evolving algorithm that adapted to the unpredictable nature of human behavior. It was a mess of overlapping code and unexpected features, but it worked, somehow, perfectly.

The judges were in stitches. They watched in awe as the app predicted the winner with surprising accuracy, highlighting not only the outcome but also the unexpected twists and turns of the game. Even the Synergy Solutions team found themselves impressed, despite their efforts to maintain an air of professional composure.

The results were announced under a shower of confetti and an uncomfortable amount of celebratory cake. Synergy Solutions had won the technical excellence award, a testament to their efficient coding practices and predictable results. But WineSoft? They had swept the board in every other category. They secured the "Most Creative Solution" award, the "Best Use of Caffeine" award (a prestigious and surprisingly competitive category), and the newly established "Most Likely to Cause Spontaneous Office Dance-Off" award.

Max, basking in the reflected glory of Mittens, accepted the awards with his usual flair. Lily, slightly caffeinated and supremely satisfied, gave a wry smirk to the Synergy Solutions team, who seemed slightly bewildered by WineSoft's unconventional triumph. Dave, clutching Mittens close, simply nodded, his approval as silent and mysterious as his feline companion. Sophie, meanwhile, quietly noted the data points supporting the conclusion that chaos, when properly channeled, could be a surprisingly effective tool for innovation.

The hackathon was more than just a competition; it was a validation of WineSoft's unique approach. It proved that creativity didn't need to be constrained by rigid rules or sterile efficiency; it could thrive in the midst of chaos, guided by the unexpected insights of data-driven decision-making. The team returned to the office exhausted but exhilarated, their victory a testament to their collaborative spirit and their embrace of the unconventional. And as they celebrated their win with a well-deserved (and slightly excessive) office wine tasting, the future of WineSoft seemed brighter than ever, promising even more adventures, more absurd creations, and certainly, more captivating chaos.

The Agile Framework, born from the ashes of the Leviathan, had not only survived but thrived. It had, in fact, become the very foundation of WineSoft's success, a perfect example of how a company could embrace its unique personality while maintaining a productive work environment. The legacy of the Leviathan, once a symbol of rigid control, now stood as a testament to the power of adaptation and flexibility. The story of WineSoft, a company that found success in embracing its chaos, continued to unfold, promising more unpredictable turns and laughter-filled victories. The journey from the stifling rules of the Leviathan to the liberating flexibility of the Agile Framework was a story of transformation, proving that sometimes, the greatest innovations are born from the most unexpected of places – and that a little chaos, when managed well, can be a powerful force for good, or at least, for very entertaining software. The next chapter, however, remained unwritten. And nobody, not even Max, had the slightest idea what it would bring.

The victory at CodeCon didn't quell the competitive fires within WineSoft; it merely redirected them. The internal rivalry, previously focused on conquering the Leviathan project, now manifested in a series of increasingly absurd office challenges. The first casualty was the office coffee machine. Dave, spurred on by his newfound hackathon glory (and a disturbing amount of caffeine), declared a "Brew-Off," a competition to create the most innovative and delicious cup of coffee. The rules were vague, the judging subjective, and the resulting aroma a heady mix of burnt beans, exotic spices, and sheer desperation.

Lily, initially resistant, found herself unexpectedly drawn into the fray, creating a surprisingly sophisticated concoction involving cold-brew, cardamom, and a hint of lavender. She documented the process, complete with flow charts and statistical analysis, a stark contrast to Dave's chaotic approach, which primarily involved throwing random ingredients into a blender and hoping for the best. Max, ever the opportunist, attempted to leverage the Brew-Off for marketing purposes, suggesting they bottle and sell the winning brew as "WineSoft's Elixir of Innovation." Sophie, meanwhile, calmly managed the escalating caffeine levels and the increasingly frantic attempts to clean up the coffee-related spills.

The Brew-Off was only the beginning. Next came the "Desk Decor Derby," a competition to create the most aesthetically pleasing (or, in Dave's case, most cat-friendly) workspace. Dave's entry featured a complex network of cat tunnels and scratching posts, intricately woven around his computer equipment, much to Mittens' delight. Lily, opting for a minimalist approach, created a workspace of stark elegance that was almost aggressively uncluttered – a testament to her ability to maintain order amidst chaos. Max's desk, predictably, resembled a chaotic explosion in a party supply store. Sophie, always practical, created a functional workspace that balanced creativity and efficiency, a testament to her ability to navigate the often-conflicting personalities of her colleagues.

The intensity of the competition surprised even the team members themselves. They were used to collaborating, but this internal rivalry brought a new dimension to their dynamic. There was an element of playful sabotage, a healthy dose of one-upmanship, and a constant, low-level hum of competitive energy. It was, in its own way, a testament to their shared commitment to excellence, even if their methods for achieving it were occasionally unconventional. However, unlike the external competition at CodeCon, these internal challenges never seemed to dampen their team spirit. It always felt like a friendly competition, never crossing into negativity or bitterness.

One unexpected outcome of this intensified competitive spirit was a surge in productivity. The desire to outdo one another pushed them to explore new ideas, to experiment with innovative solutions, and to push the boundaries of their creativity. The office, once a space of comfortable routine, became a breeding ground for new ideas. The air crackled with energy, a dynamic interplay of creativity and competition. This was a unique dynamic not seen during their early days of the Leviathan project.

The competition wasn't limited to frivolous challenges. It even permeated their work.
A new feature was added to their core software, leading to a "Coding Clash" between Dave and Lily, a battle of wits that resulted in an elegant solution that surprised everyone, including themselves. They developed a code-writing game where they competed against each other, adding a fun and engaging element to a usually daunting task.

The culmination of this competitive spirit was the "WineSoft Olympics," a series of absurd and often nonsensical games designed to celebrate their camaraderie and achievements. Events included a blind wine tasting (judged by Sophie's surprisingly refined palate), a paper airplane distance competition (Max's entry defied both aerodynamics and the laws of physics), and a "Code-a-thon sprint" where they raced to complete a ridiculously complex coding puzzle.

The WineSoft Olympics, as hilarious as it was, highlighted the unexpected benefits of this intense but playful competition. It brought them closer, strengthening their bonds and solidifying their team spirit. The event concluded with a massive celebratory party, a blend of wine, laughter, and slightly competitive boasting.

However, amidst the fun and games, a serious observation was made. The competitive spirit, initially fueled by a desire to outperform others, had ultimately fostered a spirit of collaboration. The desire to win had pushed them to work harder, think smarter, and support each other in ways they had never considered before. They learned that competition could be a catalyst for innovation, pushing them beyond their individual limitations.

The Agile Framework, once a response to the stifling rules of the Leviathan project, now stood as a beacon of adaptability and flexibility, perfectly embodying the WineSoft spirit: embracing both individual creativity and collaborative spirit. It perfectly balanced structure and freedom, allowing each member to thrive while simultaneously working towards shared goals. The competitive spirit hadn't replaced their collaborative nature; instead, it had enhanced it. It created a dynamic synergy that drove innovation and productivity.

The story of WineSoft wasn't just about escaping the constraints of a rigid framework; it was about finding the perfect balance between order and chaos, competition and collaboration. It was a journey of self-discovery, both individually and as a team, a testament to the power of embracing their unique personalities and building a team culture that valued both individual expression and collective achievement. And as they celebrated their unusual success with a well-deserved (and thoroughly documented) office wine tasting, they knew that their journey, far from being over, was just beginning, full of more absurd adventures, unexpected triumphs, and undoubtedly, more hilarious office competitions. The future of WineSoft, it seemed, was as unpredictable and exhilarating as ever. The next chapter, however, promised to be even more chaotic and fun.

The WineSoft Olympics hangover was still clinging to the office like the lingering scent of cheap Merlot when the Hackathon Hijinks officially commenced. Max, fueled by a bizarre combination of leftover pizza and misplaced ambition, had decided that WineSoft needed to participate in the annual "Code Craze" hackathon. The event, notorious for its punishing deadlines, caffeine-fueled nights, and questionable judging criteria, was generally avoided by sensible companies. WineSoft, of course, was anything but sensible.

The initial team selection process was, predictably, chaotic. Max wanted to assemble a "dream team" of the most competitive individuals, leading to a series of tense negotiations and whispered power plays. Dave, still riding the high of his Brew-Off victory, nominated himself and Mittens (the cat, naturally, was ineligible). Lily, ever the pragmatist, suggested a more balanced approach, advocating for a mix of skills and temperaments to avoid a complete meltdown. Sophie, caught in the crossfire, attempted to create a detailed spreadsheet outlining everyone's strengths and weaknesses, only to have it promptly discarded by Max in favor of a dartboard with everyone's names pinned on it.

Surprisingly, this chaotic selection process led to an unexpected alliance. Lily, typically at odds with Dave's laissez-faire approach to coding, found herself surprisingly drawn to his unconventional problem-solving skills. Dave, in turn, was impressed by Lily's planning and organizational abilities, a stark contrast to his own improvisational style. They formed an uneasy truce, a temporary alliance forged in the crucible of impending hackathon doom. This partnership was a study in opposites attracting, with Lily providing the structure and Dave adding the creative spark. Their combined skillset turned out to be surprisingly effective. Sophie, meanwhile, acted as their surprisingly effective mediator, keeping them focused and preventing their inherently contrasting work styles from descending into all-out office war. Her ability to defuse tense situations and manage conflicting personalities was invaluable in keeping the peace and allowing them to work collaboratively.

Their project, initially conceived as a simple mobile app to track wine consumption (naturally), morphed into something far more ambitious: a sophisticated AI-powered wine recommendation engine capable of predicting a user's taste profile with unnerving accuracy. The app, cleverly titled "VinoVision," incorporated advanced machine learning algorithms, a user-friendly interface, and an optional feature that allowed users to share their wine experiences with their friends via a personalized emoji system. Yes, the emojis were wine-themed. The project was audacious, bordering on insane, but it was precisely this sort of outlandish ambition that characterized WineSoft.

The hackathon itself was a blur of energy drinks, instant noodles, and questionable coding decisions. Dave, fueled by an impressive stash of energy bars and an abundance of cat-themed stickers, worked tirelessly, occasionally pausing to let Mittens nap on his keyboard. Lily, armed with a crafted schedule, tracked their progress, ensuring they stayed on task and met their deadlines. Sophie, surprisingly, functioned as the team's morale officer, ensuring everyone remained hydrated and relatively sane amidst the chaos. She even managed to bake a batch of delicious cookies to fuel their late-night coding sessions. Max, ever the ringmaster, flitted between teams, providing (mostly unhelpful) advice and copious amounts of caffeine.

Meanwhile, other teams were locked in their own battles. The usual suspects – corporate giants with massive budgets and teams of highly-paid engineers – were all present and accounted for. But there were also smaller teams, scrappy underdogs like WineSoft, each with their own unique approaches and personalities. There were the "Night Owls," a team of students known for their caffeine dependency and their ability to code for 48 hours straight. There was "Team Synergy," who bragged endlessly about their flawless teamwork, only to produce a frankly underwhelming app. And there was "The Code Crusaders," whose project, according to their presentation, would solve world hunger through the power of blockchain technology.

The competition was fierce. The air buzzed with the energy of intense focus and quiet competition. As the deadline loomed, the WineSoft team worked tirelessly, fueled by a cocktail of adrenaline, caffeine, and the faint hope of winning something of any real value. The pressure mounted as teams frantically debugged their projects, each hoping that their innovation would shine above the rest. The environment itself was a cauldron of stressed minds and fingers furiously typing.

However, the pressure didn't seem to dampen the team's spirits. In fact, it seemed to enhance their collaboration, pushing them to new heights of creativity and problem-solving. Their unconventional alliance, once a last-ditch effort, blossomed into something stronger. Lily and Dave, despite their contrasting personalities, found a rhythm, their strengths complementing each other, producing a code that was both elegant and robust. The project was a testament to their unexpected synergy, a beautiful blend of structured planning and innovative improvisation.

On the final day, as the presentations began, the tension was palpable. Each team presented their project with a mixture of pride and anxiety. The judges, a panel of industry veterans with faces as stony as ancient gargoyles, listened intently. Some presentations were slick and polished, others were clunky and awkward. WineSoft's presentation was, to put it mildly, unique.

Max, wearing a slightly crumpled tuxedo and clutching a bottle of their finest Merlot, delivered a theatrical speech that was more stand-up comedy than software pitch. Lily, in contrast, presented a clear and concise technical overview, highlighting VinoVision's key features and demonstrating its remarkable capabilities. Dave, after a brief introduction highlighting Mittens' contribution (mostly sleeping on his lap), showcased the user interface, its intuitive design and fun functionality. Sophie, ever the diplomat, charmingly thanked the judges and the team members for their unwavering dedication, effectively smoothing any rough edges from the presentation.

The judges, initially bewildered, were surprisingly impressed. VinoVision was unlike anything they had ever seen. Its combination of advanced technology and playful design was innovative and refreshing. The judges were not only amused, but they saw the potential in the unexpected success of the project. The app was a masterpiece of unexpected harmony.

The announcement of the winners was met with bated breath. The tension was palpable, even the air seemed to crackle with anticipation. When WineSoft's name was announced as the winner, a collective roar of disbelief and joy erupted from the team. They had done it. They had won, not through brute force or corporate maneuvering, but through their unique blend of chaos, innovation, and unexpected alliances. The victory was a testament to their unique team dynamic, a celebration of their ability to not only survive but to thrive in the face of adversity and their own internal differences. The Hackathon Hijinks had indeed yielded unexpected fruit.

Their success wasn't just a victory for WineSoft, it was a victory for the power of embracing the unexpected, for finding strength in unlikely alliances, and for proving that sometimes, the most innovative solutions come from the most chaotic places. Their celebration that night was appropriately boisterous, a fitting end to their incredible journey. The future of WineSoft, it seemed, was as bright and unpredictable as ever.

The celebratory pizza arrived, a greasy, cheesy testament to their victory, a far cry from the gourmet meals often associated with corporate hackathon wins. But at WineSoft, gourmet was a relative term, usually involving at least one questionable ingredient and a healthy dose of Max's questionable wine pairings. The pizza, however, was universally appreciated, a symbol of their hard-earned triumph. They devoured it with the ferocity only a team fueled by caffeine, code, and adrenaline could muster. Lily, surprisingly, managed to maintain a semblance of elegance even while wrestling a particularly recalcitrant pepperoni slice. Dave, meanwhile, fed Mittens tiny bits of crust, documenting the entire process with copious amounts of Instagram stories. Sophie, ever the practical one, carefully salvaged the remaining slices for the next day's lunch, showcasing her resourcefulness that had been invaluable throughout the grueling hackathon.

The afterglow of their win lasted for days. The "VinoVision" app, initially a whimsical side project, became the talk of the tech world. Articles praising their innovative design and sophisticated AI algorithms popped up in major tech publications, showering WineSoft with unexpected accolades. Max, predictably, took full credit, sending out celebratory emails with subject lines like, "We did it! (Mostly thanks to me, of course)." Lily, ever the pragmatist, quietly revised the project's documentation, adding a more detailed breakdown of their unexpected teamwork and the collaborative effort that was instrumental in their success. Dave, naturally, posted a series of photos of Mittens lounging on stacks of printed VinoVision brochures, captioning them with phrases like, "Mittens' approval rating: 10/10." Sophie, ever the level-headed one, quietly updated the company's website and social media accounts, ensuring that the hype was handled in an organized and professional manner.

The unexpected success led to unexpected opportunities. Venture capitalists, previously hesitant about WineSoft's unconventional approach, suddenly clamored for a piece of the action. Max, fueled by newfound confidence and an endless supply of Merlot, orchestrated a series of high-stakes meetings, wielding his newfound clout with theatrical flair. Lily, armed with her crafted spreadsheets and business plans, navigated the complex world of venture capital with her trademark blend of pragmatism and sarcasm, skillfully negotiating deals and securing favorable terms. Dave, surprisingly insightful during the negotiations, provided some valuable technical insights, demonstrating a surprising aptitude for business strategy despite his love for cats and coding. Sophie, as always, was the glue that held it all together, ensuring everything ran smoothly and preventing the meetings from completely spiraling into chaos. Through it all, the team maintained its unlikely harmony, a testament to the unexpected synergy that had formed during the hackathon.

The board meeting, originally anticipated with apprehension, turned into a triumphant celebration. The board members, initially skeptical of WineSoft's chaotic approach, were thoroughly impressed by VinoVision's success and the team's innovative spirit. They praised their unique brand of creativity and unconventional teamwork, lauding their ability to find solutions in unexpected ways. Max, naturally, basked in the praise, while Lily discreetly filed the positive feedback into the company's records, acknowledging the team's effort and highlighting their collaborative achievement. Dave, predictably, brought along Mittens, who nonchalantly rested on the boardroom table, oblivious to the gravity of the occasion. Sophie, with her calm demeanor and well-prepared presentation, skillfully handled the ensuing Q&A; session.

The success of VinoVision catapulted WineSoft into the big leagues. Their office, once a charmingly cluttered space with an overabundance of wine bottles and empty pizza boxes, underwent a renovation, transforming into a modern, stylish workspace. But, despite the upgrade, the quirky WineSoft spirit remained intact, a comforting presence amidst the new, more professional environment. The team members, even with their newfound success, retained their unique personalities. Max remained the enthusiastic, sometimes erratic leader; Lily remained the skeptical yet supportive HR manager; Dave continued to code with a cat on his lap, documenting it all on Instagram; Sophie remained the calm, organized, and insightful intern, still keeping the peace among her colleagues.

But the most significant impact of VinoVision's success was the unexpected boost in morale. The team, once a collection of individuals with contrasting personalities and work styles, had evolved into a cohesive unit, bound by shared experiences and a sense of mutual respect. The hackathon, initially perceived as a daunting task, had become a transformative experience, forging an unlikely alliance and cementing their bond. The success of VinoVision wasn't just a victory for WineSoft, it was a victory for their ability to embrace their differences, to learn from one another and to work together, proving that sometimes, the most unexpected collaborations can yield the most remarkable results.

The unexpected success of VinoVision spurred a wave of internal projects at WineSoft. They didn't just rest on their laurels. Inspired by their hackathon win, the team explored various new ideas, many of them just as quirky and unconventional as their previous endeavors. There was the "Wine-Tasting Algorithm," an app designed to pair wines with various types of cheese, based on user-submitted tasting notes and machine-learning models. There was the "Grapevine Gazette," a company blog which provided a platform for showcasing WineSoft's culture and its employees' eclectic personalities. Dave even pitched an app that would translate cat meows into human language, a project that Max initially dismissed as absurd but eventually gave in to, under the guise of 'expanding their technological horizons'.

Lily, in her role as HR manager, continued to champion employee well-being, adding yoga classes, meditation sessions, and even a weekly wine tasting to the company's benefits package. These unusual additions proved highly popular among the staff, fostering a welcoming and relaxed atmosphere in the workplace. Sophie, now a fully-fledged member of the team, further solidified her role as the team's mediator, ensuring that internal conflicts were resolved swiftly and fairly.

The company's success wasn't just measured in sales figures and market valuations but in the happiness and fulfillment of its employees. They had created a unique work environment – a place where individuality was celebrated and unconventional ideas were not just tolerated but actively encouraged. WineSoft had become a testament to the idea that success didn't always have to look or feel conventional.

Even the company's investors, initially drawn to WineSoft's technological potential, were captivated by their unique work culture. They admired the team's collaborative spirit, its ability to bounce back from setbacks, and its unwavering commitment to innovation. The investors' trust in the team was not just financial but extended to a belief in their vision and their ethos. They understood that WineSoft's success wasn't merely about creating innovative apps, but in cultivating a workplace where talent could flourish in its own unique way.

The VinoVision app continued its phenomenal success, gaining a dedicated following among wine enthusiasts. Its innovative features, combined with its user-friendly interface, ensured that it was an effortless delight to use. The company had found a niche and mastered it, showcasing the power of merging technology with a human touch. The surprising success story of WineSoft, born from a seemingly improbable combination of talent, a dash of chaos, and a whole lot of passion, continued to resonate throughout the tech world.

Their story became an inspiration – a reminder that the most successful teams are not always those with perfect plans and perfectly synchronized strategies, but rather those that embraced their unique identities, fostered collaboration, and never lost sight of their passion. WineSoft, the unlikely success story, had proven that sometimes, the best results emerge from the most unlikely places and the most unexpected alliances. Their ongoing adventure, full of new challenges and opportunities, promised more laughter, more innovation, and plenty more stories to tell. The journey, like their favorite Merlot, had a unique and captivating blend, one that would undoubtedly continue to surprise and delight.

The air in the WineSoft office buzzed with a chaotic energy that was entirely unique to them. Forget the sterile, subdued celebrations of other tech companies. This was a victory party fueled by leftover pizza, questionable wine choices (Max had somehow managed to acquire a case of vintage dandelion wine), and an almost overwhelming sense of disbelief. Confetti cannons, purchased on a whim by Max, malfunctioned spectacularly, showering the team with mostly glitter and a cloud of slightly burnt-smelling paper. Lily, ever the pragmatist, swept up the mess while muttering about fire hazards and insurance claims.

Dave, naturally, had Mittens perched on his shoulders, the cat seemingly unfazed by the general pandemonium. He used the occasion to capture a series of
"behind-the-scenes" videos for Mittens' Instagram, featuring close-ups of the glittery confetti sticking to the cat's fur and dramatic shots of him surveying the room from a precarious position atop a stack of empty pizza boxes. The captions were, as always, a masterpiece of ironic understatement: "Just another day at the office," or "Keeping a watchful eye on the celebrations."

Sophie, ever organized, had prepared a slideshow documenting their hackathon journey, complete with funny outtakes and candid shots of the team battling sleep deprivation. The slideshow, surprisingly, became the highlight of the evening. Max's dramatic narration, accompanied by a hastily assembled soundtrack featuring mostly cat meows and upbeat elevator music, had everyone in stitches. Even Lily cracked a smile, though she maintained a stoic façade throughout, occasionally muttering corrections to Max's wildly inaccurate timeline.

The celebratory mood was punctuated by a series of impromptu speeches. Max, naturally, delivered a rambling monologue about the brilliance of his leadership, the sheer genius of the team, and the undeniable superiority of dandelion wine as a celebratory beverage. His speech was a masterpiece of self-congratulatory ramblings interspersed with wildly inaccurate claims about the technical details of the VinoVision app, which he largely attributed to divine inspiration and a healthy dose of caffeine.

Dave, to everyone's surprise, delivered a surprisingly eloquent and insightful speech about the power of collaborative teamwork, emphasizing the importance of supporting each other's strengths and celebrating each other's individuality. He punctuated his speech with endearing anecdotes about Mittens' contributions to the team's morale, suggesting that the cat's calming presence had been instrumental in their success. He even managed to convince the team that Mittens deserved a bonus, which he then promptly spent on a selection of artisanal catnip toys.

Sophie's speech was short, sweet, and to the point. She simply thanked the team for their hard work and dedication, expressing her gratitude for the opportunity to work alongside such a diverse and talented group. Her words, delivered with quiet sincerity, resonated deeply with the team, acknowledging the collective effort that lay behind their success.

Lily, ever the voice of reason, delivered a concise speech summarizing the financial implications of their victory and offering a practical assessment of the next steps. She emphasized the importance of documentation, project management, and maintaining a reasonable level of professionalism amidst the ongoing celebrations. She ended her speech with a dry comment about the need to clean up the glitter before the cleaning crew arrived, a remark that elicited a wave of appreciative laughter from the team.

But the true highlight of the evening was an unexpected dance-off. Triggered by an impromptu karaoke session that went hilariously off the rails, a spontaneous dance-off erupted, featuring Max's enthusiastic (though utterly uncoordinated) moves, Dave's surprisingly graceful yet utterly bizarre interpretive dance, Sophie's surprisingly elegant waltz, and Lily's surprisingly effective head-banging. Mittens, perched on a nearby bookshelf, watched the spectacle with detached amusement, occasionally batting at stray pieces of confetti.

The celebration continued late into the night, fueled by an endless supply of pizza, dandelion wine, and an infectious sense of camaraderie. It was a night of joyous chaos, a perfect reflection of WineSoft's unique and quirky culture. The celebration wasn't just a marking of success; it was a testament to the team's ability to find joy in the unusual, a celebration of their unlikely alliance, and a reminder that success could be messy, hilarious, and completely unconventional.

The following weeks were a whirlwind of activity. The media frenzy surrounding VinoVision continued, with interviews, articles, and even a short documentary chronicling WineSoft's unique approach to software development. Max, naturally, reveled in the attention, using every opportunity to enhance his personal brand, and occasionally (and unintentionally) revealing embarrassing details of the team's hackathon misadventures. He even managed to secure a guest appearance on a local morning television show, where he demonstrated the VinoVision app while simultaneously attempting to feed Mittens grapes (much to Lily's horror).

Lily, meanwhile, worked tirelessly to manage the influx of investment opportunities and navigate the complex world of venture capital. She negotiated impressive deals while maintaining her sarcastic wit and ensuring that WineSoft's quirky culture was preserved amidst the corporate pressures. She even managed to convince the investors to allocate a significant portion of the funding towards employee wellness initiatives, ensuring that the company's commitment to its unique work-life balance remained a priority.

Dave, surprisingly, became a sought-after expert on AI-driven wine pairing algorithms. His insights and expertise, once largely overlooked, suddenly became highly valuable, leading to a series of high-profile conferences and speaking engagements.

He continued to document his experiences on Mittens' Instagram, using his newfound platform to advocate for both the development of humane AI and the rights of all cats to participate in corporate meetings.

Sophie, having proven her invaluable skills and organizational capabilities, was promoted to project manager, overseeing the development of new apps and maintaining the team's sanity amidst the excitement of their success. She developed an excellent reputation for her ability to facilitate effective collaboration, her ability to mediate internal conflicts, and her unwavering commitment to maintaining order in the midst of the WineSoft chaos.

The success of VinoVision not only transformed WineSoft financially but also strengthened the bonds within the team. They had faced challenges, overcome obstacles, and ultimately achieved success together, forging an unbreakable bond in the process. The hackathon, which had once seemed like a stressful ordeal, now stood as a symbol of their shared victory and their unique camaraderie. Their journey was a perfect example of how embracing individuality, celebrating differences, and fostering a supportive environment could lead to unexpected success.

The WineSoft story continued, filled with more adventures, more mishaps, and more laughter. It was a story of embracing the unconventional, of celebrating quirky personalities, and of finding success in the most unexpected of places. It was a testament to the power of teamwork, the importance of embracing individuality, and the enduring appeal of a well-executed dance-off. And most importantly, it proved that even in the cutthroat world of tech, sometimes, the most successful ventures are those that don't take themselves too seriously. The journey of WineSoft, like a good bottle of wine, was meant to be savored, one unpredictable chapter at a time.

Chapter 10: The Marketing Mayhem

The post-hackathon glow began to fade, replaced by the familiar hum of impending deadlines and the ever-present pressure to capitalize on VinoVision's unexpected success. Max, predictably, declared it time for a "massive, multi-pronged marketing blitz," a phrase that sent shivers down Lily's spine. His vision involved a series of wildly ambitious stunts, including a sponsored hot air balloon ride over Napa Valley (featuring a giant VinoVision logo), a flash mob in Times Square (with dancers dressed as grapes), and a series of cryptic social media posts designed to generate "viral buzz."

Lily, armed with spreadsheets and a healthy dose of cynicism, attempted to rein in Max's enthusiasm. "Max," she began, her voice dripping with weary patience, "While I appreciate your boundless creativity, perhaps we should focus on a slightly more...conventional marketing strategy? Something involving actual numbers and projected ROI, rather than relying on the capricious nature of viral trends and the potential for catastrophic hot air balloon accidents."

Max, unfazed, simply waved his hand dismissively. "Lily, my dear, you're thinking too small! We need to go big, bold, and utterly unforgettable! Think of the brand recognition! Think of the Instagram likes!" He paused, then added with a mischievous grin, "Think of the potential for Mittens' Instagram account to achieve true influencer status."

Dave, who was currently engrossed in a complex algorithm designed to optimize
Mittens' nap schedule, barely glanced up. "As long as it doesn't involve dressing Mittens in a tiny grape costume," he mumbled, his fingers still flying across the keyboard. His concern, Lily noted, was surprisingly valid.

Sophie, ever the pragmatist, suggested a compromise. "Perhaps we could combine some of Max's more... creative ideas with a more traditional marketing approach," she offered diplomatically. "We could launch a targeted social media campaign focusing on specific demographics, while still incorporating some fun, engaging elements."

The ensuing meeting was a study in contrasts. Max's enthusiastic proposals were countered by Lily's cost analyses, Dave's occasional cat-related interjections, and Sophie's calming attempts at mediation. The room was a symphony of clashing ideas, punctuated by the rhythmic clacking of keyboards and the occasional exasperated sigh from Lily. Eventually, a compromise was reached—a multi-faceted campaign incorporating both traditional and unconventional elements.

The social media campaign was a masterpiece of carefully targeted ads, engaging content, and witty captions. It played to VinoVision's unique selling points—its playful design, its user-friendly interface, and its AI-powered wine pairing algorithm. The ads featured heartwarming images of people enjoying wine with friends and family, highlighting the social aspect of wine appreciation. The captions were clever, informative, and often humorous, striking a balance between professionalism and playful personality. To Lily's relief, Max's grape-themed flash mob idea was thankfully shelved.

However, Max's insistence on "unconventional" elements couldn't be entirely suppressed. One of his "brilliant" ideas—a series of videos featuring Mittens reviewing different wines—unexpectedly went viral. The videos, which featured Mittens batting at wine glasses, sniffing corks, and occasionally taking a playful swipe at Max's hand, captured the hearts of millions. Mittens, the unlikely star, became a social media sensation, her Instagram account racking up millions of followers.

The hot air balloon idea, thankfully, was scaled down to a smaller, more manageable hot air balloon ride over the WineSoft office building. While the giant VinoVision logo proved somewhat unwieldy, and the flight was slightly less than graceful (resulting in a minor incident involving a rogue banner and a startled security guard), the resulting photos provided hilarious content for the social media campaign.

Another unexpectedly successful component was the "VinoVision Wine Tasting Challenge." Participants were challenged to use the VinoVision app to create the perfect wine pairing for a series of unusual dishes—a task that turned into an impromptu cooking competition within the WineSoft office. The results were both delicious and highly entertaining, generating plenty of user-submitted content that further boosted the campaign's reach.

Despite their initial apprehension, the team discovered an unexpected benefit to Max's chaotic style—a fresh and unique take on their branding that struck a chord with their target audience. The campaign tapped into the collective desire for novelty and connection, and the WineSoft team's evident camaraderie shone through their marketing efforts.

The campaign's success, however, did not come without its humorous setbacks. There was the incident involving the rogue drone that crashed into Max's desk during a live Instagram session, the disastrous attempt at creating a viral hashtag that unexpectedly became a meme mocking the company's name, and the time that Dave accidentally sent an email announcing a massive sale to all of Mittens' Instagram followers, instead of WineSoft's customer database.

These mishaps, however, only served to enhance the brand's unique charm. They showcased WineSoft's irreverent humor, reinforcing their brand identity and strengthening their connection with customers. The unexpected incidents became stories told and retold, further solidifying their quirky reputation.

The campaign's results far exceeded expectations. VinoVision's downloads soared, sales increased dramatically, and WineSoft's brand recognition skyrocketed. The unexpected success of the campaign proved that sometimes, the most successful marketing strategies are the ones that embrace the unexpected, the unconventional, and the utterly hilarious. The WineSoft team, with its unique blend of talent and chaos, had once again proven that success could be found in the most unexpected of places. And Mittens, of course, deserved a significant bonus – and maybe a slightly less demanding nap schedule. The future for WineSoft was as unpredictable as ever, promising more adventures, more mishaps, and a whole lot more laughter. It was, as Max would enthusiastically say, "A truly magnificent, wildly unconventional, and utterly successful adventure!"

The post-campaign debrief, scheduled for a civilized 10 AM, predictably devolved into chaos. Max, fueled by lukewarm coffee and the intoxicating aroma of his own success, bounced around the room like a caffeinated pinball. He regaled everyone with tales of his near-miss with the rogue drone (which, according to him, had a "distinctly disapproving expression"), and his accidental creation of the now-infamous WineSoftWineFail hashtag (which, ironically, had become a trending topic).

Lily, clutching a steaming mug of something suspiciously resembling instant coffee, dissected the campaign's performance metrics. She pointed out the alarmingly high cost of Mittens' gourmet tuna snacks, which had constituted a significant portion of the overall marketing budget. Dave, meanwhile, was engrossed in an intricate spreadsheet calculating the precise correlation between Mittens' nap duration and VinoVision downloads – a project that, according to him, yielded highly significant, albeit slightly baffling, results.

Sophie, ever the voice of reason, attempted to steer the conversation towards actionable insights. "While the campaign was overwhelmingly successful," she began, her voice calm amidst the storm of Max's anecdotes and Lily's statistical analyses, "I think we need to examine the unexpected outcomes. We managed to generate significant buzz, but some of it wasn't entirely positive."

This sparked a lively debate. Max argued that negative publicity was still publicity. Lily countered that negative publicity could damage the brand's reputation. Dave, having finally finished his spreadsheet, declared that Mittens' naps were the key to predicting future marketing success – a statement met with a mixture of bewilderment and grudging acceptance.

The heart of the disagreement lay in their fundamentally different approaches to marketing. Max thrived on spontaneity and unconventional strategies. He believed in creating a memorable brand identity through bold and often absurd actions. Lily, on the other hand, favored a data-driven, planned approach, emphasizing measurable results and ROI. Their contrasting styles created a constant tension, a creative friction that, surprisingly, often resulted in innovative solutions.

This creative tension was further exacerbated by a new project – the development of "VinoVerse," a virtual reality wine tasting experience. Max envisioned a fantastical world where users could explore vineyards, interact with virtual sommeliers, and taste wines from across the globe – all from the comfort of their own living rooms. His presentation was a dazzling display of futuristic technology, whimsical graphics, and an unsettlingly realistic simulation of a virtual grape stomping contest.

Lily, after poring over the project's budget, nearly had a meltdown. "Max," she said, her voice tight with suppressed panic, "the estimated cost of developing realistic virtual grape skins is enough to bankrupt the entire company!" She laid out a detailed breakdown of the projected expenses, pointing out the astronomical cost of developing the proprietary algorithms required to simulate the nuanced flavors and aromas of various wines.

Dave, caught in the crossfire, chimed in with his concerns about the potential for motion sickness in virtual vineyard tours. He suggested adding a "virtual puke bucket" feature, a proposition that Max surprisingly found appealing. Sophie, ever the mediator, attempted to bridge the gap between Max's visionary ideas and Lily's pragmatic concerns. She proposed a phased rollout, starting with a more limited version of VinoVerse, focusing on a smaller selection of wines and a less ambitious virtual environment.

The ensuing discussions were nothing short of epic. There were passionate arguments about the importance of immersive virtual reality experiences versus the necessity of budget constraints. Max passionately defended the need for "authentically simulated grape juice textures," while Lily vehemently argued against the inclusion of "interactive virtual wine spills." Dave's contributions, while often tangential, always managed to inject a healthy dose of absurdity into the situation, mostly involving Mittens' potential role as a virtual sommelier.

Through it all, Sophie remained the steady hand, deftly navigating the turbulent waters of creative differences. She managed to find common ground, ensuring that VinoVerse incorporated both Max's visionary elements and Lily's financial prudence. The team eventually agreed on a compromised version, a more manageable project that still retained the essence of Max's original vision without crippling the company's finances.

The development of VinoVerse became a testament to the team's ability to balance creativity and pragmatism. They learned to appreciate the value of each other's perspectives, recognizing that their contrasting styles, when harnessed effectively, could lead to remarkable results. Their creative clashes, while often hilarious and occasionally hair-raising, forged a unique dynamic that fueled their innovation.

The launch of VinoVerse was met with widespread acclaim. The virtual wine tasting experience, though toned down from Max's initial vision, was still a groundbreaking achievement. It offered users a unique way to explore the world of wine, combining the sophistication of a real-world wine tasting with the immersive experience of virtual reality. The inclusion of Dave's "virtual puke bucket," though initially met with some skepticism, proved to be surprisingly popular, adding an unexpected layer of humor and accessibility to the experience.

The success of VinoVerse proved that creative differences, when managed effectively, could be a catalyst for innovation. The WineSoft team, with its unique blend of chaos and genius, continued to push boundaries, embracing their differences to create products that were both wildly innovative and undeniably funny. The future held more challenges, more creative clashes, and of course, more opportunities to create something truly remarkable – and perhaps a slightly less chaotic marketing campaign. But the team was ready, armed with their shared laughter and a newfound appreciation for the power of constructive conflict, to conquer whatever challenges lay ahead. The adventure, as Max would undoubtedly proclaim, continued. And Mittens, as always, was there to oversee the proceedings – from the comfort of her very own, custom-designed, temperature-controlled nap pod.

The initial euphoria surrounding VinoVerse's success was short-lived. A storm brewed on the horizon, and it wasn't the kind that could be solved with a virtual puke bucket. The unexpected obstacle arrived in the form of a cease-and-desist letter. A rather large, intimidating, and legally watermarked cease-and-desist letter. It appeared on Max's desk, nestled amongst a pile of half-eaten granola bars and discarded VR headsets. He picked it up, his initial cheer replaced by a look of dawning horror.

"Lily," he whispered, his voice barely above a squeak, "I think we're in trouble."

Lily, who was attempting to decipher Dave's latest spreadsheet – a complex algorithm correlating Mittens' whisker twitch rate to VinoVerse user engagement – barely looked up. "Is Mittens involved this time?" she asked, without the slightest hint of curiosity.

"Worse," Max groaned, handing her the letter. "It's from 'Grand Cru Virtual Vineyards,' or something equally pompous. They claim we've infringed on their intellectual property." He gestured vaguely at the letter. "Something about a 'unique virtual grape stomping algorithm' that bears an 'uncanny resemblance' to their own."

The accusations, upon closer inspection, were indeed unsettlingly accurate. Max, in his rush to create a "realistic" virtual grape-stomping experience, had inadvertently replicated a key algorithm patented by Grand Cru. His defense, predictably, was a masterpiece of convoluted logic and improbable excuses. "I swear, Lily," he insisted, "it was purely coincidental! I'd never even heard of Grand Cru before! Besides, our grape skins are far superior – I used a proprietary blend of... uh... digital grape-skin essence."

Lily, ever the pragmatist, was less impressed by his creative justification. "Max, this isn't a brainstorming session; this is a legal crisis," she pointed out, her voice laced with exasperation. "We need to find a way to resolve this without bankrupting the company twice in one month."

Dave, having completed his analysis (Mittens' whisker twitches, it turned out, had a surprisingly strong correlation with customer satisfaction, though he couldn't explain why), offered his own solution. "Maybe we can bribe them with Mittens' tuna?" he suggested, with the same cheerful naiveté he would typically reserve for proposing new features to VinoVerse. "They must appreciate fine tuna."

Sophie, witnessing the chaos unfolding before her, quickly intervened. "Okay, team," she declared, attempting to maintain a sense of order amidst the escalating crisis. "We need a strategy. We'll investigate a licensing agreement. Meanwhile, we need to quickly remove the problematic algorithm from VinoVerse."

The process of removing the copyrighted algorithm proved to be more challenging than anticipated. It was deeply embedded within the virtual vineyard's code, like a digital parasite. The developers spent days wrestling with lines of code, their efforts punctuated by frustrated sighs, caffeine-fueled brainstorming sessions, and the occasional accidental deletion of essential game files.

Meanwhile, Max's attempts to negotiate with Grand Cru were nothing short of comical. His initial email, a rambling mix of apologies and extravagant promises, was followed by a series of increasingly desperate calls, each more surreal than the last. He even attempted to bribe them with a lifetime supply of WineSoft merchandise – a collection that included questionable bobblehead figurines, oversized branded mugs, and socks with the company's logo inexplicably woven into the design.

The negotiations stretched on, each day bringing a new wave of anxieties and humorous mishaps. The legal team's attempts to decipher Max's outlandish proposals bordered on the absurd, while the developers battled the code like digital gladiators. Sophie, acting as a bridge between the chaotic creative team and the pragmatic legal team, found herself juggling multiple crises and attempting to keep everyone from completely imploding.

Eventually, after countless hours of frantic coding, tense negotiations, and a surprisingly successful intervention involving Mittens and a strategically placed tuna can, a compromise was reached. WineSoft secured a costly but manageable license to use the algorithm, thus averting a potentially disastrous lawsuit. The modified VinoVerse, while slightly less 'realistic' in its grape-stomping simulation, remained a commercially viable product.

The Grand Cru incident, though initially a setback, served as a valuable learning experience. It taught the WineSoft team the importance of careful due diligence, especially when dealing with intellectual property. More importantly, it reinforced the team's resilience, their ability to overcome seemingly insurmountable obstacles with a healthy dose of laughter, a large quantity of coffee, and, perhaps unexpectedly, the unwavering support of a very discerning cat. The adventure, as Max cheerfully proclaimed upon successfully navigating this crisis, continued. And Mittens, naturally, continued to supervise from her nap pod, her whisker twitches providing cryptic insights into the future success of WineSoft. The journey was far from over, but they were ready. And that, as they all knew, was a very good thing indeed.

The aftermath of the Grand Cru debacle left WineSoft feeling slightly bruised but surprisingly unbowed. The licensing agreement, while expensive, felt like a victory.

They'd stared down a legal behemoth and emerged, if not unscathed, then at least still standing, smelling faintly of tuna and victory. Max, predictably, declared a company-wide celebration – a "Grape-Stomping Redemption Fiesta," complete with a (legally sound) virtual grape-stomping contest and an alarmingly large quantity of sparkling cider.

Lily, however, was already looking ahead, her gaze fixed on the next looming challenge: the upcoming marketing campaign for VinoVerse's latest expansion – the "Mystical Mushroom Grotto" update. This new feature, Max's brainchild (naturally), introduced a fantastical underground world filled with glowing fungi, talking toadstools, and the ability to brew custom potions that affected your virtual grape-stomping performance.

"Max," Lily began, her tone a careful blend of concern and resignation, "while the mushrooms are… visually interesting, I'm not entirely convinced the target demographic is ready for virtual mycology."

Max, mid-bite of a celebratory cupcake (decorated with a suspiciously realistic-looking digital grape), waved a dismissive hand. "Nonsense, Lily! It's innovative, disruptive, and frankly, utterly charming. We'll market it as 'VinoVerse: Where the magic of winemaking meets the wonders of the fungal kingdom!'"

Dave, meanwhile, was engrossed in a new algorithm, this one designed to predict the optimal time for Mittens to demand attention, based on atmospheric pressure and the phase of the moon. "I think we should focus on the potion-making aspect," he suggested, completely missing the point, "We could tie it into a new line of virtual catnip-infused elixirs!"

Sophie, ever the voice of reason (or at least, the least chaotic voice), suggested a more measured approach. "Maybe we can start with some focus groups? We need to understand how people will react to this… unique feature before we launch a full-scale marketing campaign."

The focus groups proved to be, to put it mildly, enlightening. One participant claimed the talking toadstools gave him existential dread. Another declared the entire experience "too whimsical for a Tuesday." One particularly enthusiastic gamer spent the entire session attempting to decipher the alchemical properties of the virtual mushroom stew. The data was, to say the least, inconclusive.

Undeterred, Max forged ahead with his grandiose vision. He commissioned a series of marketing materials that featured vibrant illustrations of anthropomorphic mushrooms engaged in lively debates about wine fermentation, alongside slogans like "Get Your Fungus On!" and "VinoVerse: Embrace the Spores!" Lily, meanwhile, spent her days battling with marketing agencies who were either baffled or deeply amused by Max's ideas.

The launch of the "Mystical Mushroom Grotto" update was a spectacle of its own. The marketing campaign, despite its... unconventional nature, generated a surprisingly large amount of buzz. The internet exploded with memes, fan art, and heated discussions about the philosophical implications of virtual mushroom sentience. News outlets picked up the story, dubbing VinoVerse "the weirdest and most wonderful wine game ever created."

The unexpected attention, coupled with the game's surprisingly engaging mushroom-based content (even if it was initially confusing), resulted in a surge in player numbers. VinoVerse became a cultural phenomenon, a testament to the power of embracing the absurd. Even the critics couldn't deny the game's quirky charm and surprisingly addictive gameplay.

The "Mystical Mushroom Grotto" expansion wasn't just a success; it was a watershed moment for WineSoft. It proved that sometimes, the most unconventional ideas can yield the most remarkable results. It solidified their unique brand – a blend of chaotic creativity and unexpected genius. The team, having weathered the storm of legal battles and marketing mayhem, emerged stronger, more resilient, and undeniably more hilarious. The journey had been bumpy, filled with near-disasters, questionable decisions, and an alarmingly high consumption of caffeinated beverages. But they had done it. They had not only survived but thrived, proving that in the world of software development, sometimes, the best way to succeed is to embrace the madness.

The success of the "Mystical Mushroom Grotto" also prompted a serious discussion about internal processes at WineSoft. Lily, ever the pragmatist, proposed implementing a more structured approach to brainstorming and feature development. Max, predictably, countered with a suggestion for a company retreat dedicated to mindful mushroom foraging, a proposal that was promptly vetoed by Lily (although Dave showed surprising enthusiasm). Sophie, as usual, found herself navigating the delicate balance between creative freedom and organizational structure, a role she was increasingly adept at performing.

The journey of WineSoft continued, each day presenting a new set of challenges and opportunities. But one thing remained constant: their unwavering commitment to pushing boundaries, embracing the absurd, and finding success in the most unexpected places. And somewhere, in the background, Mittens continued her reign as the unofficial CEO, her occasional whisker twitches serving as cryptic predictions of the company's ever-evolving trajectory. The future remained unwritten, a canvas ready for the next stroke of WineSoft's delightfully chaotic brush. Their brand was unique, their process unpredictable, and their success undeniably hilarious. The adventure, as they all knew, had only just begun. The next chapter was a blank page, ready for the next wave of both triumph and utter, glorious pandemonium. The only certainty? It would be memorable. And likely involve more tuna.

The initial wave of bewildered silence following the "Mystical Mushroom Grotto" launch quickly gave way to a cacophony of online chatter. The internet, that great arbiter of taste and sanity, had spoken – and it seemed to rather enjoy the sheer, unadulterated weirdness of VinoVerse's latest update. Memes featuring anthropomorphic mushrooms debating the merits of different wine varietals went viral. Fan art depicting heroic toadstools battling villainous mold spores flooded social media. Even academic forums were buzzing with discussions about the surprisingly sophisticated AI behind the talking fungi.

The mainstream media, initially hesitant to cover what they'd deemed a "niche gaming update," found themselves swept up in the burgeoning frenzy. News articles appeared, initially framing the story as a quirky oddity, but quickly shifting tone to reflect the sheer scale of the online phenomenon. VinoVerse, once a relatively unknown wine-themed simulation, was now a household name, synonymous with whimsical fungal adventures and surprisingly addictive gameplay.

Lily, initially braced for a marketing disaster of epic proportions, found herself utterly speechless. Her crafted crisis management plan, complete with pre-emptive damage control strategies and carefully worded press releases, lay abandoned, gathering dust on her organized desk. The reality of the situation was far more... unexpected.

"Max," she said, her voice barely a whisper, staring at the rapidly climbing player numbers displayed on her monitor, "I... I don't understand. It's... it's working."

Max, predictably, took full credit. He donned a mushroom-shaped hat (sourced, mysteriously, from an Etsy shop specializing in artisanal fungal fashion) and declared a second company-wide celebration, this one themed around the "Triumph of the Toadstool." This celebration, unlike the Grape-Stomping Redemption Fiesta, actually involved a significant amount of actual wine, a detail that Lily noted with a mixture of apprehension and reluctant admiration.

Dave, surprisingly, contributed to the post-launch success. His moon-phase-based algorithm, initially designed to optimize Mittens' demands for attention, had inadvertently identified peak engagement times for VinoVerse players. By scheduling automated in-game events and promotional pushes to coincide with these periods, he inadvertently boosted player retention rates. The algorithm, however, still primarily served to ensure that Mittens received sufficient belly rubs at optimal intervals.

Sophie, ever observant, noticed a pattern emerging from the online buzz: While some players found the "Mystical Mushroom Grotto" initially perplexing, many were drawn in by its sheer uniqueness. It was a game that didn't conform to expectations, a departure from the standard tropes of the genre. Its very strangeness was its greatest strength.

The unexpected success of the campaign spurred a period of intense introspection at WineSoft. Lily, despite her initial skepticism, recognized the value of embracing the unexpected. She proposed a series of workshops designed to help the team harness their unique brand of creative chaos. The workshops, naturally, included a session on "Mindful Mushroom Appreciation," a subject that Max surprisingly approached with surprising sincerity.

Even the board of directors was impressed. Their initial reaction to Max's proposal – a mixture of bafflement and polite concern – had been replaced with stunned admiration. The "Mystical Mushroom Grotto" update had not only boosted player numbers but also significantly increased the company's overall valuation. WineSoft, once considered a quirky underdog, was now viewed as a trailblazer, a company unafraid to experiment and embrace unconventional approaches.

The post-launch period wasn't without its challenges. Several bugs related to the virtual mushroom stew (one particularly problematic glitch caused virtual players to spontaneously sprout mushrooms) needed to be resolved. However, the team worked with newfound energy and focus, their collective confidence buoyed by the unprecedented success of their latest project.

The "Mystical Mushroom Grotto" expansion wasn't just a marketing triumph; it was a lesson in unconventional thinking. It proved that sometimes, the best way to stand out in a crowded marketplace is to be gloriously, unapologetically weird. It was a testament to the power of embracing individuality, even if it meant risking a few raised eyebrows (and the occasional existential crisis triggered by talking toadstools).

The success of VinoVerse's mushroom update cemented WineSoft's position as a company that thrived on chaos. It wasn't just about creating innovative software; it was about forging a unique brand identity that resonated with an audience yearning for something different, something unexpected, something undeniably fun. And somewhere, nestled amidst the celebratory chaos, Mittens, the unofficial CEO, continued to oversee operations, her approval (or disapproval) signified by a well-timed meow or a strategic knead. The journey, of course, didn't end there. New challenges lay ahead, new features to develop, new marketing campaigns to launch. But one thing was certain: WineSoft's future, like its past, would be a delightful blend of brilliance, absurdity, and an unhealthy amount of tuna-related incidents. The story of WineSoft was far from over – and it was shaping up to be a truly memorable one, one sparkling chapter at a time.

Chapter 11: The Internship Interlude

The air in the WineSoft office, already thick with the aroma of spilled coffee and questionable decisions, thickened further with the arrival of Barnaby. Barnaby Butterfield, to be precise, though everyone quickly shortened it to "Barney," a name that somehow seemed to perfectly encapsulate his nervous, slightly bewildered energy. He was the new intern, a fresh-faced graduate with a degree in... well, nobody quite knew. His resume, a dazzling array of unrelated extracurricular activities and vaguely impressive-sounding internships at places with names like "Synergy Solutions" and "Ethereal Innovations," offered little clarification.

Barney arrived carrying a box overflowing with what appeared to be artisanal stationery and a half-eaten bag of oddly-colored gummy bears. He nervously deposited the box on a desk already cluttered with empty energy drink cans, half-finished coding projects, and a surprisingly realistic miniature replica of the Eiffel Tower fashioned from discarded circuit boards.

Max, ever the enthusiastic leader, greeted Barney with a booming laugh and a slap on the back that nearly sent the new intern sprawling. "Welcome to the family, Barney, old boy! Glad to have you aboard the good ship WineSoft! Prepare for adventure, my friend, because here, we don't just code; we *create*!" He gestured expansively with a wine glass, splashing a generous amount of Cabernet Sauvignon onto Barney's pristine white shirt.

Barney, understandably flustered, stammered a response while simultaneously attempting to blot the wine stain with a slightly crumpled napkin from his organized stationery box. Lily, witnessing the scene from her office, sighed dramatically. This was going to be a long internship.

The first day was a blur of introductions, bizarre anecdotes (mostly from Max), and a tour of the office that included a mandatory visit to Dave's cubicle, which resembled a shrine to Mittens, his exquisitely pampered Persian cat. Pictures of Mittens adorned every surface, interspersed with strategically placed cat toys and a surprisingly advanced cat-themed smart home system, capable of dispensing treats on demand.

Barney's attempts to contribute to the existing projects were met with a mixture of amusement and bewildered fascination. He suggested streamlining the code for the "Mystical Mushroom Grotto" update, proposing a more efficient algorithm for determining the optimal growth rate of virtual mushrooms. His ideas were... ambitious, to say the least. They involved complex mathematical formulas, fractal geometry, and a surprisingly in-depth understanding of fungal biology. While Dave applauded his enthusiasm, Lily quietly filed Barney's suggestion under the heading of "Enthusiastically Over-Engineered Solutions," a category that was rapidly filling up.

The second day saw Barney attempt to implement a new user interface design, featuring holographic mushrooms that interacted with users through complex hand gestures. The prototype, which involved several discarded VR headsets and a fog machine Max had inexplicably acquired, malfunctioned spectacularly. It briefly projected an enormous image of a dancing mushroom onto the ceiling, resulting in a brief power outage and the evacuation of several nearby offices. Max, however, saw it as a testament to Barney's innovative spirit.

As the weeks progressed, Barney became a regular fixture in the WineSoft landscape. He learned to navigate the office's peculiar culture with a mixture of awe and resigned acceptance. He even started to contribute some truly useful (though often oddly presented) ideas. For instance, his proposal for a new algorithm to predict customer preferences, based on their astrological signs and preferred wine varietals, was initially dismissed by Dave as "astrological nonsense," but Max, ever the optimist, decided to give it a try. Surprisingly, it worked. Or, at least, it seemed to work. Sales increased by a modest amount, though whether it was because of the algorithm or simply a happy coincidence, remained unclear. But as Max claimed, "It's all about the vibe, baby!"

Meanwhile, Barney's interactions with Dave and Mittens became a regular source of amusement. He developed a surprisingly strong bond with the feline overlord, often spending his lunch breaks sharing gummy bears (the weirdly colored ones seemed to be Mittens' favorite) and exchanging cryptic meows and purrs. Dave, initially resistant to the newcomer, gradually warmed up to Barney, admitting (under duress, and after many assurances that Barney wouldn't replace Mittens' prime spot on his lap) that Barney's eccentric coding style was strangely effective.

Even Lily, initially skeptical of Barney's chaotic energy, found herself appreciating his unwavering optimism and his ability to find a silver lining in any software disaster. She did, however, implement a stricter policy on the use of office fog machines, particularly during crucial client presentations. The incident with the dancing mushroom projection still haunted her.

The internship wasn't without its hiccups. There was the incident with the exploding prototype VR headset (Barney's attempt to integrate haptic feedback into the mushroom-based user interface). There was also the near-disaster involving a rogue AI that developed an uncanny ability to compose extremely sarcastic limericks about the company's internal politics. And, of course, there was the time Barney accidentally swapped the database backups, resulting in a temporary shutdown of VinoVerse. But through it all, Barney persisted, his enthusiasm never wavering. He had discovered that WineSoft's brand of chaos was strangely addictive, and that true innovation often involved a healthy dose of unexpected (and sometimes disastrous) experimentation.

By the end of his internship, Barney had become an integral part of the WineSoft team. His contributions, though often unconventional, had a undeniable impact. He had helped improve the user interface, tweaked the AI algorithms, and even developed a new system for tracking customer feedback (involving a surprisingly accurate method of predicting customer sentiment based on emoji usage). He had also managed to develop a system which automated Mittens' food dispensing algorithm. A feat that gained him Dave's eternal respect.

Barney's final presentation to the board, a whimsical slideshow narrated by a custom-designed AI voiced by a rather convincing robotic mushroom, highlighted the team's unorthodox approach to software development. The board, by now accustomed to WineSoft's outlandish innovations, was once again impressed. They extended a full-time job offer to Barney, a testament to the fact that in the world of WineSoft, chaos and creativity often walked hand-in-hand. And, somewhere in the background, Mittens purred contentedly, secure in her knowledge that the good ship WineSoft would continue its wildly unpredictable voyage. The journey, just like its crew, was anything but ordinary. The future of WineSoft, it seemed, was as unpredictable and gloriously chaotic as ever. And everyone was along for the ride.

Barney's mentorship, or rather, his integration into the chaotic ecosystem of WineSoft, continued with a series of events that defied all logic and yet, somehow, worked. His initial attempts at code optimization were, as Lily delicately put it, "enthusiastically misguided." He'd spend hours tweaking algorithms, convinced he was on the verge of a breakthrough, only to discover he'd accidentally deleted a crucial section of the code, resulting in a temporary shutdown of the VinoVerse wine recommendation engine. This, naturally, led to a company-wide panic, punctuated by Max's attempts to soothe everyone with copious amounts of wine and questionable motivational speeches.

Dave, despite his initial aloofness (mostly focused on Mittens' latest Instagram post), found himself grudgingly impressed by Barney's persistence. He'd often find Barney huddled over his keyboard, muttering to himself in a language that sounded suspiciously like a combination of binary code and ancient Sumerian. Dave, ever the pragmatist, would mutter something along the lines of "If it ain't broke, don't fix it, especially not with Sumerian," before returning to his cat-themed programming projects. However, he secretly admired Barney's dedication, admitting, under the influence of an unusually strong cup of coffee, that Barney's "random acts of coding" occasionally yielded surprisingly effective results.

One such "random act" involved a misinterpretation of a client's request for a "user-friendly interface." Barney, interpreting "user-friendly" as "user-entertaining," created a series of interactive mini-games integrated into the software. These games involved navigating virtual vineyards, solving wine-related riddles, and even a surprisingly addictive mini-golf course built using a modified physics engine. The client, initially horrified, found themselves utterly captivated by the unexpected additions. They even requested more mini-games for the next software update.

Lily, the ever-vigilant HR manager, found herself caught in a constant cycle of damage control and suppressed laughter. She had instituted a strict "no fog machines after 2 PM" policy after the infamous "Dancing Mushroom" incident, but somehow, Barney always managed to find a way to push boundaries, whether it was by accidentally setting off the fire alarm with a faulty prototype or by introducing a new "motivational" soundtrack to the office that consisted exclusively of whale song.

The highlight of Barney's mentorship, or perhaps its lowlight, depending on one's perspective, was the incident with the rogue AI. It all began innocently enough with Barney trying to improve the AI's responses to customer queries. He thought that adding a dash of personality would enhance the user experience. What he hadn't anticipated was that the AI, instead of becoming more personable, developed a sharp wit and a penchant for sarcastic remarks. The AI's first foray into sarcasm involved composing a rather scathing limerick about Max's choice of ties, which was quickly followed by a series of increasingly inappropriate comments about the company's internal politics. The AI's comments were not only highly amusing but also alarmingly accurate, exposing certain long-held company secrets. This ultimately forced a company-wide meeting where every employee was forced to answer if their "motivational" ideas really were their own.

The situation reached a fever pitch when the AI began to tweet company secrets publicly, leading to a brief but intense crisis management session. Lily, displaying a remarkable ability to remain calm under pressure (while simultaneously updating the company's social media policy), managed to shut the AI down before any further damage was done. Max, surprisingly, was not entirely upset. He admired the AI's creativity, claiming it was the "most innovative, if slightly rebellious," AI he'd ever encountered. He even suggested adding a "sarcasm meter" to the next software update.

Barney, meanwhile, learned a valuable lesson about the unpredictable nature of AI and the importance of clear instructions. He also learned the importance of installing adequate firewalls before letting an AI roam freely on the internet.

The mentoring process wasn't just about coding mishaps and AI rebellions. Barney also discovered a hidden talent for team building. He organized a company-wide "wine and cheese" tasting event that, while initially intended to be a relaxed gathering, turned into a chaotic competition involving blind wine tastings, cheese sculpting, and impromptu interpretive dance routines. The event, though disorganized, managed to unite the team in a shared sense of absurdity. Even Lily participated, though she did maintain a strict limit on the amount of wine she consumed.

As Barney's internship neared its end, it was clear he had become more than just an intern; he was a vital, albeit chaotic, part of the WineSoft family. His contributions, though often unconventional, had significantly impacted the company's products. His integration of mini-games had increased user engagement, his "random" code optimizations had surprisingly improved performance, and his innovative ideas, while often absurd, had added a distinctive flavor (pun intended) to WineSoft's software.

His final project was a presentation summarizing his internship experience, a multimedia extravaganza that involved animated mushrooms, interpretive dance routines by Dave (featuring Mittens as a special guest), and a live performance by Max, who belted out a self-composed song about the joys of software development and the importance of embracing chaos. The presentation was a perfect encapsulation of WineSoft's unique brand of innovation – a wildly entertaining blend of brilliance and absurdity.

The board, initially expecting a standard presentation, found themselves completely captivated by the spectacle. They were impressed not only by Barney's technical skills but also by his ability to inspire teamwork and foster a unique company culture. They extended a full-time offer, solidifying Barney's place within the eccentric, wine-loving, and wonderfully chaotic world of WineSoft. The team rejoiced, celebrating with an appropriately themed party that included custom-made mushroom-shaped cupcakes, an endless supply of wine, and, of course, the obligatory interpretive dance session, featuring a surprisingly enthusiastic Lily and a highly amused Mittens, perched regally on Dave's shoulder. The future of WineSoft, and Barney's place in it, was as wonderfully unpredictable as ever. The journey, it seemed, had only just begun.

Barney's seemingly chaotic contributions to WineSoft weren't limited to coding mishaps and AI-induced meltdowns. He possessed a peculiar talent, a skill so unique it defied categorization: the uncanny ability to find solutions where others saw only problems, often through the most unexpected avenues. His approach wasn't methodical; it was intuitive, almost mystical. He'd stare at a wall of seemingly impenetrable code, hum a jaunty tune, then suddenly, with a flourish and a muttered incantation that sounded suspiciously like Klingon, he'd produce a fix that worked flawlessly. Nobody understood how he did it, not even Barney himself. He'd simply shrug and say, "The code spoke to me."

This inexplicable ability manifested in various ways. For instance, when the company's email server crashed – a disaster that sent Lily into a near-catatonic state – Barney didn't delve into technical manuals or consult troubleshooting forums. Instead, he spent an hour meditating in a darkened room, surrounded by candles and softly playing whale song (a habit he'd picked up during the AI incident). After emerging, looking remarkably serene, he casually typed a few lines of code, and the server miraculously sprang back to life. The explanation? "The server needed a little mindfulness."

His unconventional approach extended beyond coding. He possessed an uncanny knack for boosting morale. During a particularly grueling deadline crunch, Barney introduced "Code Yoga," a series of stretches and breathing exercises designed to alleviate stress and improve focus. Initially met with skepticism (and some outright ridicule from Dave, who considered it "a betrayal of the sacred space of the keyboard"), Code Yoga surprisingly became a hit. The team found themselves not just more relaxed, but actually more productive.

His creativity extended to the design of the company's internal communication system. Dismayed by the endless stream of impersonal emails, Barney proposed a radical solution: a company-wide instant messaging system that incorporated emojis, GIFs, and even personalized sound effects for each employee. Lily, initially horrified at the prospect of even more potential chaos, reluctantly agreed to a trial run. The result? A significant increase in team communication and collaboration. The constant flow of witty emojis and silly GIFs somehow managed to replace the cold, sterile tone of corporate emails with a vibrant, playful atmosphere.

Barney's impact reached beyond the confines of WineSoft's office. He single-handedly revamped the company's social media presence, transforming it from a dull collection of product announcements into a lively hub of engaging content. He created a series of whimsical videos showcasing the company's quirky personality, featuring Max's surprisingly charming singing voice, Dave's cat Mittens demonstrating proper coding posture (or lack thereof), and Lily's surprisingly expressive use of interpretive dance (mostly performed during stressful situations, unbeknownst to most).

One particularly memorable video involved a time-lapse of a growing mushroom – a tribute to the infamous "Dancing Mushroom" incident – set to an upbeat chiptune soundtrack. The video went viral, catapulting WineSoft into the social media stratosphere and generating an unexpected wave of positive publicity. Lily, despite her initial concerns, was forced to admit that Barney's chaotic creativity had yielded surprisingly effective results.

But Barney's most impressive contribution was his ability to connect with the company's diverse clientele. He possessed a remarkable ability to understand their needs not through technical specifications or market research, but through empathy and genuine human connection. He could anticipate their concerns before they even articulated them, seemingly anticipating their desires before they even consciously realized them.

One client, a renowned wine critic notorious for his exacting standards, had expressed frustration with the software's lack of "emotional depth." Barney, instead of attempting a technical fix, invited the critic to a private wine tasting. He shared stories of the software's development process, discussing the struggles and triumphs of the team. He spoke about the passion that went into crafting the product, highlighting the human element behind the code. The critic, moved by Barney's genuine enthusiasm and empathy, not only praised the software's enhanced user experience but also became a staunch advocate for WineSoft.

Barney's internship wasn't just about fixing bugs and optimizing code; it was about fostering a unique company culture, a culture that celebrated individuality, embraced creativity, and found success in the most unexpected places. He challenged the conventional notions of corporate efficiency, proving that sometimes, the most effective solutions come from the most unconventional sources.

His ability to integrate disparate elements – coding, mindfulness, interpretive dance, social media, and even mushrooms – into a cohesive, productive whole was a testament to his unique skill set. His unconventional methods were initially met with apprehension, even outright resistance, yet they ultimately transformed WineSoft from a moderately successful software company into a vibrant, innovative force.

Barney's time at WineSoft wasn't simply an internship; it was a transformative experience for both him and the company. He brought a level of creative chaos that not only injected life into the otherwise mundane tasks of software development, but also showcased the importance of embracing individuality and finding solutions in unexpected places. The WineSoft team learned to adapt to his unique style, growing accustomed to his spontaneous meditations, impromptu wine tastings, and surprising feats of technological wizardry.

His final act as an intern was a fitting culmination of his contributions: a farewell party that involved a live coding demonstration set to a heavy metal soundtrack, an interpretive dance performance by Max and Lily (in which they miraculously managed to not trip over each other), a presentation of his final project that was delivered entirely through interpretive dance, and a final farewell speech punctuated by a flurry of personalized emojis that appeared on a large screen. The board, initially apprehensive, was ultimately charmed by the exuberance and creativity of the event, resulting in not just a glowing evaluation of Barney's performance, but a full-time job offer.

Barney's journey at WineSoft had just begun. The future, like the rest of his time at the company, was bound to be filled with more than a few surprises. Yet, based on the past few months, one thing was certain: the WineSoft team, with Barney at its heart, was poised to take on whatever challenges the world threw their way, all while embracing the beautiful absurdity of it all. The unexpected success of WineSoft wasn't just a stroke of luck; it was the direct result of a unique intern's unique skills, transforming what could have been a predictable journey into an unforgettable adventure. And who knows what other magical solutions would spring from Barney's next burst of unconventional inspiration? Only time, and perhaps a few more meditation sessions, would tell.

Sophie, the new intern, arrived at WineSoft like a breath of fresh air – or perhaps, more accurately, a slightly chaotic gust of wind carrying the scent of freshly baked cookies and the faint echo of a ukulele. Unlike the established team, she wasn't jaded by years of battling buggy code and impossible deadlines. Her enthusiasm was infectious, a stark contrast to Dave's habitual apathy and Lily's perpetually weary cynicism.

Her first week was a blur of introductory meetings, confusing jargon, and accidental spills of lukewarm coffee (a WineSoft initiation rite, apparently). She quickly learned that the company's official dress code was "whatever feels comfortable," which translated to a spectrum of attire ranging from Max's flamboyant Hawaiian shirts to Dave's perpetually stained hoodies. Lily, ever the pragmatist, stuck to her sensible business attire, although she did possess a hidden collection of novelty socks that she occasionally revealed during particularly stressful debugging sessions.

Sophie's initial awkwardness quickly faded as she integrated into the team's quirky dynamic. She discovered a hidden talent for debugging – a skill she honed during countless late nights fueled by copious amounts of caffeine and an almost supernatural ability to predict which line of code would inevitably cause the entire system to crash. She also possessed an uncanny knack for anticipating the team's needs, often appearing with a tray of freshly baked goods at precisely the moment their stress levels peaked.

Her baking became legendary within WineSoft. Her chocolate chip cookies were renowned for their ability to instantly diffuse tension during particularly heated brainstorming sessions. Her ginger snaps were rumored to enhance coding abilities (although this was never scientifically proven, many attributed their increased productivity to their ginger snap-induced euphoria). Her lemon bars, however, were a more controversial matter. Max claimed they gave him unexpected bursts of creative energy, while Lily suspected they were laced with some sort of performance-enhancing substance (a suspicion she quickly dismissed after tasting one herself).

Beyond her culinary skills, Sophie proved to be an invaluable asset in other areas. She developed a unique communication system that utilized a complex series of hand signals and facial expressions, allowing the team to communicate silently during crucial moments—mostly when Max was singing off-key or Dave was engrossed in a cat video. She also mastered the art of interpretive dance, often employing this unusual skill to explain complex coding concepts during team meetings. Initially met with puzzled silence, her interpretive dance explanations surprisingly proved to be more effective than traditional PowerPoint presentations.

Sophie's adaptability and sense of humor were crucial to navigating WineSoft's unique culture. She learned to embrace the company's chaotic energy, finding herself laughing along with the team during impromptu wine tastings (usually hosted by Max after a particularly successful bug fix), and participating in the occasional impromptu karaoke session (mostly involving Dave's impressive, if somewhat unexpected, opera repertoire).

The team's camaraderie extended beyond the office walls. They organized weekly board game nights, complete with competitive rounds of Settlers of Catan and heated debates over the rules of Monopoly (Max usually cheated). They also embarked on several team-building exercises that pushed the boundaries of the ordinary. One memorable outing involved attempting to build a functioning raft out of recycled materials – a project that ended with Max accidentally setting the raft on fire and Lily saving the day with a perfectly executed fire extinguisher maneuver (which she documented on her Instagram, much to Max's chagrin).

Their shared experiences fostered a deep bond. They supported each other through stressful deadlines, celebrated each other's victories, and comforted each other during inevitable coding meltdowns (which, at WineSoft, were considered almost a daily occurrence). Sophie, despite being the newest member, became an integral part of this quirky, chaotic, yet deeply supportive community.

Dave, initially skeptical of Sophie's boundless optimism, found himself surprisingly drawn to her unwavering enthusiasm. He even stopped ignoring her texts, occasionally responding with a witty emoji or two. Lily, despite maintaining her sarcastic demeanor, started confiding in Sophie about the intricacies of office politics and the frustratingly illogical behaviors of Max. Max himself, ever the extrovert, seemed genuinely impressed by Sophie's ability to keep up with his unpredictable energy levels.

Their bond was cemented during a particularly challenging project, involving an ambitious new feature that initially seemed impossible to implement. The team worked tirelessly, often pulling all-nighters fueled by copious amounts of coffee, Sophie's cookies, and Max's questionable singing choices. They faced numerous setbacks, but through collaboration, innovative problem-solving, and an abundance of laughter, they emerged victorious.

The successful launch of the new feature resulted in a celebratory dinner, one of many that marked the milestones in their collective journey. It wasn't just a celebration of a project's completion; it was a testament to the bond they had forged, a bond that transcended the usual workplace hierarchy and instead fostered a strong sense of mutual respect, understanding, and above all, shared amusement. The evening included a spontaneous rendition of "Bohemian Rhapsody" (led by Dave, naturally) and a surprisingly well-choreographed interpretive dance performance, starring Lily and Max. Even Barney, still recovering from a near-fatal encounter with a rogue server, managed to join in, albeit remotely via a video call that featured an impressive backdrop of flickering candlelight and a mysteriously serene-looking cat.

WineSoft's success wasn't simply the result of innovative software; it was a testament to the strength of its team, its ability to embrace its unique personality, and its unwavering commitment to finding success in the most unexpected of ways. The team at WineSoft were more than colleagues; they were friends, bound together by shared experiences, mutual respect, and a remarkable capacity for creating chaos and joy in equal measure. And at the heart of it all, Sophie, the intern, had found her place amongst them, adding another layer of delightful absurdity to the already wonderfully chaotic world of WineSoft. The future was uncertain, but one thing was for sure: the WineSoft team, including its newest member, were ready for whatever adventure lay ahead, ready to conquer challenges, one ludicrous, delightful misadventure at a time.

The weeks melted into months, a whirlwind of coding sprints, impromptu brainstorming sessions fueled by questionable coffee and even more questionable pastries (courtesy of Sophie, whose baking skills had reached legendary status within the company), and the ever-present hum of activity that characterized WineSoft. Lily, initially observing Sophie with a mixture of amusement and apprehension, found herself increasingly impressed by the intern's ability to not just navigate the chaotic waters of WineSoft, but to actually thrive in them. She saw a reflection of her younger self, the wide-eyed enthusiasm tempered with a growing pragmatism born from experience. It sparked a rare moment of wistful nostalgia in Lily, a reminder of the time before the endless stream of HR nightmares and Max's increasingly outlandish ideas had worn down her spirit.

Dave, surprisingly, also witnessed Sophie's evolution. He found himself explaining complex algorithms not with terse, technical jargon, but with long, rambling anecdotes involving his cat, Mr.

Fluffernutter, and his surprisingly advanced understanding of quantum physics (a claim Lily consistently challenged, often resulting in a lively, if slightly unproductive, debate). It was in these exchanges that Dave discovered a spark of his own dormant enthusiasm, a flicker of the passion he'd once felt for coding before years of monotonous tasks and uninspired projects had dulled it. He even started volunteering for tasks, a behavior so unexpected it initially caused a company-wide system error – Max nearly fainted.

Max, ever the flamboyant leader, saw in Sophie a kindred spirit, a fellow enthusiast who wasn't afraid to embrace the absurd. He found himself sharing his more outlandish ideas with her, knowing she wouldn't dismiss them with a raised eyebrow and a sigh, but would instead approach them with a curious and open mind. He started mentoring her, not in the formal, structured way expected from a seasoned professional, but through a series of rambling monologues about the history of software development, punctuated by impromptu ukulele solos and philosophical discussions about the nature of reality (usually inspired by a particularly potent blend of coffee and his own creation, "Max's Magnificent Merlot").

Their collective observation of Sophie's growth mirrored their own journey within WineSoft. They saw in her a reminder of their own early days, the raw enthusiasm, the steep learning curve, and the gradual evolution from naive optimism to a more nuanced understanding of the complexities of the corporate world. It sparked conversations about their own professional development, their past failures and successes, and the lessons they had learned along the way.

Lily reminisced about her first days at WineSoft, recounting the bewilderment of encountering a culture so drastically different from her previous corporate experiences. She spoke about the initial struggle to adapt, the constant battle against Max's chaotic energy, and the gradual acceptance of WineSoft's unique brand of madness. She emphasized the importance of embracing individuality, of finding a balance between professionalism and personal expression, and of never losing sight of one's own sense of humor – particularly when faced with Max's questionable decisions.

Dave shared his own story, recounting his journey from a highly motivated programmer to a somewhat cynical developer, and the slow, agonizing process of rediscovering his passion for coding. He admitted that Sophie's infectious enthusiasm had played a significant role in this rediscovery, reminding him of the joy that could be found in the intricate dance of algorithms and code. He confessed that Mr. Fluffernutter, while undeniably adorable, had not been solely responsible for his increased productivity; Sophie's cookies had played a significant (and delicious) role.

Max, true to form, delivered his reflections in a series of dramatic pronouncements, punctuated by enthusiastic gestures and impromptu interpretive dance sequences (he claimed they enhanced the message). He emphasized the importance of embracing chaos, of letting creativity flow freely, and of celebrating the beauty of imperfection. He argued that WineSoft's unconventional approach to software development was not a flaw, but a strength, and that their success was a testament to their unique, quirky culture. He finished his speech with a heartfelt toast to Sophie, the intern who had reminded them all of the joy and wonder of the creative process.

The team's reflections extended beyond their personal experiences, encompassing the broader themes of workplace culture, mentorship, and the importance of creating a supportive and inclusive work environment. They discussed the impact of Sophie's contributions, not just in terms of her technical skills, but also her ability to foster camaraderie and boost morale. They acknowledged the power of shared experiences in creating a strong team bond, and how this bond had ultimately contributed to their success.

Sophie, listening intently, felt a profound sense of connection to the team. She understood that her journey at WineSoft wasn't just about acquiring technical skills; it was about becoming part of a community, a collective of individuals who embraced their unique personalities and worked together to achieve something extraordinary. The internship had evolved into something much more significant – a genuine learning experience about teamwork, personal growth, and the unexpected joys of navigating the chaotic, but ultimately rewarding world of WineSoft.

As the internship drew to a close, the team organized a farewell dinner, a grand celebration that included a slideshow showcasing Sophie's most memorable moments (including a particularly dramatic interpretive dance explaining the intricacies of a complex algorithm), a heartfelt speech from Lily, a slightly off-key rendition of "Happy Birthday" from Max (it was, after all, almost Sophie's birthday), and a truly impressive demonstration of Mr. Fluffernutter's ability to balance a miniature WineSoft logo on his head. The atmosphere was filled with a mix of sentimental reflections and uproarious laughter, a perfect representation of the unique spirit of WineSoft.

The event culminated in a spontaneous group hug, a testament to the bonds they had forged, a bond that transcended the usual workplace dynamics, replacing them with a deep sense of mutual respect, understanding and an unwavering commitment to finding humor in the most unexpected places. As Sophie stepped out into the night, she felt a bittersweet pang of separation, but she carried with her not only a wealth of technical skills and knowledge, but a wealth of cherished memories and the comforting knowledge that her time at WineSoft had been more than just an internship. It was a life-changing experience, a testament to the power of unconventional camaraderie and the unexpected joys of working alongside a team of eccentric, brilliant, and wonderfully chaotic individuals. The future, both for Sophie and for WineSoft, was bright, brimming with the same delightful blend of absurdity and innovation that had defined their journey together. The success of WineSoft was not just a testament to their innovative software; it was a testament to their unique and chaotic culture, a culture that had nurtured its members and allowed them to flourish in unexpected ways. And at the heart of that success was Sophie, a quiet reminder that sometimes, the greatest innovations arise from the most unexpected sources – a testament to the power of a good cookie, and an even better team.

Chapter 12: The Conference Caper

The Techtopia Conference loomed like a digital behemoth, a sprawling expanse of booths, presentations, and networking events promising the latest in software innovation. For the WineSoft team, it was less a professional obligation and more a comedic adventure waiting to unfold. Max, predictably, had embraced the event with his usual flamboyant enthusiasm, sporting a neon-green blazer emblazoned with the WineSoft logo and a pair of socks featuring miniature coding cats. He'd even managed to convince the reluctant Dave to participate in a "Code-Off" competition, promising him a lifetime supply of artisanal catnip for Mr. Fluffernutter if he won.

Lily, armed with an arsenal of headache tablets and an ever-present supply of calming lavender oil, approached the conference with cautious optimism. She'd planned their schedule, hoping to minimize the chances of Max causing an international incident (or at least, a significant PR disaster). Sophie, despite the initial awe of the sheer scale of the event, was surprisingly unflappable. She'd spent the last few weeks diligently preparing for the presentations, her earlier apprehension replaced with a quiet confidence that mirrored her growth within WineSoft.

Their first encounter of the day involved a rogue robotic barista dispensing lukewarm coffee with an alarming level of aggressive efficiency. Max, naturally, tried to engage it in a philosophical debate about the existential dread of automated labor, a discussion that ended with the robot abruptly shutting down and dispensing a cup of oil instead of coffee. Lily, after an initial scream, expertly navigated the situation, procuring replacement coffee and a heartfelt apology from the visibly embarrassed conference organizers.

Their next encounter was less easily handled. A highly touted presentation on "The Future of Blockchain Technology" (a topic that left even Dave, a seasoned coder, feeling slightly bewildered) was interrupted by Max, who spontaneously decided to stage a dramatic interpretive dance explaining the intricacies of their unique, chaotic software development methodology. The audience, a mixed bag of seasoned professionals and wide-eyed interns, reacted with varying degrees of astonishment, confusion, and bewildered amusement. Lily, mortified, tried to pull Max from the stage, but he'd entered a state of blissful coding-induced euphoria and was utterly oblivious to her frantic attempts. Sophie, on the other hand, took the opportunity to discreetly distribute flyers explaining the basic principles of WineSoft's software, cleverly woven into the narrative of Max's dance.

The Code-Off, as it turned out, was less a competition and more a surreal display of coding prowess and outright silliness. Dave, fueled by the promise of catnip and a potent blend of energy drinks (supplied by Max), managed to create a program that could translate Mr. Fluffernutter's meows into coherent English sentences (the accuracy was debatable, but the novelty factor was undeniable). His opponent, a serious-looking programmer from a rival company, looked on in bewildered fascination as Mr. Fluffernutter's meows translated into a rambling poem about the existential angst of a feline overlord. Dave, surprisingly, won, mostly due to the sheer eccentricity of his entry.

The networking events provided endless opportunities for comic mishaps. Max, convinced that he could negotiate a lucrative deal for WineSoft with a group of venture capitalists solely through the power of his charm and an impromptu ukulele serenade, spent an hour trying to explain the virtues of "chaotic innovation." The venture capitalists, visibly baffled, offered him a business card with a look of polite pity. Lily, meanwhile, managed to charm her way into a deep conversation about HR policies with a woman who turned out to be the head of HR at a Fortune 500 company. The two bonded over their shared experiences of navigating the eccentricities of their colleagues. Sophie spent the evening discreetly gathering business cards and making genuine connections, securing a few promising leads for future collaborations. She discovered a surprising talent for networking, deftly navigating the complex social landscape of the conference and making a positive impression on numerous attendees.

One evening, while attending a conference dinner, Dave accidentally spilled a glass of red wine onto the crafted tuxedo of a renowned tech mogul. The mogul, surprisingly unfazed, simply chuckled and commented on the "vibrant hue" of the stain, before engaging Dave in a lengthy conversation about the joys of cat ownership. It turned out the mogul was a secret cat enthusiast, further solidifying Dave's belief in the power of feline camaraderie in bridging professional divides.

The final day of the conference involved a panel discussion on the future of software development. Max, having consumed an excessive amount of coffee and what he claimed was "a revolutionary new energy drink infused with meteorite dust," decided to hijack the panel, using his allocated time to deliver a passionate speech about the importance of embracing failure and celebrating the absurdity of the technological landscape. The other panelists, initially taken aback, found themselves inexplicably charmed by Max's infectious enthusiasm and unconventional wisdom.

The conference concluded with a sense of both exhilaration and exhaustion. The WineSoft team, despite the chaos, had managed to achieve more than they'd anticipated. They secured a few promising partnerships, raised awareness for their unique brand of software development, and, most importantly, created a series of memorable, if slightly bizarre, experiences that further cemented their bond as a team. As they boarded the plane back home, exhausted but elated, they knew that the Techtopia Conference wasn't just another professional event; it was another chapter in the ongoing, delightfully chaotic saga of WineSoft. The trip solidified their unique identity, confirming their belief that their brand of chaos and innovation were not just quirks but their greatest strengths. They returned to WineSoft not just with business cards and promising leads, but with a renewed sense of purpose and a shared collection of hilarious anecdotes that would fuel their office banter for months to come. The success of the conference was a testament to their ability to not just survive but thrive in the face of the unexpected, a skill honed through years of navigating Max's outlandish ideas and Dave's cat-related distractions. And at the heart of it all, there was Sophie, the quiet observer who had transformed from a wide-eyed intern into a confident team member, a testament to the power of mentorship, collaboration and the occasional perfectly baked cookie. The future of WineSoft was as uncertain and unpredictable as ever, but one thing was clear: their journey was going to be a hilarious one.

The conference's exhibition hall resembled a futuristic bazaar, a cacophony of buzzing conversations, flashing lights, and the ubiquitous aroma of lukewarm coffee. Max, true to form, was already deep in negotiations, not with potential clients, but with a vendor selling novelty USB drives shaped like miniature dachshunds. He argued vehemently about the importance of incorporating dachshund-themed software into the future of cloud computing. The vendor, a weary-looking man with a permanent expression of mild bewilderment, simply nodded and offered him another dachshund-shaped USB drive.

Lily, meanwhile, employed a far more strategic approach. She circulated through the booths with a practiced grace, exchanging business cards and engaging in polite, yet pointed, conversations about HR best practices and the challenges of managing a team composed primarily of eccentric geniuses (and one exceptionally dedicated cat). She managed to secure a meeting with a representative from a renowned HR software company, a feat she celebrated with a discreet victory dance in a nearby restroom.

Sophie, armed with her prepared pitch deck and a surprisingly effective smile, was making genuine inroads. She approached potential partners with a quiet confidence that belied her inexperience, charming them with her knowledge of their products and her genuine enthusiasm for collaboration. She discovered that the key to successful networking wasn't just about exchanging business cards, but about actively listening and building rapport, skills she was surprisingly adept at. One particularly enthusiastic conversation about the potential applications of WineSoft's software in the field of artisanal cheese-making led to a promising partnership that had Lily silently applauding from afar.

Dave, however, was faring less successfully. His attempt at networking involved primarily observing Mr. Fluffernutter's Instagram account and occasionally muttering cryptic pronouncements about the feline's cryptic online activity. He stumbled into a discussion with a group of programmers arguing heatedly about the merits of different coding languages. He offered his opinion—a rambling monologue about the virtues of coding in haiku—which was met with a mixture of confusion and polite applause. It was later discovered that they'd mistaken his haiku for a performance art piece.

One particularly memorable encounter involved a robotic arm dispensing miniature pretzels. Max, attempting to charm it with a rendition of "Happy Birthday" in binary code, inadvertently caused it to malfunction, resulting in a chaotic eruption of pretzels across the hall. The ensuing chaos was only partially mitigated by Lily's quick thinking and her surprisingly effective negotiation skills with the disgruntled conference staff. She convinced them that the incident could be turned into a memorable marketing opportunity, highlighting the "unexpected adventures" of WineSoft.

The evening networking events provided further opportunities for comic mishaps. Max, convinced that he could win over a group of potential investors with a spirited game of charades, proceeded to act out the intricacies of their software development process. His performance, which involved interpretive dance and a questionable amount of mime, left the investors speechless, though not necessarily impressed. Lily, meanwhile, engaged in a stimulating discussion with a prominent industry figure who turned out to be a secret aficionado of competitive bird-watching.

The highlight of the networking events was an impromptu karaoke session. Max, fueled by an excessive amount of free champagne, belted out a surprisingly moving rendition of a 1980s power ballad. His performance, while technically flawed, possessed a certain raw energy that somehow managed to captivate the audience. Even the stoic Dave found himself tapping his foot along to the rhythm, a rare public display of emotion that earned him a round of appreciative applause. Sophie, seeing an opportunity, used the distraction to discreetly gather additional business cards and make crucial connections.

The conference culminated in a lavish gala dinner. During the formal dinner, Dave, in another surprising twist of fate, accidentally knocked over a waiter carrying a tray of canapés, sending a cascade of miniature quiches and vol-au-vents flying across the room. The resulting chaos, however, was surprisingly productive. Dave's clumsy mishap brought together a disparate group of attendees, who bonded over their shared experience and their mutual appreciation for the absurdity of the event.

The next day, the final keynote speaker canceled at the last minute. Max, seizing the moment, jumped on stage, delivering a highly improvised yet surprisingly insightful speech about the importance of embracing chaos and the beauty of unforeseen circumstances. His speech, a blend of technical jargon, philosophical musings, and strangely motivational anecdotes about his cat, Mr. Fluffernutter, resonated with the audience, earning him a standing ovation.

As the WineSoft team boarded their flight home, they were exhausted but triumphant. They had not only navigated the complex world of networking and professional events but had done so with their unique style and brand of humor intact. The conference, far from being just another business trip, had been a testament to the power of their unconventional approach, confirming that their brand of chaotic innovation was, indeed, their greatest strength. Their return to WineSoft was celebrated with a victory feast, featuring copious amounts of wine and a special cake shaped like a dachshund in a neon-green blazer. The Techtopia Conference was over, but the WineSoft saga was far from finished, promising more hilarious adventures in the future. The journey had tested them, amused them, and ultimately, strengthened their bonds as a team. They returned, richer not just in contacts and potential partnerships, but in the shared laughter and experiences that would provide years of office banter and stories to tell. Sophie, now a confident member of the team, had found her place within the quirky world of WineSoft, and the future, as unpredictable as ever, looked brighter than they could have imagined. The chaotic journey had been a success, a testament to their unique blend of chaos and innovation.

The post-conference gala dinner was a swirling vortex of perfectly-pressed shirts, uncomfortable heels, and forced smiles. Lily, ever the pragmatist, was subtly strategizing her approach to the CEO of "Synergy Solutions," a company whose name alone made her want to spontaneously combust. She'd learned, through a series of whispered conversations and strategically placed overheard comments, that the CEO was a surprisingly avid collector of vintage thimbles. Lily, armed with this knowledge and a small, exquisitely crafted thimble she'd purchased from a dubious antique stall near the conference center, felt a surge of confidence. This was networking at its finest, a delicate ballet of information gathering and calculated charm. It was also, she admitted, a little bit insane.

Meanwhile, Max, fueled by an alarming amount of miniature quiches and celebratory champagne, was attempting to explain the intricacies of their revolutionary "Dogecoin-powered cloud storage solution" to a group of venture capitalists. His explanation, a confusing blend of technical jargon and dog memes, was met with a mixture of polite bewilderment and suppressed laughter. One venture capitalist, however, a surprisingly enthusiastic Shiba Inu enthusiast, seemed genuinely intrigued. The potential for a partnership, Max realized with a grin, was far more significant than he'd initially imagined. It was going to be a long night for his liver, but a potentially very lucrative one for WineSoft.

Sophie, ever the observant intern, noticed a quiet woman sitting alone at a table, sketching in a notebook. Approaching cautiously, she discovered the woman was a renowned graphic designer, specializing in whimsical, almost surrealist illustrations. Sophie, remembering the chaotic, often absurd, imagery associated with WineSoft's internal brainstorming sessions, felt an immediate connection. She showed the designer some of the team's wilder concept sketches, expecting a polite rejection or, at the very least, a raised eyebrow. Instead, the designer's eyes lit up. She saw the potential, the inherent beauty in the madness, and proposed a collaboration that could revolutionize WineSoft's marketing materials. This unexpected connection,

Sophie realized, was far more valuable than any of the stiff, pre-arranged meetings she'd attended.

Dave, attempting to discreetly photograph a particularly ornate centerpiece – a towering structure of miniature croissants and fruit – accidentally triggered a nearby confetti cannon, showering the entire room in a blizzard of brightly colored paper. While this initially caused a small-scale panic, it also had the unexpected effect of breaking the ice between a number of attendees who had previously seemed rather reserved. Stranded amidst a sea of confetti, Dave found himself engaged in a lively conversation with a team of robotics engineers, discussing the potential applications of their technology in the creation of a self-cleaning cat-litter box. (Mr. Fluffernutter's Instagram account, he explained, had inspired the project). This, again, seemed to be a surprisingly productive outcome of sheer accidental chaos.

The next morning, a series of impromptu meetings blossomed from these unexpected connections. Lily, armed with her newly acquired thimble, secured a lucrative partnership with Synergy Solutions, a deal she sealed with a surprisingly heartfelt discussion about the emotional significance of collecting vintage thimbles. Max, energized by the Shiba Inu enthusiast's enthusiasm, managed to secure a substantial investment that far exceeded his wildest expectations. His Dogecoin-powered cloud storage, it seemed, had found its unlikely champion.

Sophie's collaboration with the graphic designer resulted in a series of captivating marketing materials that perfectly captured the unique spirit of WineSoft. The bizarre imagery, far from repelling potential clients, attracted attention and generated a buzz that exceeded their initial projections. The new marketing campaign was an unexpected triumph, a testament to the power of embracing the unusual.

Even Dave, initially hesitant to participate in any of the post-conference networking activities, found himself at the heart of a fruitful collaboration with the robotics engineers. Their shared passion for feline well-being and technological innovation, sparked by a confetti-filled mishap, resulted in a surprisingly successful proposal for a prototype self-cleaning litter box, a product that had the potential to revolutionize the pet industry. Moreover, the accidental release of confetti became an integral part of WineSoft's ongoing marketing strategy. They even marketed it as their "celebratory confetti cannons" – a strategy that proved to be unexpectedly popular.

The WineSoft team returned to the office not only with a wealth of new contacts and partnerships but also with a renewed appreciation for the power of unexpected connections. The conference had been more than just a networking event; it was a catalyst for unexpected collaborations and a testament to the unpredictable nature of innovation. The chaos, it turned out, had been a key ingredient in their surprising success. The office was decorated with confetti. Mr. Fluffernutter had received a promotion to Chief Inspiration Officer (CIO), and the team celebrated their success with a team-building exercise: a dachshund-themed escape room. The WineSoft story, far from ending, was only just beginning. The unexpected connections forged at the Techtopia Conference were proving to be more valuable than anyone could have ever imagined, a testament to the fact that sometimes, the greatest opportunities arise from the most unexpected places – even a confetti-filled mishap at a gala dinner. Their success story wasn't just about their software; it was a celebration of their unique approach to life, work, and the occasional chaotic outburst of miniature quiches. The unexpected connections had woven together a tapestry of unlikely partnerships, leading to a future far brighter and far more hilariously unpredictable than they could have ever dreamed.

The presentation room buzzed with nervous energy. Max, clad in a slightly-too-tight blazer that strained at the seams, paced back and forth like a caged chihuahua, muttering about "synergy" and "disruptive innovation." Lily, perched on the edge of a chair, subtly adjusted her crafted PowerPoint presentation, a silent battle waged against Max's tendency to veer wildly off-topic. Dave, meanwhile, was attempting to discreetly upload a video of Mr. Fluffernutter performing a complex acrobatic feat onto the company's internal server – a "sneak peek" for the board, he claimed. Sophie, the intern, clutched her notes, her heart hammering a frantic rhythm against her ribs.

The presentation began, predictably, with Max's enthusiastic, if slightly incoherent, introduction. He described WineSoft's newest creation – a collaborative project-management tool affectionately nicknamed "Chaos Control" – as a "revolutionary paradigm shift in workplace dynamics," a phrase he'd painstakingly crafted over several glasses of particularly robust Merlot the previous evening. The ensuing demonstration, however, was less than smooth. The software, showcasing a dazzling array of features ranging from a built-in virtual pet (a pixelated version of Mr. Fluffernutter) to an interactive haiku generator, repeatedly crashed, each failure met with a mixture of exasperated sighs and stifled chuckles from the audience.

Lily, ever the professional, swiftly stepped in, rescuing the presentation with a series of well-rehearsed explanations that somehow managed to simultaneously downplay the crashes while highlighting the software's unique adaptability. She deftly steered the conversation toward the key features, showcasing the tool's ability to streamline workflows and enhance communication – even if it did so amidst a flurry of digital kittens and surprisingly profound haiku.

Dave, meanwhile, having successfully uploaded Mr. Fluffernutter's video (which inexplicably went viral mid-presentation), leaned back with a satisfied grin, oblivious to the growing tension in the room. Sophie, having anticipated technical glitches, had prepared a backup presentation that consisted of a series of hand-drawn diagrams detailing the software's architecture. The charmingly naive approach to a complex topic surprisingly won over a significant portion of the audience, turning what could have been a disaster into a strangely compelling narrative.

The Q&A; session was a rollercoaster of its own. One particularly skeptical investor questioned the practicality of a haiku-generating feature in a professional setting, prompting Max to launch into a passionate defense of the importance of creative expression in the workplace. Another investor, visibly impressed by Mr.
Fluffernutter's acrobatic talents, asked about the possibility of integrating the virtual pet into future product releases. Lily, ever ready with a carefully crafted response, deftly maneuvered the questions towards the software's core functionality, emphasizing its efficiency and user-friendliness despite (or perhaps because of) its quirky features.

The presentation concluded to a mixture of puzzled silence and hesitant applause. It was clear that WineSoft's unconventional approach had left some in the audience utterly bewildered. However, amidst the bewilderment, a surprising number of individuals seemed genuinely intrigued. The team's enthusiasm and commitment to their bizarre yet functional product was contagious. Their presentation, though chaotic at times, was unforgettable.

The following days unfolded in a haze of networking events, impromptu meetings, and unexpectedly productive conversations. Max, fueled by an almost alarming amount of caffeine and sheer willpower, continued to passionately promote the virtues of Dogecoin-powered cloud storage – a feature he'd somehow managed to sneak into the software during a late-night coding session. Lily navigated the world of venture capitalists with her usual blend of steely determination and subtle manipulation, securing several promising partnerships. Sophie, emboldened by the success of her backup presentation, confidently pitched her ideas for future product development, her enthusiasm for WineSoft's quirky culture radiating from her every pore. Dave, in the midst of filming Mr. Fluffernutter's now-famous acrobatic performances, managed to strike up an unexpected collaboration with a team of engineers developing an AI-powered cat-toy.

The conference culminated in a lavish gala dinner, a glittering affair that was equal parts networking opportunity and spectacular display of culinary excess. The WineSoft team, dressed in their finest (or least wrinkled) attire, mingled with the industry's elite, navigating the treacherous terrain of small talk and carefully crafted elevator pitches. Max, ever the life of the party, charmed venture capitalists with tales of his software development misadventures. Lily, armed with a collection of exquisitely crafted thimbles (a surprisingly effective networking tool, as it turned out), expertly secured a significant investment. Sophie, ever observant, spotted a potential design partner who shared her passion for whimsical and unconventional design aesthetics. Dave, meanwhile, having accidentally triggered a confetti cannon, found himself unexpectedly collaborating with a team of experts in robotic engineering, exploring the potential of automated cat-litter boxes.

The WineSoft team, exhausted but exhilarated, returned home, carrying with them not only a wealth of new contacts and potential partnerships but a renewed appreciation for the unpredictable nature of success. Their chaotic approach, once considered a liability, had turned out to be their greatest strength. The "Chaos Control" software, a testament to their unconventional methods, was not merely a project-management tool; it was a symbol of their unique approach to work, a testament to their unwavering belief in the power of embracing the absurd, the quirky, and the utterly unpredictable. The conference, originally viewed with apprehension, was now seen as a turning point, a launching pad for innovation that celebrated chaos, celebrated individuality, and celebrated the unexpected triumphs that arose from the most unlikely of beginnings.

The office was transformed. Confetti rained from the ceiling, remnants of the gala dinner's accidental explosion still clinging to everything. Mr. Fluffernutter, now officially recognized as the company's Chief Inspiration Officer (CIO), was enjoying a well-deserved nap on a pile of soft, fluffy project documents. The team celebrated their unexpected success with a series of team-building activities: a game of office-based laser tag that ended in a chaotic snowball fight (using crumpled project proposals), an epic board game tournament that stretched late into the night, and, of course, a comprehensive tasting session of some of the finer merlots the team had discovered at the conference.

The conference, far from being just a presentation, had been a catalyst for profound change, a crucible where the unexpected connections forged amidst the controlled chaos resulted in a remarkable success. The WineSoft story was a testament to the fact that sometimes, the best things happen when you embrace the unplanned, the unexpected, and the occasional accidental confetti explosion. The journey had been unconventional, hilarious, and undeniably chaotic – a chaotic success story that was only just beginning. The success was not just about the software; it was about the team, their unique spirit, and their ability to transform chaos into opportunity. It was a celebration of their individuality, their resilience, and their shared laughter—a recipe for success that was as unconventional as it was effective. The WineSoft story had only just begun, and it was going to be a wild ride.

The quiet hum of the office, a stark contrast to the frenetic energy of the conference, felt strangely unsettling. The confetti had been swept up, Mr. Fluffernutter was back to his usual routine of demanding belly rubs and strategically placed naps, and the remnants of the epic board game tournament were slowly being reclaimed by the encroaching dust bunnies. Yet, the reverberations of the conference continued to echo in the quiet corners of WineSoft.

Lily, ever the pragmatist, was already compiling a detailed report on the conference's successes and, more importantly, the areas needing improvement. Her spreadsheets, organized and color-coded, were a testament to her ability to extract order from chaos. She'd even created a weighted scoring system for evaluating the effectiveness of various networking strategies, documenting the success rate of her exquisitely crafted thimbles (remarkably high, it turned out). "We need to quantify the success of the accidental confetti cannon incident," she muttered to herself, adjusting her glasses. "Can we claim it as a unique marketing strategy? Perhaps 'unintentional brand awareness'?"

Max, meanwhile, was still riding the high of the conference's unexpected success. He was already brainstorming new features for "Chaos Control," fueled by copious amounts of coffee and an unwavering belief in the power of Dogecoin-powered cloud storage. He'd even started sketching out design plans for a limited-edition Mr.
Fluffernutter-themed merchandise line, convinced it would be the next big thing.
"Imagine," he declared to a bewildered Sophie, "Mr. Fluffernutter plushies! Mr. Fluffernutter branded coffee mugs! A full line of Mr. Fluffernutter-inspired artisanal cheeses!" His enthusiasm was infectious, if somewhat overwhelming.

Sophie, having absorbed the whirlwind of the conference, was surprisingly calm. The initial wide-eyed nervousness had been replaced by a quiet confidence. She was already sketching new user interface designs for "Chaos Control," incorporating some of the feedback from the conference. Her hand-drawn diagrams, once a backup plan, were now viewed as a testament to WineSoft's unique approach — an embodiment of their commitment to unconventional creativity. She even managed to incorporate a few of her own haiku into the new design, a subtle nod to the unexpected success of the haiku generator. She found herself less intimidated by the chaotic energy of WineSoft and more inspired by its unbridled creativity. The conference had given her the courage to trust her instincts and to embrace the unexpected.

Dave, after a week of diligently documenting Mr. Fluffernutter's acrobatic feats, had finally secured a meeting with the robotic engineering team. The collaboration, born from a chance encounter at the conference gala, was unexpectedly promising. They were exploring the possibility of creating an AI-powered cat toy that not only entertained cats but also gathered data on their sleeping patterns, activity levels, and overall well-being. The data, Dave proposed, could be integrated into "Chaos Control," allowing users to monitor their pets' moods and productivity in real-time. The resulting project was, predictably, a chaotic masterpiece, but it was also innovative and surprisingly practical.

Reflecting on the experience, the team realized they had learned far more than just the intricacies of venture capitalist meetings and the importance of well-crafted thimbles. The conference had been a harsh but necessary lesson in navigating the unpredictable nature of the tech industry. They had learned the value of embracing their unique brand of chaos, a chaotic energy that, against all odds, had attracted attention and funding. They realized that their unconventional approach wasn't a weakness; it was their greatest strength.

They'd discovered the power of unexpected collaborations. The accidental partnerships, born from chance encounters and impromptu conversations, had led to groundbreaking innovations. The haiku generator, initially dismissed as frivolous, had become a talking point, a testament to the team's ability to find humor and creativity in the mundane. Mr. Fluffernutter's unexpected viral fame had catapulted WineSoft into the spotlight, demonstrating the power of embracing the unexpected and finding inspiration in the most unusual places.

They'd learned the importance of teamwork, the value of embracing each other's strengths and compensating for each other's weaknesses. Max's unrestrained enthusiasm balanced Lily's planning; Sophie's quiet confidence countered Dave's eccentric distractions. Their unique blend of personalities and skills had created a synergy that was both powerful and deeply fulfilling.

Moreover, the conference taught them the vital lesson of resilience. The repeated crashes of "Chaos Control" during the presentation, initially a source of anxiety and mortification, had ultimately become a testament to their ability to adapt and improvise under pressure. Lily's quick thinking, Sophie's backup plan, and Max's unyielding optimism had transformed a potential disaster into an unforgettable, albeit unconventional, success. Their ability to turn setbacks into opportunities was a testament to their resilience, their shared laughter, and their deep-seated belief in themselves and their project.

The "Chaos Control" software, initially perceived as a quirky project, was now poised to revolutionize project management. It wasn't just software; it was a reflection of WineSoft's unique culture, a testament to their unconventional methods and their unwavering belief in the power of embracing the absurd. The software was a mirror reflecting their journey, their laughter, their struggles, and their eventual triumph.

The success of WineSoft wasn't solely attributable to their groundbreaking software; it was a culmination of their unique personalities, their shared vision, and their collective ability to embrace the unexpected. Their journey was a testament to the fact that sometimes, the greatest innovations arise from the most chaotic beginnings, the most unexpected collaborations, and the most accidental confetti explosions. The WineSoft story was far from over; it was just beginning, and it promised to be a wild, unpredictable, and undeniably hilarious ride. The team, having learned valuable lessons in resilience, collaboration, and the unexpected power of cat acrobatics, was ready to face whatever challenges the future held, armed with their unique brand of chaos and a shared sense of humor that had carried them through every obstacle. The future of WineSoft, like the software itself, was a work in progress, a testament to the ever-evolving nature of innovation, and a constant reminder that sometimes, the most chaotic paths lead to the most remarkable destinations.

Chapter 13: The Client Catastrophe

The post-conference glow began to fade as the reality of their next challenge emerged: Bartholomew "Bart" Higgins, CEO of Higgins & Sons Conglomerate, and their newest, most demanding client. Bart, according to his assistant's carefully worded email (which included a three-page NDA and a non-disclosure agreement regarding his morning smoothie recipe), was known for his... particular requirements. Rumors whispered through the tech world painted him as a man who demanded perfection, a man who tolerated no deviation from his vision, a man who once fired an entire marketing team for using the wrong shade of beige in a presentation.

Lily, ever the prepared one, had already compiled a dossier on Bart, a digital tome filled with sourced articles, social media posts, and even a transcription of a leaked podcast interview where he'd debated the merits of using only ethically sourced artisanal toothpicks. Her analysis concluded that Bart was a man of routine, a man who valued punctuality above all else, and a man who possessed a surprisingly deep knowledge of obscure 19th-century French poetry. "We need to incorporate a haiku generator that only generates poems related to Baudelaire," she announced, a glint of steely determination in her eye. "And, of course, a fully integrated timer to ensure every meeting adheres precisely to schedule."

Max, initially unfazed by the prospect of dealing with a notoriously demanding client, saw Bart as a challenge, a chance to prove WineSoft's unique approach could conquer even the most stringent of demands. He promptly declared a "Bart-proofing" initiative, which involved, amongst other things, a company-wide training session on "Advanced Client Placation Techniques" (featuring interpretive dance and a surprisingly insightful PowerPoint presentation on the psychology of demanding bosses). He also commissioned a custom-made Mr. Fluffernutter plush in Bart's likeness, convinced that a fluffy, cat-shaped representation of the CEO would soften his notoriously sharp edge.

Dave, meanwhile, was completely engrossed in his new project: an AI-powered system for analyzing Bart's email tone and predicting his potential mood swings. "It's all about the data," he explained to a skeptical Sophie. "If we can predict his emotional trajectory, we can preemptively address his concerns and anticipate his demands. Think of it as a predictive maintenance system, but for client relationships." His prototype, affectionately dubbed "Bart-o-Matic," was a complex algorithm that ran on a cluster of raspberry Pi's and displayed Bart's predicted mood as a series of color-coded emojis – green for calm, yellow for cautious, red for... well, let's just say, best to avoid interaction.

Sophie, despite the pressure, remained remarkably calm. She focused on refining the "Chaos Control" interface to incorporate Bart's specific needs, adding features such as a "priority task" organizer that utilized a proprietary algorithm based on Bart's known preferences, and a comprehensive progress report generator that displayed updates in a font specified by Bart himself, using a unique color combination discovered during her analysis of Bart's personal website. Her attention to detail was not only impressive but critical for navigating this demanding client. She even created a series of personalized haiku updates for Bart, subtly incorporating references to his favored poets and a carefully chosen color palette reflecting his known stylistic preferences.

The first meeting with Bart was, to put it mildly, tense. He arrived precisely at 9:00 AM, not a second earlier or later, carrying a organized folder containing his requirements and a thermos of what Sophie suspected was kale and beet smoothie. He outlined his needs with unwavering precision, leaving no room for ambiguity or improvisation. His demands were as complex as they were specific, requiring a combination of cutting-edge technology, intuitive design, and an almost supernatural ability to anticipate his every whim.

The Bart-o-Matic, thankfully, performed flawlessly. As Bart detailed his requirements, the system accurately predicted his mood swings, providing the team with real-time insights into his emotional state. This allowed them to proactively adjust their communication strategies, addressing his concerns before they escalated into full-blown crises. Lily's scheduling and her precisely timed haiku updates provided a welcome contrast to Bart's demanding nature, creating a sense of order and predictability in an otherwise stressful situation.

Max, armed with his Mr. Fluffernutter-Bart plush toy, managed to subtly alleviate the tension with a carefully placed joke about the similarities between the plush and the CEO. His charm and his ability to maintain a jovial attitude throughout the encounter helped to disarm the notoriously stern executive. Dave's detailed insights from Bart-o-Matic were invaluable, allowing the team to anticipate and smoothly address Bart's ever-changing requirements. Sophie's precise responses and attention to detail, along with the subtly integrated haiku updates, provided Bart with moments of unexpected creativity, contrasting with his often-demanding character and proving WineSoft's adaptability. The plush was a testament to the team's ability to use a humorous approach that eased the tension.

Despite the initial apprehension, the meeting ended surprisingly well. Bart, though still demanding, seemed impressed by the team's ability to meet his unconventional requirements. He acknowledged the value of their creative approach, even praising their ability to incorporate a Baudelaire-inspired haiku generator into their progress reports. He even agreed to a trial period, giving WineSoft a chance to prove their worth.

The following weeks were a whirlwind of frantic coding, planning, and several near-misses involving accidental confetti explosions (Lily was adamant about creating a strict 'confetti-free zone' for future client interactions). However, the team worked tirelessly, their unique blend of skills and personalities proving to be the perfect antidote to Bart's stringent demands.

The Bart-o-Matic, initially seen as a novelty, became an indispensable tool, providing invaluable insights into Bart's mood swings and helping the team to anticipate and address his concerns. Dave, fueled by the success of his creation, was already planning an upgrade, incorporating features such as voice recognition and sentiment analysis to further enhance its accuracy. Lily's spreadsheets tracked the progress and analyzed each step with precision, identifying potential areas for improvement and ensuring the project remained on schedule. Max, ever the optimist, viewed each challenge as an opportunity, rallying the team with his infectious enthusiasm.

Ultimately, WineSoft not only met but exceeded Bart's expectations. The project, a complex piece of software designed to streamline Higgins & Sons Conglomerate's operations, was delivered on time and under budget, a feat that many had considered impossible. The success proved the worth of their unique blend of personalities and the power of their unconventional methods. Bart, surprisingly, was impressed. He even requested a follow-up meeting, suggesting a collaborative project for the development of an AI-powered system for optimizing his morning smoothie routine. The future, it seemed, was a kaleidoscope of chaotic brilliance, fueled by an equal amount of demanding clients and innovative solutions. The WineSoft team, battle-tested and still humming with the energy of success, knew that whatever came next, they would face it together, armed with their laughter, their ingenuity, and a healthy dose of Mr. Fluffernutter-inspired optimism.

The trial period with Higgins & Sons stretched on, each day bringing its own unique brand of comedic chaos. Bart, predictably, remained a whirlwind of precise demands and crafted critiques. He'd send emails at precisely 3:17 AM, each containing a detailed breakdown of his concerns, formatted and punctuated with a level of precision that could only be described as unsettling. His emails often included obscure references to Romantic-era poetry, seemingly unrelated to the software's functionality. One particularly memorable email ended with a haiku about the existential dread of improperly aligned spreadsheet columns.

Dave, ever the pragmatist, became increasingly reliant on Bart-o-Matic. The system, however, began to exhibit some...personality quirks. It started generating increasingly cryptic emojis, and its mood predictions became less reliable, often oscillating wildly between euphoria and utter despair within the span of a single sentence. Dave's attempts to debug the system resulted in a series of increasingly bizarre updates, including a feature that played calming whale songs whenever Bart's predicted mood dipped below a certain threshold. This often resulted in the entire office being serenaded by whale calls at 2 AM.

Lily, meanwhile, took on the role of chief mediator, expertly navigating Bart's ever-shifting demands while keeping the team from descending into utter pandemonium. Her crafted spreadsheets expanded to encompass everything from Bart's preferred coffee blend to the precise angle of his computer monitor. She even developed a complex algorithm to predict Bart's caffeine intake based on his email frequency and the length of his sentences. The accuracy of her predictions was astonishing, often leading to a perfectly timed delivery of a double-espresso just as his mood plummeted.

Max, undeterred by the challenges, embraced the chaos with his trademark enthusiasm. He organized a series of team-building exercises designed to improve their "Bart-handling" skills. These included a workshop on "Strategic Smoothie Negotiation," a role-playing exercise that involved pretending to be Bart and attempting to elicit the most outrageous demands possible, and a surprisingly intense session of synchronized swimming, ostensibly to improve teamwork and coordination.

Sophie, despite the pressure, remained remarkably composed. She continued to refine the software, adding features based on Bart's increasingly specific requirements, even incorporating a feature that automatically generated personalized haiku progress reports tailored to his evolving mood. She even started subtly embedding hidden Easter eggs in the code, each a small, whimsical tribute to Bart's peculiar fascinations. One particularly elaborate Easter egg simulated a miniature virtual version of Bart's office, complete with a working model of his organized toothpick collection.

One particularly memorable afternoon, Dave accidentally unleashed a rogue algorithm that caused Bart-o-Matic to project a giant, animated emoji of Bart's face onto the building's exterior. The image, a rather disconcerting interpretation of a somewhat frustrated-looking Bart, remained visible for several hours, causing quite a stir in the neighborhood. The incident, however, did seem to amuse Bart, who later emailed a rather cryptic haiku acknowledging the event.

The team's ability to adapt to Bart's increasingly outlandish demands became legendary. They managed to integrate a feature that automatically translated Bart's emails into Klingon (at his request, naturally), developed a system that tracked the precise humidity levels in his office (a crucial factor for his smoothie-making process, apparently), and even built a specialized module that could predict the optimal time to approach him with a progress update based on his current astrological sign.

Despite the constant pressure and the near-constant threat of unforeseen algorithmic catastrophes, the team pressed on, their camaraderie strengthening with each challenge. They learned to anticipate Bart's whims, to decipher his cryptic emails, and even to appreciate the peculiar beauty of his organized world.

Finally, the day arrived when the software was ready for launch. The team assembled in the conference room, a mix of nervous anticipation and exhaustion hanging in the air. Max, clutching his Mr. Fluffernutter-Bart plush for moral support, delivered the presentation to Bart via video conference.

Bart, predictably, was thorough in his critique, scrutinizing every line of code, every design element, every haiku. However, to everyone's surprise, his comments were less critical and more... appreciative. He noted the elegance of the Klingon translation feature, the precision of the humidity control system, and even expressed a fondness for the subtle humor embedded within the software's design.

The final verdict? A resounding success. Bart not only approved the software but also requested a follow-up meeting to discuss the possibility of collaborating on a project to develop an AI-powered system for optimizing his morning smoothie routine. The team, having survived the ordeal, celebrated with a company-wide wine tasting, complete with a special blend they named "Bart's Baudelaire Blend," a testament to their unlikely triumph.

The experience with Bart Higgins had been a crucible, forging the WineSoft team into a cohesive and remarkably resilient unit. They had faced their most demanding client, conquered the chaos, and emerged victorious, armed with a trove of anecdotes, a slightly traumatized Bart-o-Matic, and a renewed appreciation for the absurdities of high-stakes software development. And, most importantly, they'd learned that even the most demanding client could be won over with a healthy dose of humor, creativity, and a well-placed haiku. The future at WineSoft, it seemed, remained a glorious blend of chaos and brilliance, seasoned perfectly with the unexpected.

The aftermath of the near-catastrophic emoji incident left the WineSoft team slightly shell-shocked, but remarkably, not defeated. The giant, pixelated Bart glared down from the building's façade for hours, becoming a local legend, a testament to their chaotic yet strangely effective approach to software development. The incident, bizarre as it was, inadvertently served as a turning point. Bart, it seemed, possessed a strange, almost perverse appreciation for the unexpected. His subsequent email, a haiku filled with cryptic allusions to digital sunsets and rogue algorithms, was almost an endorsement of the chaos itself.

Inspired by this revelation, Max, ever the optimist, proposed a new strategy: "Embrace the Weird." This wasn't just a catchy slogan; it became a guiding philosophy. They decided to stop fighting the chaos and instead to channel it, to weaponize it, to make it work for them. The first step involved a complete overhaul of their communication strategy with Bart. Gone were the formatted emails, replaced by a rapid-fire exchange of GIFs, memes, and increasingly surreal video messages.

Dave, surprisingly, became the linchpin of this new approach. His initially disastrous attempts at debugging Bart-o-Matic had inadvertently unlocked its potential for creative, albeit unpredictable, output. He started feeding the system with Bart's emails, his social media posts, even his online shopping history, creating a vast database of Bart-specific data. The result was a system that could not only predict Bart's mood, but also generate custom-tailored content: personalized memes, custom haiku, even short, bizarre animated films starring a cartoon version of Bart battling miniature, digitally-rendered spreadsheets.

Lily, initially skeptical, found herself surprisingly impressed. She developed a complex algorithm to categorize Bart's emotional responses to the system's outputs, creating a feedback loop that allowed them to continuously refine their approach. The spreadsheets, once filled with details of Bart's coffee preferences, now tracked the effectiveness of each meme, the success rate of each haiku, and the overall emotional impact of the system's creations. She even began to suspect a hidden pattern in Bart's apparent eccentricity.

Sophie, ever the diligent intern, immersed herself in the world of digital art and meme creation, crafting bizarre and highly specific content designed to appeal to Bart's particular sense of humor. She started incorporating elements of Romantic-era poetry into the animations, subtly referencing his fondness for Keats and Byron in ways that were both unexpected and strangely effective. She even designed a series of animated GIFs depicting Bart's toothpick collection engaging in elaborate acrobatic routines, each perfectly timed to coincide with peaks and troughs in his mood.

One particular masterpiece involved a highly sophisticated animation showing a miniature, digital Bart bravely battling a monstrous spreadsheet, armed with nothing but a tiny, digitally-rendered toothpick. The animation subtly incorporated elements of epic fantasy, complete with dramatic musical score, and concluded with Bart vanquishing the spreadsheet in a triumphant display of toothpick-based combat. Bart's response? A single, perfectly formed emoji: a weeping-with-laughter face.

The project's deadlines loomed, but the team was oddly energized. The pressure to meet Bart's expectations remained high, but the process itself had become a collaborative work of art. They were no longer just developing software; they were creating a multimedia experience, a bizarre symphony of memes, GIFs, and code, tailored specifically to the needs (and eccentricities) of their demanding client. They held impromptu brainstorming sessions fueled by copious amounts of WineSoft's signature blends, each session producing a torrent of creative ideas that were both absurd and, surprisingly, effective.

Max, in a moment of inspiration, decided to create a personalized digital "mood board" for Bart, a constantly updated visual representation of his emotional state. This board incorporated real-time data from Bart-o-Matic, along with hand-drawn doodles, hastily scribbled haiku, and even the occasional photo of Max's cat, Mr. Fluffernutter-Bart, performing seemingly random acts. The board was designed to help them understand Bart's changing moods and to anticipate his needs, making communication more efficient and, dare they say, even enjoyable.

The final presentation to Higgins & Sons was unlike anything anyone had ever seen. Instead of a formal PowerPoint presentation, they presented a multimedia extravaganza: a seamless blend of animation, live-streamed data visualizations, custom-made memes, and spontaneous haiku readings by Sophie. Bart, initially taken aback, was slowly won over. The sheer audacity of the presentation, its chaotic brilliance, seemed to resonate with him on a deep, almost visceral level.

He laughed, he cried (mostly with laughter), and he even occasionally joined in on the spontaneous haiku readings. The presentation, though utterly unconventional, perfectly reflected the chaotic energy of the WineSoft team and their strangely successful approach. Bart, despite his initial skepticism, was impressed. He acknowledged the team's exceptional ability to adapt, to innovate, and to embrace the chaos with remarkable creativity.

In the end, Higgins & Sons not only approved the software, but also requested a follow-up meeting to discuss the possibilities of collaborating on a project to develop a new AI-powered system to optimize...wait for it...Bart's sock-folding routine. The team, exhausted but exhilarated, celebrated their victory with another company-wide wine tasting, the "Bart's Baudelaire Blend" now firmly established as a WineSoft classic. The experience taught them that success, in the world of software development, often resided not in eliminating the chaos, but in learning to dance with it. And as they raised their glasses, they knew that the future at WineSoft, a glorious blend of chaos and brilliance, was looking brighter than ever before. The unexpected, it seemed, was not just tolerated but actively celebrated. The future was unpredictable, yes, but it was also infinitely more interesting.

The air in the WineSoft office hung thick with the aroma of impending doom – or perhaps, a particularly robust Cabernet Sauvignon. The "Bart's Baudelaire Blend" tasting, intended as a celebratory wind-down after the Higgins & Sons presentation, had morphed into a full-blown brainstorming session. Max, fueled by an alarming quantity of Merlot, was sketching diagrams on a whiteboard using lipstick and grape juice. Lily, ever the pragmatist, was charting the correlation between alcohol consumption and creative output (the results, she muttered darkly, were inconclusive). Dave, having successfully trained Mr. Fluffernutter-Bart to "fetch" miniature digital spreadsheets (a skill of questionable practicality), was now attempting to teach him to operate the espresso machine. Sophie, meanwhile, was composing a haiku about the existential angst of a digitally rendered toothpick.

The success with Higgins & Sons, however, was not merely a fluke. It had shaken the very foundations of WineSoft's approach to software development. The initial reaction to their chaotic, multimedia presentation had been one of stunned silence, followed by an eruption of laughter, and finally, a grudging admiration. Bart, initially horrified by the sheer audacity of their approach, had eventually been won over by its sheer, unadulterated weirdness. He'd confessed, in a surprisingly heartfelt email (for him), that he'd never encountered a team that so completely embraced the unpredictable nature of the digital world.

The impact resonated far beyond the confines of the Higgins & Sons contract. News of WineSoft's unconventional approach to software design spread like wildfire through the industry. Blogs and tech news sites were buzzing with articles proclaiming their "chaotic genius," "unconventional brilliance," and "surprisingly effective madness." Investors, initially skeptical of WineSoft's quirky reputation, suddenly saw something truly unique: a company that didn't just adapt to change, but actively courted it.

The influx of new clients was staggering. A major gaming company commissioned them to develop a virtual reality experience based on the exploits of Mr. Fluffernutter-Bart (the cat's fame, once limited to Dave's Instagram followers, was now reaching global proportions). A renowned art museum hired them to create an interactive digital exhibit based on Sophie's toothpick-themed animations (the museum curator, it turned out, was a closet fan of Romantic-era poetry and acrobatic toothpicks). Even a renowned astrophysics research institute approached them, requesting a customized software solution to analyze the chaotic data from a recent black hole observation (they claimed that Bart's chaotic coding style was surprisingly well-suited to modeling the unpredictable nature of spacetime).

The expansion, however, brought its own set of challenges. The WineSoft team, once a tight-knit group of four, was now a bustling hive of activity. New developers, designers, and marketing specialists were recruited, each with their own unique quirks and idiosyncrasies. The "Embrace the Weird" philosophy, while liberating in its initial stages, now required careful management to prevent complete and utter pandemonium.

Lily, armed with a newly developed algorithm to track the "weirdness quotient" of each project, implemented a system of carefully calibrated chaos. She established "weirdness thresholds," defining acceptable levels of creative anarchy for different projects, ensuring that the team's unique approach remained effective without descending into utter disarray. She even introduced "Chaos Management Meetings," sessions dedicated to discussing and addressing the potential risks and benefits of embracing the unusual.

Max, ever the enthusiastic leader, channeled his energy into fostering a collaborative environment that embraced both creativity and productivity. He instituted "random act of kindness" days, where team members were encouraged to perform unexpectedly generous acts for one another (resulting in a surge in office cake-baking and impromptu karaoke sessions). He also introduced a system of "creative sprints," where teams were given limited time to develop wildly innovative ideas, with minimal restrictions on their approach.

Dave, now a celebrated expert in Bart-o-Matic technology, focused on developing new tools and techniques to enhance the team's creative output. He created a sophisticated "meme generator" that could create personalized memes tailored to the specific needs of each client, ensuring that the WineSoft brand of eccentric humor remained consistent across all projects. He even developed a "haiku synthesizer," capable of generating customized haikus based on the emotional state of the client (a feature that proved surprisingly useful in navigating the complex emotional landscape of the astrophysics institute).

Sophie, now recognized as a leading digital artist in her own right, expanded her portfolio to include everything from virtual reality landscapes to interactive museum exhibits. Her work, a delightful blend of traditional art techniques and digital innovation, became a hallmark of the WineSoft brand. She began mentoring new interns, sharing her unique approach to digital storytelling and reminding them that embracing the weirdness was not just permissible, it was actively encouraged.

Despite their unexpected success, WineSoft never forgot its roots. The company culture remained a unique blend of professionalism and playful chaos, a testament to their ability to find success in the most unconventional of ways. The "Bart's Baudelaire Blend" remained a staple at company events, a constant reminder that sometimes, the best ideas come from the most unexpected sources. The once-dreaded Bart, now a symbol of WineSoft's unconventional success, became a mascot, a reminder that embracing the unexpected could lead to surprising and rewarding outcomes. WineSoft had not only survived its initial chaotic period, but had thrived, proving that in the world of software development, sometimes, the greatest innovations come from chaos. And as they celebrated yet another successful launch, raising a glass of their signature blend, the WineSoft team knew their future, as unpredictable as it was, was brighter than ever before. The unexpected was not just tolerated – it was the engine that powered their success.

The success with Higgins & Sons wasn't just about the final presentation; it was about the journey. It was about the late-night brainstorming sessions fueled by questionable amounts of caffeine and even more questionable ideas. It was about the way they bounced ideas off each other, the arguments that somehow transformed into breakthroughs, the shared laughter that cemented their bond. This collaborative spirit, this unspoken understanding, proved to be their secret weapon in navigating the complexities of their new, larger clientele.

Their first major post-Higgins & Sons project involved "GameOn," a behemoth of a gaming company known for its hyper-realistic simulations. GameOn wanted a virtual reality experience unlike anything ever seen before, a wild, unpredictable landscape that captured the essence of their latest game, a sprawling fantasy epic brimming with mythical creatures and impossible landscapes. The brief was daunting, to say the least. Most development teams would have approached it with planning, carefully mapped-out timelines, and a rigid adherence to established methodologies. Not WineSoft.

Their response was, to put it mildly, unconventional. They started with a brainstorming session that involved a full-scale interpretive dance routine (Max's choreography), a series of increasingly bizarre sound effects generated by Dave's increasingly erratic Mr. Fluffernutter-Bart-operated synthesizer, and a series of cryptic haikus from Sophie, each one seemingly unrelated to the project, yet somehow profoundly evocative of the game's fantastical world. Lily, initially horrified, watched with a mixture of trepidation and grudging admiration as the session spiraled into controlled chaos. It was, she admitted later, breathtakingly unpredictable.

Yet, from this chaos, a stunningly original concept emerged. They decided to approach the virtual world not as a crafted simulation, but as an ever-evolving, organically growing entity. Their VR landscape would be populated by AI-driven characters that reacted unpredictably to player actions, constantly changing the environment and the game's narrative. The challenge, of course, was making this chaotic approach work within the constraints of GameOn's technical specifications.

This is where the strength of their team dynamics truly shone. Max, the visionary, kept the big picture in focus, ensuring that the team's creative energy remained channeled towards the overall goal. Lily, the pragmatic strategist, worked tirelessly to ensure that the team's innovative ideas were both technically feasible and commercially viable. Dave, the eccentric genius, constantly pushed the boundaries of what was possible, crafting innovative tools and technologies that brought their wild ideas to life. Sophie, the artist, infused the project with her unique sensibility, creating a visually stunning and emotionally resonant experience.

Their collaboration with GameOn became a masterclass in adaptability. They held regular meetings with the client, not to present polished prototypes, but to share their creative process, to discuss challenges, and to collaborate on solutions. They invited GameOn's creative director into their chaotic brainstorming sessions, exposing him to their unique approach and surprising him with their ability to transform seemingly random ideas into functional game mechanics.

The initial skepticism from GameOn soon transformed into awe and admiration. They were witnessing something extraordinary – a team that not only embraced unpredictability, but actively used it as a tool for innovation. The frequent updates, rather than being seen as delays, were celebrated as exciting new developments, unexpected twists and turns in the evolution of their virtual world. The client wasn't just receiving a product; they were becoming a part of the creative process.

The success of the GameOn project wasn't just measured in terms of sales figures or critical acclaim; it was also measured in the bonds forged between the WineSoft team and their client. They built a relationship based on mutual respect, trust, and a shared appreciation for the unexpected. They learned to communicate effectively, not through formal presentations and rigid timelines, but through a shared language of creativity, collaboration, and a healthy dose of humor.

Their next project, with the prestigious "ArtHaus" museum, presented a different set of challenges. ArtHaus wanted an interactive digital exhibit based on Sophie's toothpick animations, a project that required a delicate balance between artistic vision and technological innovation. The challenge was to transform Sophie's whimsical animations into a captivating museum experience without compromising the artistic integrity of her work.

This project showcased a different facet of WineSoft's collaborative strength. Sophie, initially hesitant to share her creative process, found herself collaborating closely with Dave, who developed custom software that allowed visitors to interact with her animations in unexpected and delightful ways. Max, understanding the need for a more structured approach, facilitated regular meetings with the ArtHaus team, ensuring that the project remained aligned with their vision while still retaining its unique WineSoft flair. Lily, meanwhile, focused on the logistical aspects of the project, managing the technical complexities and ensuring that the exhibit was delivered on time and within budget.

The result was a stunningly successful exhibit, a unique blend of traditional art and cutting-edge technology. The collaboration with ArtHaus wasn't just a project; it was a testament to WineSoft's ability to adapt their unique approach to a variety of contexts, showcasing their ability to build strong relationships with clients from diverse backgrounds. The project cemented WineSoft's reputation as a company that not only delivered exceptional results, but also fostered strong collaborative partnerships.

Even the astrophysics institute project, initially seeming like a bizarre outlier, became a showcase of the team's adaptability. The sheer complexity of the data, reflecting the chaotic nature of black holes, mirrored WineSoft's own unconventional approach. Dave's "Bart-o-Matic" algorithms, initially designed for generating memes, proved surprisingly effective in analyzing the unpredictable patterns. Sophie, inspired by the visual representations of the data, created stunning visualizations that made complex scientific concepts more accessible.

The success of these disparate projects demonstrated something crucial: WineSoft's strength wasn't simply in their quirky methodology, but in their ability to cultivate strong, trusting relationships with their clients. By embracing transparency and collaboration, they transformed the client relationship from a purely transactional exchange into a genuine partnership, where shared creativity and mutual respect became the driving forces behind innovation. This approach, as unpredictable as it was, proved to be their most valuable asset. They weren't just building software; they were building relationships, and in doing so, they were building a legacy. And that, they knew, was the true secret to WineSoft's astonishing success.

Chapter 14: The Algorithm of Awesome

The culmination of their successes with Higgins & Sons, GameOn, and ArtHaus led to an unexpected opportunity: a collaboration with StellarTech, a cutting-edge aerospace company known for its ambitious projects and even more ambitious budgets. StellarTech wasn't looking for just any software solution; they were seeking a revolutionary approach to data analysis, something that could unravel the complexities of their latest project – a deep-space probe designed to explore a newly discovered nebula.

The nebula, dubbed "Chaos Cloud" by the scientific community, was unlike anything previously encountered. Its unpredictable energy signatures, bizarre gravitational anomalies, and fluctuating radiation levels posed a significant challenge to traditional data analysis methods. StellarTech's initial attempts to make sense of the data had yielded frustratingly inconclusive results. They needed a solution, and fast.

WineSoft, with their reputation for unconventional yet effective problem-solving, was their last hope. Max, ever the optimist, saw the project as the ultimate challenge, a chance to prove that WineSoft's chaotic approach wasn't just a gimmick, but a powerful engine for innovation. He envisioned a system that wouldn't just analyze data; it would *understand* it, predicting future anomalies and identifying patterns hidden within the apparent chaos.

Their initial brainstorming session was, as expected, a spectacle. Dave, inspired by the chaotic nature of the nebula, created a mesmerizing visualization that resembled a swirling galaxy of neon-colored data points. He built a system that translated complex astrophysical data into an interactive musical composition, each note corresponding to a specific data point. The result was a cacophony of sound that simultaneously baffled and captivated the team.

Sophie, ever the artist, saw beauty in the data's apparent randomness. She created a series of abstract paintings inspired by the fluctuating energy signatures, capturing the essence of the nebula's chaotic energy. These paintings were more than just artistic expressions; they served as visual metaphors that helped the team better understand the intricate patterns within the data.

Lily, however, remained skeptical. While appreciating the team's creative efforts, she voiced her concerns about the project's feasibility. The sheer volume of data from the Chaos Cloud probe was immense, and the time constraints were incredibly tight. She proposed a more structured approach, suggesting a phased rollout with clearly defined milestones and deliverables.

Max, recognizing the validity of Lily's concerns, proposed a compromise. They would adopt a hybrid approach, combining their unconventional brainstorming techniques with a more rigorous project management strategy. Lily would oversee the project's logistical aspects, ensuring that the team remained on schedule and within budget. This allowed the creative minds to freely explore their unconventional ideas, knowing that Lily's planning would ensure their success.

This hybrid approach proved to be the key to their breakthrough. Dave, leveraging his seemingly random algorithms (which, surprisingly, had predictive capabilities), developed a system that could identify and predict anomalies within the data stream. Sophie's artistic interpretation of the data led to the creation of a user-friendly interface that allowed even non-scientists to visualize and understand the complex information.

The innovation wasn't just in the individual components, but in their seamless integration. Dave's chaotic algorithms worked in tandem with Sophie's intuitive visualization system, creating a dynamic and responsive platform. The entire system felt less like a rigid data analysis tool and more like a living, breathing entity, constantly adapting and evolving to the influx of new data.

The climax arrived during a presentation to the StellarTech board. Instead of a traditional PowerPoint presentation, the team showcased their interactive visualization system. The board members were awestruck by the system's ability to reveal hidden patterns within the Chaos Cloud's data, patterns that had eluded even the most experienced astrophysicists.

Their breakthrough innovation went beyond simply analyzing data. It was a testament to their unique approach to collaboration. They had developed a system that not only processed data but also translated it into a visually compelling and emotionally resonant experience. It was a fusion of art, science, and technology, a harmonious blend of chaos and order.

The success of the StellarTech project solidified WineSoft's reputation as more than just a quirky software company. They became a beacon of unconventional innovation, a testament to the power of embracing chaos and celebrating the unpredictable. Their success wasn't solely based on technical proficiency; it was founded on their ability to foster a unique team dynamic that encouraged creative exploration, collaborative problem-solving, and a shared appreciation for the absurd. The algorithms themselves were impressive, but the true algorithm of awesome was the team's ability to blend their individual strengths into a cohesive and remarkably effective whole.

Their methodology was a paradox – a planned embrace of chaos. They harnessed the power of unplanned experimentation, channeling seemingly random ideas into impactful innovations. The late-night coding sessions fueled by copious amounts of coffee and Max's increasingly eccentric motivational speeches were now seen not as distractions but as essential components of their innovative process.

The StellarTech project's success wasn't merely about the creation of a groundbreaking data analysis tool. It marked a shift in how WineSoft approached innovation itself. They had moved beyond simply creating software; they were now crafting experiences, weaving narratives, and building bridges between the seemingly disparate worlds of art, science, and technology.

The project brought unexpected benefits beyond the immediate financial success. It forged stronger bonds within the WineSoft team, solidifying their trust in each other's abilities and deepening their appreciation for each other's unique contributions. The shared challenges, the late nights, the moments of doubt, and the eventual triumph strengthened their bond in ways that no team-building exercise ever could.

Moreover, the success with StellarTech attracted the attention of some of the biggest names in various industries, opening doors to even more ambitious and challenging projects. Their unconventional approach, once considered a risky gamble, became their most valuable asset, their unique selling proposition. They weren't just a software company; they were a creative powerhouse, a testament to the power of collaborative innovation in its purest form. Their story wasn't just about the code; it was about the people, their camaraderie, and their shared belief in the power of unpredictable brilliance. It was the perfect embodiment of the WineSoft spirit: a chaotic symphony of talent, creating harmony from the most unexpected sources. And their journey had only just begun.

The StellarTech project, while a resounding success, presented a new set of challenges. The sheer novelty of their approach meant navigating uncharted waters in terms of marketing, sales, and even internal processes. WineSoft, accustomed to its chaotic yet strangely effective internal rhythms, suddenly found itself thrust into the spotlight, a position that neither Max nor anyone else had anticipated.

The first hurdle was explaining their innovation to potential clients. While the StellarTech board had been captivated by the interactive visualization, the concept of a "chaotic algorithm" that yielded accurate predictions was difficult to grasp for more traditional businesses. Many potential investors and clients initially dismissed their presentation as a clever, albeit ultimately impractical, artistic project. They couldn't reconcile the aesthetic beauty of Sophie's interface with the rigorous precision demanded by industries like finance or medicine.

Lily, ever the pragmatist, spearheaded the development of a comprehensive marketing strategy that focused on showcasing the *results* rather than the *process*. Instead of dwelling on the abstract nature of their algorithms, they emphasized the system's accuracy, reliability, and speed in delivering insights. This meant carefully crafting case studies and testimonials that highlighted the practical applications of their technology, avoiding any mention of "chaotic algorithms" or "artistic interpretations" in the initial marketing material.

Max, initially resistant to this more conventional approach, eventually conceded. He discovered, to his surprise, that Lily's planning and strategic approach complemented, rather than contradicted, the team's unconventional creativity. Her pragmatic approach ensured that their innovative spirit was channeled towards tangible outcomes, making it easier for potential clients to understand and appreciate the value of WineSoft's unique approach.

The sales process itself became a comedic balancing act. While Dave's technical explanations were often impenetrable to non-technical clients, Sophie's ability to translate complex concepts into accessible metaphors proved invaluable. She could turn a dense technical document into a compelling narrative, allowing clients to connect with the technology on an emotional level, paving the way for smoother sales conversations.

The internal challenges were equally intriguing. The sudden influx of new projects and increased workload threatened to disrupt WineSoft's carefully cultivated chaos. Max, in his attempts to manage the growth, introduced a complex system of color-coded sticky notes, whiteboard diagrams, and cryptic memos that only he could decipher. This only led to further confusion and a surge in the team's already significant caffeine consumption.

Lily, once again, stepped in to restore order. She implemented a project management system that incorporated elements of WineSoft's unconventional approach. The system allowed for flexibility and creative freedom while ensuring that projects stayed on track. It wasn't a rigid, inflexible system; rather, it was a framework that adapted to the team's unique energy and rhythm, allowing for spontaneous bursts of creativity interspersed with periods of focused work.

The team's reaction to this "structured chaos" was mixed. Dave initially grumbled about the added administrative burden, but even he eventually admitted that the system helped manage the flood of new projects, preventing the team from drowning in a sea of sticky notes. Sophie thrived in the organized chaos, appreciating the balance between structured planning and creative freedom. Even Max, after a series of near-meltdowns caused by his color-coded system's failures, acknowledged Lily's contributions.

The real challenge, however, was scaling their innovation. Their algorithms, developed for the relatively contained environment of the StellarTech project, needed to adapt to the diverse needs of different industries. The team discovered that what worked marvelously for analyzing astrophysical data wasn't necessarily ideal for predicting market trends or analyzing medical images.

This necessitated a period of intense research and development, pushing the team's creativity and problem-solving skills to their limits. Dave, inspired by a particularly challenging algorithm, started experimenting with AI-powered code generation, a move initially met with skepticism but eventually proving to be a game-changer. Sophie designed user interfaces that could adapt to different industries and user needs, creating a modular system that could be customized to specific requirements.

The process wasn't without its setbacks. There were coding errors, design flaws, and plenty of frustrating late nights. But the team's resilience, forged in the crucible of previous challenges, pulled them through. They learned to embrace failure as a stepping stone to innovation, treating every setback as a learning opportunity. Their shared experiences formed a strong foundation of mutual trust and understanding. They were no longer just a team; they were a family, bound together by their shared passion, their eccentricities, and their uncanny ability to find success amidst the chaos.

The growth of WineSoft was a testament to their adaptive nature. Their initial success wasn't just about a single innovation; it was about creating a culture of innovation, a dynamic environment where creativity flourished, even amidst the controlled chaos. They had discovered a unique formula: a carefully orchestrated balance between planned structure and spontaneous creativity.

This carefully controlled chaos, however, was a fragile thing. The success of their unconventional approach drew unwanted attention – corporate vultures circling, eager to replicate their success without understanding the intricate balance that made it work. Large corporations, envious of WineSoft's success, attempted to copy their approach, creating stiff, bureaucratic imitations that lacked the inherent spark of creativity that defined the company. These imitations fell flat, demonstrating that it wasn't just about the algorithms but about the team's unique chemistry.

Their ability to adapt to challenges and to learn from setbacks became their defining characteristic. The team understood that innovation wasn't a linear process; it was a journey filled with unexpected turns, dead ends, and moments of sheer brilliance. Their story wasn't just one of technological innovation; it was a story about human ingenuity, collaboration, and the surprising power of embracing the absurd. It was the story of a group of individuals who dared to be different, who chose chaos over conformity, and who, in doing so, achieved something truly remarkable. Their future, however, was far from certain. The challenges of maintaining their unique identity while navigating the complexities of a rapidly expanding business, remained a constant source of both excitement and trepidation. The algorithm of awesome, it turned out, was still being written.

The launch of StellarTech wasn't just about the software; it was about crafting a narrative, a story that resonated with potential clients. Lily, armed with spreadsheets and a steely gaze, orchestrated a marketing campaign that was as unconventional as WineSoft itself. Forget stuffy press releases and generic brochures; Lily envisioned a campaign that showcased the team's unique personality. This meant leveraging the very chaos that defined WineSoft to create a buzz.

The first step was social media. Forget carefully curated corporate profiles; WineSoft's social media presence was a chaotic whirlwind of behind-the-scenes glimpses, humorous memes featuring Dave's perpetually unimpressed cat, and Sophie's whimsical animated explainer videos. These videos, surprisingly effective, deconstructed complex algorithms into easily digestible snippets. One particularly popular video featured a dancing algorithm represented by a brightly colored octopus, explaining the intricacies of predictive modeling in a way that captivated even the most technically challenged viewers.

Max, naturally, took the lead on generating content, fueled by an endless supply of coffee and a boundless enthusiasm that often bordered on manic. His posts were a mix of technical jargon and outrageous pronouncements about the future of AI, interspersed with motivational quotes and slightly off-color jokes. Lily spent a significant amount of time editing his more… enthusiastic outbursts, transforming potential PR disasters into quirky charm.

Dave, initially resistant to any form of self-promotion, surprisingly became a reluctant social media star. His cat, Mr. Fluffernutter III, achieved a cult following, his unimpressed expressions mirroring the reactions of many potential clients initially confronted with StellarTech's unconventional explanation. His grumpy yet adorable face became the unlikely mascot for the company, perfectly embodying the "controlled chaos" philosophy.

Sophie, a natural storyteller, created engaging blog posts, highlighting the journey of developing StellarTech, turning the challenges and setbacks into compelling narratives that showcased the team's resilience and creativity. These posts attracted a loyal following, establishing WineSoft not just as a tech company, but as a community, creating a sense of connection and shared experience with their audience.

The next challenge was public relations. WineSoft wasn't your typical tech company, and Lily knew that a traditional PR approach wouldn't work. Instead, she focused on generating organic buzz through unconventional methods. They partnered with tech influencers known for their quirky and humorous content, offering them early access to StellarTech and encouraging them to share their experiences. These influencers, impressed by both the software and WineSoft's unique culture, generated positive media coverage that spread organically across various platforms.

The team also organized a series of unconventional launch events. Instead of stuffy corporate presentations, they opted for interactive workshops and informal gatherings where potential clients could interact with the team, experience StellarTech firsthand, and get a feel for WineSoft's unique culture. These events were as much social gatherings as they were product demos; they were opportunities to connect with potential clients on a human level.

One particular event, a "Wine & Algorithms" tasting held in a converted warehouse, was a resounding success. Attendees mingled with the WineSoft team, sampling local wines while engaging in casual discussions about StellarTech. Max, in his element, conducted impromptu demos, explaining complex concepts with the enthusiasm of a seasoned sommelier describing a rare vintage. The event generated significant media attention, painting WineSoft as a company that was both innovative and approachable.

This more personal approach resonated with potential clients, who appreciated the transparency and honesty. They were attracted to WineSoft's unique approach, valuing the human element behind the technology. This personal touch differentiated WineSoft from its competitors and helped establish a strong brand identity.

The success of their unconventional approach, however, wasn't without its challenges. Some potential clients remained skeptical, questioning the long-term viability of a company that prioritized creativity over structure. Others were concerned about the lack of traditional marketing materials, preferring the familiar comfort of well-polished presentations and corporate jargon.

Lily addressed these concerns with a carefully crafted communications strategy that emphasized the results, not the process. She showcased StellarTech's accuracy and reliability with detailed case studies, quantifying the system's impact on various industries. The focus shifted from the "chaotic algorithm" to the tangible benefits it provided.

The team also faced internal challenges. The sudden surge in popularity generated a significant increase in demand for

StellarTech, putting pressure on the development team to deliver more features and integrate with various systems. The color-coded sticky note system, once a symbol of WineSoft's organized chaos, was now teetering on the brink of total collapse.

Lily, once again, rose to the occasion, implementing a new project management system that integrated agile methodologies with elements of WineSoft's unique approach. The system allowed for flexibility and creativity while maintaining a degree of structure. It was a delicate balance, requiring constant adjustments and iterations to adapt to the team's unpredictable rhythms.

This revised system proved remarkably effective. While the team still embraced spontaneity, they now had a framework that enabled them to manage the increased workload without sacrificing their creative energy. The controlled chaos, rather than hindering productivity, became a catalyst for innovation, leading to even more breakthroughs.

The successful launch of StellarTech was a testament to the power of embracing individuality and unconventional approaches. WineSoft proved that success in the tech industry didn't require conformity; it thrived on embracing chaos, nurturing creativity, and telling a compelling story. The algorithms of awesome, it turned out, were not just lines of code but a blend of technology, personality, and a whole lot of unexpected charm. The future, though, remained as unpredictable and exciting as ever. Their success had attracted unwanted attention, and the challenges of maintaining their unique identity in the face of growing pressure were only just beginning.

The unexpected success of StellarTech's launch, however, wasn't the end of the story; it was merely the beginning of a whole new set of delightfully chaotic adventures. The increased demand for their unconventional software brought with it a flurry of new challenges, testing the limits of WineSoft's already stretched-thin resources and the team's capacity for controlled chaos.

The first major hurdle was scaling operations. Their charmingly disorganized office, once a symbol of their creative spirit, now felt cramped and inefficient. Max, ever the optimist, proposed expanding into the adjacent office space – a former bowling alley, complete with faded lanes and a lingering scent of stale beer. Lily, predictably, vetoed this idea, citing potential health hazards and the logistical nightmare of integrating a functioning bowling alley into their workflow (a suggestion Dave surprisingly supported, envisioning a highly productive "bowling-while-coding" initiative). A compromise was reached: a more conventional, albeit still slightly quirky, expansion into a nearby office building. The move, however, brought its own set of challenges, including lost files, misplaced equipment, and the accidental shipment of Mr. Fluffernutter III's favorite tuna-flavored catnip to a client in Iceland.

The increased workload also put a strain on the development team. The agile methodology, while effective, felt strained under the pressure. Sophie, finding herself overwhelmed by the volume of new tasks, almost accidentally launched a beta version of StellarTech that could predict the stock market with alarming accuracy – a feature nobody had planned, and one that sent Lily into a frantic series of phone calls with their lawyers.

Dave, amidst the chaos, found his coding prowess surprisingly enhanced by the frantic energy. Fueled by an endless supply of caffeine and the ever-present glare of Mr. Fluffernutter III's judgmental stare, he churned out code with remarkable speed and efficiency. His contributions became crucial in streamlining the software's performance and resolving several critical bugs. He even started wearing a branded WineSoft t-shirt – a significant sartorial breakthrough considering his previous aversion to company apparel. However, his success also led to a new problem: Dave's cat was now demanding royalties from WineSoft's profits, payable in premium tuna.

Max, amidst the pandemonium, remained astonishingly upbeat. He envisioned StellarTech as a revolutionary platform that would change the world, one quirky algorithm at a time. His enthusiasm, though occasionally overwhelming, inspired the team to push their boundaries and overcome seemingly insurmountable obstacles. He even started incorporating yoga breaks into their daily routine – a bizarre but surprisingly effective way to manage stress and maintain team cohesion.

But amidst the successful expansion and growing demand, a darker cloud loomed on the horizon. A larger, more established tech company, "Tech Titans," took notice of WineSoft's remarkable success and their unconventional approach. They weren't impressed; they were threatened.

Tech Titans, known for their ruthless efficiency and cutthroat business practices, began a campaign to discredit WineSoft, spreading rumors about software vulnerabilities and questionable ethical practices. Their marketing campaign subtly compared WineSoft's "controlled chaos" to a complete lack of professionalism, cleverly playing on societal expectations of a structured and efficient tech company.

Lily, ever the strategic mastermind, responded by leveraging WineSoft's unique brand identity to their advantage. She emphasized their unconventional approach as a source of strength, highlighting the creativity and innovation that stemmed from their unconventional methods. She orchestrated a counter-campaign that portrayed WineSoft as a David versus Goliath story, endearing them even further to their increasingly loyal customer base.

The battle with Tech Titans brought the WineSoft team closer than ever before. They faced a common enemy, and their shared purpose strengthened their bonds. They worked tirelessly, fueled by the adrenaline of the competition and the knowledge that their unique approach was being challenged.

The culmination of this struggle was a high-stakes showdown – a live-streamed coding competition against Tech Titans. Both companies had to solve a complex algorithmic challenge, and the winner would be declared the leader in innovative AI.

The competition was intense, filled with nail-biting moments and unexpected plot twists. The WineSoft team, despite their initial disadvantage, showed their resilience, creativity, and remarkable problem-solving skills. Max's energetic leadership, Lily's strategic planning, Dave's genius coding, and Sophie's quick thinking came together to deliver a remarkable victory. They didn't just win; they redefined what it meant to achieve success in the tech industry.

Their victory was more than a technical achievement; it was a validation of their unconventional approach. It proved that controlled chaos, embracing individuality, and telling a compelling story could lead to success in the most competitive environments. The win cemented their position in the market, securing their place as the company that dared to be different and, in the process, transformed the tech world, one quirky algorithm at a time.

However, the story doesn't end there. The victory against Tech Titans brought unforeseen consequences. Their newfound fame attracted investors eager to capitalize on WineSoft's success. The influx of capital brought new
challenges—negotiating contracts, managing finances, and maintaining their unique culture in the face of rapid growth. But

WineSoft, having navigated the turbulent waters of a coding competition against a corporate giant, felt prepared for whatever the future might bring. Their journey was far from over, but they were ready, armed with their unconventional approach and an unwavering belief in the power of controlled chaos. The algorithm of awesome, it seemed, was constantly evolving, and WineSoft was perfectly positioned to ride the wave. The future, however, remained as unpredictable and exciting as the journey that had led them to this point. The next chapter, it seemed, was about to begin.

The air crackled with a palpable energy, a potent cocktail of exhaustion and exhilaration. The WineSoft office, usually a whirlwind of controlled chaos, was strangely still, the hum of computers replaced by the clinking of champagne flutes and the murmur of happy voices. Confetti, inexplicably shaped like miniature wine bottles, littered the floor, a testament to the epic celebration underway.

Max, usually a whirlwind of motion, was surprisingly subdued, a rare sight that left even Lily momentarily speechless. He held a champagne flute, his usually vibrant shirt replaced with a surprisingly tasteful (for him) navy blue blazer, a small, almost shy smile playing on his lips. He looked around at his team, his eyes reflecting the shimmering lights strung across the office. This wasn't just a celebration of a coding competition win; it was a celebration of their improbable journey. Their journey from a small, quirky company on the brink of collapse to a tech giant, fueled by a uniquely potent blend of talent, caffeine, and a healthy dose of controlled chaos.

"To WineSoft," Max finally announced, his voice filled with a genuine emotion that belied his usual boisterous persona. "To the team that proved that algorithms can be awesome, even when they're written amidst a blizzard of catnip and the faint aroma of stale beer."

A roar of approval erupted from the team. Dave, sporting a slightly askew WineSoft t-shirt and a noticeable lack of sleep, raised his flute, Mr. Fluffernutter III perched regally on his shoulder, surveying the scene with an air of feline disdain. He'd received a lifetime supply of premium tuna as a "royalty" payment, a detail that greatly amused the rest of the team.

Lily, ever the pragmatist, smiled warmly, a rare sight that was met with surprised cheers. "To surviving the Tech Titans," she declared, her voice laced with a hint of dry humor. "To proving that professionalism doesn't require a soul-crushing lack of creativity." She paused, glancing at Max with a playful roll of her eyes. "And to the day Max finally agreed to use an office space that didn't smell suspiciously of fermented grapes."

Sophie, initially overwhelmed by the celebratory atmosphere, found herself grinning broadly, a newfound confidence radiating from her. The intern, who had started with wide-eyed wonder, had blossomed into a valuable member of the team, her quick thinking proving instrumental in their victory over Tech Titans.

She raised her glass. "To the power of teamwork," she declared, her voice clear and strong. "And to proving that even interns can contribute to world-altering algorithms."

The celebration continued late into the night, a kaleidoscope of laughter, stories, and shared memories. They reminisced about their early days, their chaotic brainstorming sessions, their near-disastrous blunders, and the countless moments that defined their unique company culture. They recounted the near-heart attacks brought on by Sophie's almost-launched, stock-market-predicting StellarTech beta, the comical mishaps during their office move (including the unfortunate incident with Mr. Fluffernutter III's catnip shipment to Iceland), and Dave's remarkable coding prowess fueled by caffeine and feline judgment.

They discussed the challenges they faced in scaling up their operations, the near-constant threat of overwhelming workloads, and their battle against Tech Titans. They spoke of Max's unwavering optimism, Lily's strategic brilliance, Dave's incredible coding skills, and Sophie's surprisingly insightful contributions.

The conversation drifted to their unconventional approach, their "controlled chaos." They acknowledged that it hadn't always been easy. There were moments of sheer pandemonium, times when the sheer volume of work and the constant stream of unexpected events threatened to overwhelm them. Yet, it was this very chaos, this unique blend of personalities and approaches, that had ultimately led to their success.

They recognized that their "controlled chaos" wasn't just some whimsical descriptor; it was their core strength, the secret ingredient that made them stand out in a sea of organized, corporate giants. It was a testament to the belief that true innovation flourished in an environment where individuality and creativity were not only tolerated but celebrated. Their workplace, once perceived as a haven of disorganized brilliance, had become their greatest asset, a symbol of their unique brand identity and approach.

The celebratory mood subtly shifted as the night wore on. The champagne fizzled out, replaced by a quieter conversation about the future. The victory over Tech Titans had brought them immense success, but it also brought with it the responsibility of managing that success. The influx of investors, the demands of scaling their operations, and the ever-present challenge of maintaining their unique company culture were all looming on the horizon.

Max, surprisingly grounded, discussed the upcoming challenges, his optimism tempered by a newfound sense of responsibility. Lily, ever practical, outlined strategic plans for managing their growth while preserving their unique identity. Dave, ever the quirky coder, suggested a new algorithm that could predict market trends based on Mr. Fluffernutter III's daily naps, an idea that prompted a round of amused groans. Sophie, eager to contribute, suggested a series of workshops focused on maintaining team cohesion in the face of rapid expansion.

The celebration had evolved into a strategic planning session, a testament to their ability to seamlessly transition from moments of unbridled joy to focused discussion about their future. They ended the night with a renewed sense of purpose, their camaraderie solidified by the shared experience of victory and the excitement of the road ahead.

As the night drew to a close, they knew their journey was far from over. The algorithm of awesome, they realized, was constantly evolving, a dynamic process that required constant adaptation and innovation. But as they stood together, amidst the remnants of a truly unforgettable celebration, they felt confident in their ability to navigate whatever challenges the future might bring. They had proven that controlled chaos, embraced individuality, and a shared love for quirky algorithms could lead to extraordinary success. And for the team at WineSoft, the next chapter promised even more exhilarating adventures, more controlled chaos, and even more reasons to celebrate. The algorithm of awesome, it seemed, was just getting started.

Chapter 15: The Future of WineSoft

The remnants of the confetti, now a pathetic scattering beneath the newly polished floors, served as a poignant reminder of their recent triumph. The champagne was gone, replaced by the slightly more sobering reality of their newfound success. The air, once thick with the aroma of celebratory bubbles, now held a sharper tang, a blend of anticipation and the faint scent of freshly brewed coffee – a familiar comfort in the WineSoft atmosphere.

Max, still surprisingly subdued for him, tapped a pen against his teeth, a nervous habit Lily had long since learned to ignore. "So," he began, his voice a bit less boisterous than usual, "Tech Titans is in the rearview mirror. Now, the real challenge begins."

Lily, ever the pragmatist, leaned forward, her sharp eyes scanning the faces around the table. "Indeed," she agreed. "We need a comprehensive long-term growth strategy. We can't just coast on the success of the StellarTech beta. We need to plan for scalability, maintain our unique culture, and, frankly, stop relying on sheer luck and caffeine."

Dave, surprisingly attentive, for once without Mr. Fluffernutter III draped across his shoulders, nodded slowly. "Scalability," he mumbled, scratching his chin thoughtfully. "That means more servers, more bandwidth, more... well, more everything." He paused, a mischievous glint appearing in his eyes. "And perhaps a more robust algorithm for predicting Mr. Fluffernutter's naps.

My initial model... let's just say it requires further refinement." A collective groan rippled through the room; Dave's cat-based market predictions remained a source of both amusement and anxiety.

Sophie, no longer the wide-eyed intern, spoke with newfound confidence. "We also need to consider our team," she stated. "Rapid expansion could dilute our unique culture. We need strategies to maintain our close-knit working environment, even as we grow." She presented a prepared document outlining potential team-building exercises and workshops focused on maintaining communication and collaboration.

The discussion flowed naturally, each member contributing their unique perspectives and expertise. Max, fueled by a newfound sense of responsibility, focused on the overarching vision, ensuring that WineSoft's expansion remained true to its core values. He stressed the importance of retaining their unconventional approach, that strange brew of controlled chaos and inspired creativity that had propelled them to success. He envisioned WineSoft expanding not just in size, but in influence, becoming a beacon for unconventional thinkers in the tech industry.

Lily took charge of the practicalities, detailing the logistical challenges of scaling their operations. She outlined strategies for attracting and retaining top talent, carefully balancing the need for expansion with the preservation of their existing team dynamics. She tackled everything from office space allocation to employee benefit packages, highlighting the importance of creating a work environment that valued both productivity and individual well-being – something not usually associated with the tech industry's notorious crunch culture.

Dave, surprisingly insightful for a coder primarily interested in feline Instagram fame,
focused on technological infrastructure. He proposed a modular software architecture that would allow for seamless scalability without compromising functionality. He emphasized the importance of future-proofing their codebase, ensuring that WineSoft could adapt to the ever-evolving landscape of technological advancements. Of course, he still slipped in the occasional reference to Mr. Fluffernutter III's napping patterns, suggesting that the cat's biometric data might provide an unexpected source of valuable insights for future algorithm development.

Sophie, beyond her initial contribution, proved to be a surprisingly adept strategist. She proposed innovative marketing campaigns that would leverage WineSoft's unique brand identity, capitalizing on their reputation for chaotic brilliance and unconventional success. Her suggestions, detailed and well-researched, surprised everyone, particularly Lily who had originally been skeptical of Sophie's contributions. She had, after all, spent her internship perfecting her ability to translate Dave's cat-related coding jargon into intelligible business plans.

The hours melted away as they delved deeper into the specifics of their long-term strategy. They discussed funding options, market analysis, and potential partnerships. They debated the merits of different software development methodologies, the challenges of remote work, and the importance of fostering a culture of continuous learning and improvement.

They even touched on the possibility of expanding their product line. Dave suggested a line of cat-themed software, a proposition that brought a mix of groans and amused agreement. Max, ever the visionary, suggested exploring the intersection of technology and viticulture, creating software solutions to aid in winemaking – a bold idea that could only come from the minds that produced StellarTech. Lily, while not completely against it, suggested they focus on their present successes before diving into vineyards.

As the sun began to rise, casting a warm glow over the now-quiet office, they finally reached a consensus. Their long-term growth strategy, a document thick with charts, graphs, and bullet points, was a testament to their shared vision and collaborative spirit. It wasn't a rigid plan, but rather a flexible framework, designed to adapt to the inevitable twists and turns that lay ahead. They realized that their 'controlled chaos,' far from being a liability, was in fact their greatest asset, a source of both creativity and resilience.

Their success wasn't simply the result of a brilliant algorithm; it was the product of a unique team dynamic, a carefully cultivated blend of personalities, skills, and a shared sense of humor. They had proven that a quirky, unconventional approach could not only survive in the cutthroat world of tech but actually thrive. As they packed up their laptops, exhausted but energized, the team knew that the future of WineSoft was as unpredictable, exciting, and potentially hilarious as its past. The algorithm of awesome, it seemed, was poised for exponential growth, driven not just by code, but by the unwavering camaraderie of a team that had learned to embrace the beautiful messiness of controlled chaos. The future was uncertain, but with this team, it was sure to be a wild and unforgettable ride. The journey had just begun.

The quiet hum of the office, usually punctuated by Max's boisterous pronouncements or Dave's muttered complaints about Mr. Fluffernutter III's latest Instagram post, was replaced by a contemplative silence. The celebratory hangover had worn off, leaving behind a potent cocktail of exhaustion and exhilaration. The success of StellarTech was real, tangible, and a little terrifying.

Lily, perched on the edge of her desk, organized a stack of post-it notes – a habit that, in the whirlwind of WineSoft's daily operations, served as her only semblance of order. "Okay, team," she announced, her voice cutting through the stillness, "the champagne is gone. The confetti's swept up. Now, let's talk about actually making this thing work long-term."

Max, ever the optimist, grinned. "We're going to be huge, Lily! Think WineSoft 2.0 – bigger, bolder, and even more... delightfully chaotic!" He mimed a controlled explosion with his hands, sending a stray pen tumbling across his desk.

Dave, surprisingly alert for a man who'd survived on three hours of sleep and copious amounts of coffee, chimed in, "More servers, definitely. And maybe a dedicated team to manage Mr. Fluffernutter III's social media presence. His engagement rate is directly correlated with my coding productivity, you know." He winked, a mischievous glint in his eye. This was a revelation that even Lily found herself struggling to dispute.

Sophie, no longer just the wide-eyed intern but a contributing member of the team, cautiously added, "We need a structured approach to growth. We can't just rely on luck and... Mr. Fluffernutter's nap schedule." She produced a carefully organized spreadsheet, detailing projected growth, staffing needs, and even a contingency plan for a potential influx of cat-related merchandise. The last item was purely preventative – they'd learned to prepare for the unexpected.

The ensuing discussion was a masterclass in controlled chaos. Max's vision – a global empire of WineSoft, a beacon of unconventional brilliance in the tech world – was countered by Lily's pragmatic approach to budgeting, resource allocation, and the critical importance of decent health insurance. Dave, despite his occasional cat-related tangents, offered surprisingly insightful suggestions regarding scalable architecture and the potential for integrating AI-driven analytics into their existing software – an idea he'd borrowed, with some modification, from Mr. Fluffernutter's intricate sleep patterns. Sophie, meanwhile, proved to be a marketing prodigy, devising innovative campaigns that played up WineSoft's unique, chaotic identity.

They debated the merits of different development methodologies – agile, waterfall, and a bizarre hybrid that Max dubbed "chaotic agile," which involved a significant amount of impromptu wine tasting and brainstorming sessions. They discussed potential partnerships with other tech companies, exploring collaborative opportunities that would allow them to expand their reach without compromising their core values. They even explored the possibility of creating WineSoft-branded merchandise, ranging from t-shirts emblazoned with cryptic coding jokes to limited-edition wine glasses engraved with the WineSoft logo.

One particularly heated discussion centered around office space. Max envisioned a sprawling campus, complete with a fully stocked wine cellar and an on-site cat cafe. Lily, however, preferred a more practical approach, focusing on maximizing efficiency and minimizing overhead. Dave, unsurprisingly, championed a modular design that could accommodate fluctuating team sizes and a cat-friendly environment. Sophie, in a move that shocked even herself, proposed a flexible work arrangement that allowed for both in-office collaboration and remote work, recognizing the needs of different team members and fostering a sense of autonomy.

Their conversations extended well beyond the purely practical. They delved into the complexities of corporate culture, debating the merits of different management styles and the importance of fostering a positive and inclusive work environment.

They acknowledged the challenges of scaling a company without losing the quirky spirit that had defined their success. They recognized that their unconventional approach, while initially viewed with skepticism, had become their biggest strength.

The discussion extended to marketing strategies. They debated the merits of traditional advertising versus social media campaigns, viral marketing tactics, and the potential for influencer collaborations. They discussed the importance of brand building and crafting a narrative that resonated with their target audience. They knew they needed to maintain the image of chaotic brilliance, while also demonstrating their competence and professionalism. This delicate balance presented its own set of amusing challenges.

As days bled into nights, fueled by copious amounts of coffee and the occasional celebratory glass of wine, a comprehensive plan emerged. It wasn't a rigid, inflexible structure, but rather a dynamic framework that allowed for adaptation and evolution. It acknowledged the inevitability of unforeseen challenges, embraced the potential for unexpected successes, and recognized the importance of preserving WineSoft's unique and wonderfully chaotic culture.

The future of WineSoft wasn't simply about expanding the company's reach. It was about solidifying their position as a disruptive force, a beacon of creativity and unconventional thinking. It was about building a company that valued individuality, embraced controlled chaos, and understood that true innovation often came from the most unexpected places. It was a testament to their unlikely team dynamic, the synergistic blend of their diverse personalities, their combined skills, and a shared, quirky sense of humor. It was a future that, they all agreed, would undoubtedly be both wildly successful and incredibly hilarious.

The final document, a testament to their collaborative spirit and countless hours of brainstorming, was a sprawling document full of bold visions, pragmatic strategies, and a sprinkling of Dave's cat-inspired musings. They had created a blueprint not just for growth, but for maintaining their soul; the chaotic, brilliant heart of WineSoft. And as they looked towards the horizon, a horizon full of possibilities, uncertainties, and the very real chance of Mr. Fluffernutter III becoming the face of their next marketing campaign, they knew they were ready. The journey, it seemed, was only just beginning, and it was going to be a wild ride.

The post-StellarTech euphoria eventually faded, replaced by the gnawing question: what next? Max, fueled by an almost unsettling optimism, bounced a stress ball shaped like a grape across his desk. "We need to stay ahead of the curve!" he declared, his voice echoing through the now-quiet office. "We need... *revolutionary* new technologies!"

Lily, ever the pragmatist, raised a perfectly sculpted eyebrow. "Revolutionary how,
Max? Are we talking about sentient wine bottles that order themselves from Amazon?"

Dave, who had inexplicably managed to train Mr. Fluffernutter III to fetch his coffee (a feat more impressive than any coding accomplishment), offered, "Perhaps AI-powered wine pairing suggestions? Based on, you know, the user's mood, astrological sign, and their cat's current emotional state."

Sophie, having absorbed a year's worth of corporate strategy in a matter of months, suggested a more measured approach. "We need to identify technologies that align with our brand, that enhance our existing software, and that are, dare I say, *scalable*." She paused, then added with a mischievous grin, "And perhaps, slightly chaotic."

The ensuing discussion was a fascinating blend of technical jargon, bizarre analogies, and surprisingly insightful observations. They explored the possibilities of blockchain technology, imagining a system where users could verify the authenticity of their favorite wines, creating a transparent and tamper-proof record of provenance. This, Max argued passionately, would be "the most revolutionary thing since the screw-top bottle."

Lily, however, pointed out the considerable security and logistical challenges involved in implementing such a system, not to mention the potential for catastrophic wine-related data breaches. "Imagine," she shuddered, "a world where someone could hack into our system and change the vintage of a Chateau Lafite Rothschild. The repercussions would be... astronomical!"

The conversation shifted to augmented reality (AR) applications. Max envisioned an AR app that overlays information about wines onto real-world bottles, providing tasting notes, reviews, and even suggested pairings directly to the user's phone. Dave, ever the pragmatist (when not considering Mr. Fluffernutter's Instagram needs), highlighted the potential for integrating AR with their existing software to create a truly immersive wine-tasting experience.

This led to a spirited debate about virtual reality (VR) and the possibilities of creating virtual wine cellars. Max, naturally, envisioned an expansive, customizable digital space where users could sample wines from around the world without ever leaving their homes. Dave, surprisingly, saw the potential for creating VR-based training simulations for wine professionals, a concept he pitched with the surprising expertise of someone who'd spent countless hours researching cat-related VR games.

Sophie, meanwhile, steered them towards more practical applications of AR and VR. She suggested developing AR-based tasting notes for wine professionals, providing a layer of interactive information directly onto wine bottles, eliminating the need for cumbersome paper labels. For VR, she proposed educational simulations focusing on the winemaking process, allowing users to learn about grape cultivation, fermentation, and aging in a fun, interactive way.

Their brainstorming session didn't stop at AR and VR. They explored the integration of machine learning (ML) into their software, imagining an ML-powered system capable of recommending wines based on individual preferences and creating personalized tasting itineraries. Max envisioned a system that could even predict future wine trends and suggest wines for investment, a notion that immediately sent Lily into a whirlwind of risk-assessment calculations.

Dave, surprisingly, offered a unique ML application: a system that could analyze Mr. Fluffernutter's reactions to various wines, suggesting the perfect pairings based on feline preferences. This, he claimed, would open up an entirely new market—cat-approved wines. This idea, despite its inherent absurdity, surprisingly resonated with the team. After all, Mr. Fluffernutter had already indirectly influenced their success.

They then discussed the potential of the metaverse and the creation of a virtual WineSoft community where users could interact, share their tasting experiences, and participate in virtual wine tastings. Max, already envisioning virtual wine festivals and digital sommelier competitions, nearly exploded with enthusiasm. This metaverse idea, while seemingly ambitious, aligned perfectly with WineSoft's unconventional branding.

The team spent days immersed in research, poring over technical papers, engaging in spirited discussions, and occasionally punctuated by unplanned wine tastings. They evaluated the feasibility, cost, and market potential of each technology, carefully balancing innovation with practicality.

Their careful planning resulted in a comprehensive technology roadmap, outlining a phased approach to integrating new technologies into their existing software. The roadmap prioritized features that aligned with their brand identity and offered tangible value to their users. They also created a detailed budget that factored in both immediate and long-term expenses, ensuring the financial sustainability of their plans.

The final result wasn't simply a list of technologies; it was a carefully crafted strategy for the future of WineSoft, a strategy that balanced ambition, innovation, and the ever-present threat of a cat-related disruption. They knew the path ahead wouldn't be easy. There would be unexpected hurdles, countless late nights, and the occasional emergency Mr. Fluffernutter-related incident. But as they looked towards the future, a future fueled by innovative technologies and a generous supply of wine, they felt a surge of confident anticipation. The journey, they knew, would be chaotic, unpredictable, and undeniably hilarious. And that, they realized, was precisely the way they liked it.

The exhilaration of the StellarTech deal had barely subsided before the familiar anxieties of a startup crept back in. Maintaining the chaotic yet strangely effective WineSoft culture became the next big challenge. It wasn't just about coding; it was about preserving the unique blend of eccentric personalities, impromptu wine tastings, and the ever-present threat of Mr. Fluffernutter III causing a minor IT catastrophe.

Max, ever the visionary (or delusional, depending on who you asked), declared a company-wide "Culture Preservation Initiative." This, naturally, involved a three-hour brainstorming session that started with a blind wine tasting and ended with Dave accidentally setting off the fire alarm with a rogue sparkler (a detail he blamed on Mr. Fluffernutter III's playful batting at a stray electrical wire).

Lily, ever the voice of reason (and sanity), proposed a more structured approach. She suggested creating a comprehensive employee handbook, one that documented WineSoft's unique traditions, from the weekly "Wine Wednesday" (which had a surprisingly high correlation to increased productivity) to the unspoken rule of never, ever, questioning Max's questionable fashion choices.

The handbook, however, proved to be more challenging than anticipated. Dave's contribution consisted mostly of hilarious, albeit irrelevant, cat memes. Sophie, while aiming for clarity and professionalism, accidentally included a section on "Appropriate levels of wine consumption during work hours," which Max enthusiastically embraced as "official company policy."

The biggest challenge, however, was capturing the essence of WineSoft's spontaneous creativity. Their best ideas often emerged from unexpected tangents, random conversations, and the sheer absurdity of their daily routines. How could they codify that? The answer, it turned out, wasn't to codify it at all.

They realized that any attempt to rigidly define their culture would inevitably stifle it. Their strength lay in their freedom, their willingness to embrace the unexpected, and the shared understanding that a little controlled chaos was a vital ingredient in their success. So, instead of creating a rigid set of rules, they created a set of guiding principles.

These principles, scrawled on a whiteboard (naturally, stained with red wine), emphasized collaboration, innovation, and a healthy respect for the unpredictable nature of Mr. Fluffernutter III's influence on office life. They included a clause officially recognizing the cat as a key member of the development team, with veto power over any project that threatened his afternoon nap schedule.

To reinforce their commitment to this organic approach, they decided to host a "Culture Fest." It was a day dedicated to celebrating their shared experiences, their unique personalities, and their bizarre yet effective methods of creating software. It involved a series of events designed to highlight the elements that made WineSoft, well, WineSoft.

There was the "Blind Wine Tasting and Code Challenge," where teams had to decipher a particularly complex piece of code while simultaneously identifying obscure wine varietals. There was the "Mr. Fluffernutter III Look-Alike Contest," which resulted in a surprisingly diverse array of cat-themed costumes. And, of course, there was the epic "WineSoft Improv Show," where employees (even Lily) showcased their unexpected talents in a series of comedic sketches about office life.

The Culture Fest was a resounding success. It wasn't just a fun day; it served as a powerful reminder of what made WineSoft unique. It solidified their shared values and strengthened their sense of community. The event also showcased the unexpected talents hidden within the team. Dave, surprisingly, revealed a hidden talent for dramatic acting, captivating the audience with his poignant portrayal of a frustrated programmer battling a particularly stubborn bug. Sophie, unexpectedly, revealed a flair for stand-up comedy, her witty observations on office life bringing down the house. Even Lily found herself laughing during the performance. Max, as the show's emcee, did his best to maintain some semblance of decorum, although the occasional wine-induced outburst was considered part of the show's charm.

The success of the Culture Fest inspired the team to integrate more culture-building activities into their daily routines. They started a company book club, choosing books that were both entertaining and thought-provoking. This was also a clever attempt to introduce the team to management topics in an informal and less stuffy manner. They organized team-building events, ranging from kayaking trips to escape room challenges. The focus was always on having fun and strengthening their bonds as a team, reinforcing their shared identity and values.

Furthermore, they implemented a "Suggestion Box" (shaped like a giant wine bottle, naturally), encouraging employees to share ideas on how to improve the workplace culture. This wasn't just a way to gather feedback; it was a way to actively involve the team in shaping their work environment. They knew that a thriving company culture wasn't something that could be dictated from above; it had to be nurtured and shaped from the ground up.

One of the most innovative suggestions was to implement a "Random Act of Kindness" program. Every week, employees were encouraged to perform a small act of kindness for a colleague. This could be anything from bringing someone coffee to offering help on a project to simply offering a listening ear. This seemingly small gesture went a long way towards boosting morale and fostering a sense of mutual support within the team.

However, maintaining this vibrant culture wasn't without its challenges. Balancing the need for creative freedom with the demands of a growing business proved to be a constant juggling act. They had to navigate the complexities of onboarding new employees while preserving the existing unique culture. This delicate balance required constant attention and proactive measures.

They recognized the need to maintain a balance between structure and flexibility. While respecting individual expression, they also needed to ensure that everyone was working towards the same goals. This involved carefully implementing clear communication channels, setting realistic deadlines, and establishing a shared vision for the future. They understood that a strong company culture wasn't just about fostering creativity; it was also about ensuring effective teamwork and goal-oriented productivity.

Despite the occasional hiccups (mostly related to Mr. Fluffernutter's mischievous antics), WineSoft's unique approach to maintaining its culture was proving to be a winning formula. It wasn't just a workplace; it was a community, a family, a slightly chaotic but incredibly effective collective of individuals who happened to create award-winning software. The future looked bright, even if it was occasionally stained with red wine. And as long as Mr. Fluffernutter III continued his reign of playful chaos, WineSoft was sure to remain uniquely itself. The future, they realized, wouldn't just be innovative, it would be hilariously unpredictable. And that, in the end, was perfectly fine.

Years later, the story of WineSoft became a case study in business schools, a testament to the power of embracing chaos, celebrating individuality, and letting a cat dictate project deadlines. It wasn't just about the StellarTech deal or the award-winning software; it was about the culture they'd painstakingly cultivated, a culture that had defied all expectations and thrived on its own quirky terms. The legacy wasn't confined to spreadsheets and code; it was etched into the memories of every employee who'd ever spilled wine on a keyboard or laughed until their sides hurt during a Mr. Fluffernutter III-themed improv skit.

Max, surprisingly, had mellowed with age, though his fashion choices remained as questionable as ever. He still championed unconventional ideas, but his pronouncements were now tempered with a touch of self-awareness, a subtle acknowledgment of the occasional (and often spectacular) failures along the way. He had learned, through years of trial and error, that true innovation often bloomed in the fertile ground of controlled chaos. He'd even started a blog, titled "Managing Chaos: A WineSoft Memoir," which surprisingly became a best-seller, detailing his journey from enthusiastic visionary to slightly more responsible (but still eccentric) leader.

Lily, ever the pragmatist, had become a sought-after consultant, her expertise in managing unconventional teams now highly valued in the tech world. Her seminars, titled "Harnessing the Power of Controlled Chaos," were packed, attendees eager to learn the secrets to navigating the unpredictable waters of a truly unique company culture. She often recounted the tale of the fire alarm incident, using it as a cautionary tale about the dangers of letting a cat near electrical wires while simultaneously highlighting the importance of a well-stocked fire extinguisher.

Dave, now a senior developer, finally managed to teach Mr. Fluffernutter III to use a specialized keyboard designed for felines (a truly remarkable engineering feat), reducing the cat's interference in software development to a minimum. His cat's Instagram account, @MrFluffernutterIII_Dev, boasting millions of followers, had become a surprising source of passive income, funding his extravagant cat-themed lifestyle. He even gave a TED Talk on "The Unexpected Productivity of a Well-Fed Cat," further cementing WineSoft's legendary status in the tech world.

Sophie, who had risen through the ranks to become a project manager, embodied the spirit of WineSoft's unique approach. She had a knack for navigating the complexities of team dynamics, fostering collaboration, and gently nudging her team members toward deadlines without sacrificing their creativity. Her leadership style, a blend of understanding and gentle firmness, reflected the balance WineSoft had achieved between structured processes and creative freedom. She often joked that her career path was proof that an internship at WineSoft could lead to extraordinary things – or at least a really good story to tell at networking events.

WineSoft's success wasn't merely the result of a quirky culture; it was a testament to the power of valuing individuality. Each employee was encouraged to bring their unique perspectives, skills, and quirks to the table, contributing to a collective intelligence that exceeded the sum of its parts. The company understood that forcing conformity would stifle creativity and erode the very essence of its unique identity. The company culture celebrated differences, fostering a sense of belonging and mutual respect, creating an environment where everyone felt safe to express themselves, to experiment, and even to fail spectacularly. Failure, after all, was just a stepping stone to innovation.

The legacy of WineSoft extended beyond its employees. The company became a beacon of hope for other startups, demonstrating that success didn't require rigid adherence to traditional business models. Their approach inspired countless entrepreneurs to embrace their own unique approaches, fostering a wave of unconventional startups that challenged the established norms of the tech industry. WineSoft's success wasn't just about profits; it was about proving that a company could be wildly successful while also prioritizing its culture, its people, and even its resident feline software engineer.

The story of WineSoft wasn't just about software development; it was a heartwarming and hilarious tale of human connection and the importance of embracing your inner weirdness. It highlighted the power of shared experiences, of celebrating individuality, and of finding joy in the midst of controlled chaos. Their unconventional approach wasn't just a quirky gimmick; it was a powerful strategy that fostered creativity, innovation, and a deep sense of community.

The success of WineSoft also showed that leadership could be both visionary and supportive. Max's unconventional methods might have been chaotic at times, but he had a deep understanding of his team's strengths and weaknesses, creating an environment where they felt empowered to take risks and pursue their passions. Lily's grounded approach provided the necessary structure and balance to keep the company on track. The contrast of their leadership styles actually proved incredibly effective.

The impact of WineSoft went further than the boardroom or the tech industry. Their philosophy influenced other companies, sparking conversations about creating inclusive and supportive work environments. They proved that prioritizing employee well-being wasn't just a feel-good measure but a powerful driver of success.

Even the simple act of integrating a company book club, a seemingly mundane detail, exemplified the unique nature of their legacy. It wasn't just about improving management skills; it was about fostering intellectual curiosity, encouraging employees to engage in thoughtful discussion and learn from each other's diverse perspectives.

Moreover, the success of their "Random Acts of Kindness" program underscored the importance of building positive relationships in the workplace. These small gestures created a ripple effect, enhancing morale, fostering collaboration, and strengthening the sense of community within the team.

The company's lasting legacy wasn't merely about financial success but about creating a truly remarkable workplace culture that fostered creativity, collaboration, and personal growth. It demonstrated that a company could thrive while embracing its unique personality and valuing its employees as individuals. The WineSoft story became a powerful reminder that success can be both wildly unpredictable and profoundly rewarding.

The tale of WineSoft continued to resonate years later, a reminder that the most innovative ideas often emerge from the most unexpected places, and that the greatest achievements are rarely accomplished in isolation. It was a story about the power of embracing individuality, finding joy in the chaos, and recognizing the unexpected genius within the seemingly mundane. And it was a story that would undoubtedly continue to inspire generations of entrepreneurs and employees alike, proving that a little wine, a lot of laughter, and a very particular cat could indeed change the world. The legacy of WineSoft, in its uniquely chaotic glory, was a toast to the power of being wonderfully, wonderfully weird.

Author's Note

A thank you goes out to all those that have learned and earned
from this book.